SQUARING THE EARTH

K. T. Steele

SQUARING THE EARTH

This is a work of fiction. All of the name, characters, organizations, and events portrayed in this novel are either a product of the author's imagination or are used fictitiously. Any resemblance to actual events, locales or persons, living or dead, is coincidental.

SQUARING THE EARTH

Cover art and design by Kim Dingwell

ISBN 9798856242569

For Indy

Chapter One

Raid

The Toxic Garden of Iocaste Proper's sprawling Arboretum was filled to the brim with poisonous plants. These fairly benign toxic radials could be found in any of the wild back bowls of Iocaste's mountain ranges, but they were a rare sight here in the middle of the city. In spring and summer, the Garden would have been packed to the brim with day-trippers here to see the flowers in all their brilliant colors and fractal symmetry. This fall day found it nearly deserted, the most spectacular plants having lost their blooms and gone dormant as the weather grew colder.

Up ahead, a pair of unSkilled girls were daring each other to touch the death poinsettia, one of the few flowers that bloomed this time of year. Its hazardously bright red and gold bracts warned away herbivores even as the spiraling fractal geometry of its leaves and petals drew in pollinators and mesmerized those who looked at it.

"Bad idea," Raid said out loud as the girls upped the ante from touching the toxic flower to licking it.

They both jumped, looking at him with wide eyes, then dashed away giggling behind their hands.

<You should have let them lick it,> Mordred said in thoughtspeak.

<That would have been mean,> Raid answered. He hadn't felt Mordred arrive and even now as he looked with his Skills, couldn't get a sense of him. Mordred had always had a stronger Skillset than Raid, but not by a lot. Raid had never been able to see through Mordred's sight shields, but he'd always been able to feel his creche brother's psychic presence. Now he heard nothing but Mordred's voice. It felt like dealing with a high aught, and that put Raid on edge.

<But warranted,> Mordred replied, unaware of Raid's disquiet. <Anyone who wants to lick toxic radial should get first-hand experience why they shouldn't.>

<You wanted to meet?> Raid demanded, his unease making his voice sharp.

Mordred's sight shield expanded to encompass Raid, allowing them to see each other while making them invisible to the unSkilled and any Skilled with a lower aught rank than Mordred.

Both of them had been born to House of Carnage and bore the distinctive stamp of their House. The pale skin, black hair, and a similar set to their facial features. They also had blood-red eyes. Like the brilliant colors of the toxic radials, the jewel-bright irises of the Skilled Houses were a warning that their members should not be trifled with.

At this moment, Mordred looked exhausted, and distress colored his psychic scent.

<What happened?> Raid asked, all other concerns wiped away in the face of Mordred appearing so worn.

<Matriarch Katio culled the creche,> he answered dully.

<She… What?> Raid couldn't wrap his head around that statement. <Why? How many?>

<All of them.>

The enormity of that tilted the world on its axis and for a moment Raid thought he would be pitched into the sky. <Why?> The word came out barely a whisper in his mind.

<To strengthen the House.>

It took a moment before Raid could form words. <Strengthen the House? By killing the entire next generation? How does that help anything?> Culling had always been practiced by the Skilled Houses. There would always be those who posed a significant threat to themselves or those around them and were culled before they could cause damage – or worse damage in some cases. It was only in the last decade that Katio, Matriarch of House of Carnage, had started culling anyone she deemed too weak. The first one to die to her new ideal had been their creche brother Nico.

<She's old,> Mordred answered, his voice was expressionless,

as if he'd felt the same rage and shock that Raid did and had been hollowed out by it. <She was alive when Shadow and Wind went extinct. She thinks the same thing will happen to Carnage.>

<Of course it's going to happen to Carnage, she just culled the entire creche!> All the children. All the infants. Anyone who hadn't yet settled into their adult aught rank. Raid felt ill. The other Matriarchs wouldn't have intervened – each House was law unto itself – but others within Carnage had influence. <The High Inquisitor? The Witch Angels? They all just stood by?>

<The High Inquisitor protested but she wasn't strong enough to stop it. The Witch Angels… there aren't that many of them left and they're already stretched thin maintaining the Border. They may not even know yet.>

Raid ran his hands through his straight black hair. For the first time, he was glad that Mordred had sent him off on this Soth-forsaken recon mission; it meant he wouldn't be in the House – or even on the Mountain – when the Witch Angels found out what happened.

There were some basic Skills that every Skilled shared, regardless of House or aught rank. They could all hear and use thoughtspeak, sharpen their senses, and cast shields for protection or stealth. They were also physically stronger and more durable than the unSkilled.

Each House also had its specific Skillsets. Earth, Water, Ice, and Fire had control over their various elements. House of Viridae could encourage plants to grow and concoct incredible medicines and poisons from what they could coax out of their gardens and forests. Some had less well-defined abilities like House Animachea and their conjoined consciousness or Bone who seemed to have little bits of Skills from all the Houses which they recombined in ways that allowed them to heal.

Then there was Carnage. In media the unSkilled called them the Assassins House, filled with killers and murderous thieves. Their Skillsets focused on stealth, stalking, and ambush, and their instincts could be far more predatory than the other Houses. The Inquisitors used those Skills to track down and dispatch dangerous part-bloods who lived outside House jurisdiction, though recently High Inquisitor

Bester had been expanding her sphere of influence to include strictly unSkilled dilemmas and concerns as well.

Also born from Carnage were the Witch Angels. All of them were Ten aught, the strongest rank among the Skilled. Fierce, solitary, and territorial in the extreme, almost all to a one had removed themselves from the Mountain, choosing instead to live along the Border and keep Oceanea's dangerous Native wildlife from crossing into human lands.

Among the unSkilled, the horror stories about the Witch Angels had grown to monolithic proportions where they were viewed as unholy terrors and uncontrollable harbingers of death. The reality was not that terrible but still exceedingly dangerous and not to be crossed lightly. If any of the Witch Angels had had a child in the creche, then the Matriarch didn't have many days left among the living. The Witch Angels would plant her in the rose garden along with anyone else who chose to side with her.

Those thoughts carried the two of them along the meandering path of the Toxic Garden. They passed a bed full of jack skulls. The flowers that dried on the vine had the appearance of skulls and sounded like they were whispering as the crisp autumn wind blew through them.

<So now what?> Raid asked, finally breaking the silence.

<Keep doing what you were sent to do,> Mordred answered tiredly. <The safest place to be right now is off the Mountain.>

Off the Mountain. Not just out of House of Carnage but off the entire Mountain. Mordred expected the Witch Angels' retaliation to spill over onto anything nearby. Raid himself had just been thinking the same thing but it was worse to hear someone else say it.

<About the creche,> Raid clarified because for the moment he didn't care all that much about the mission.

<They've already been sung back to the land. The High Inquisitor saw to it.>

<That's…> Good. It wasn't good. They shouldn't be dead at all.

<Better than what Nico got,> Mordred finished for him.

Nico's body had simply vanished, discarded in the back bowls for the carrion eaters because he was now considered too weak, and a proper burial would have been a disgrace to the House.

<She really culled them all?> Raid asked, half hoping Mordred would say 'Just kidding!' but he'd always been too serious for jokes or pranks.

<Yeah,> Mordred said, his voice heavy. <Her senility has turned into catastrophic delusions of grandeur.>

That was putting it mildly. <Have you told Cain yet?>

Mordred shook his head. <Telling him next.>

Their other creche brother Cain had been sent to Daal the same way Raid had been sent to Ashveil. Their jobs were to infiltrate the unSkilled extremist group calling itself True Human. The High Inquisitor worried that the group was a danger to the Skilled and that Animachea's Enforcers weren't taking them seriously enough. Given what Katio had just done however, the biggest danger to the Skilled right now seemed to be themselves.

<Will you be alright?> Raid asked. If House of Carnage wasn't a safe place for him or Cain, it wasn't going to be safe for Mordred either. His Skills were a little stronger than theirs, but not by enough.

<It'll be fine,> he said shortly.

Raid didn't push it.

They came back towards the entrance of the Toxic Garden.

Raid felt like there was more he should say. Something about the horror of what had happened to the creche, or what had happened to Nico six years ago. There was also Mordred's entrance, and how his Skills had felt stronger than before. Raid was about to ask, but Mordred spoke first.

<Stay safe,> he said, lifting his sight shield from Raid and disappearing.

Raid's thoughts and words tangled, everything wanting to come out at once, and so no words came out at all. All he managed to say was, <You too.>

Mordred didn't answer.

Raid wrapped himself in a sight shield of his own, and left the Arboretum and its Toxic Garden, before heading back to his new home in the unSkilled logging town of Ashveil.

Chapter Two

Maggie Reeves
Six Months Later

Maggie Reeves led her beginners' class through their warm-down drills. Already the kids had made so much progress since they'd started a few weeks ago. They closed out with a bow over folded hands and the traditional 'stay in peace' farewell. Then the serious faces burst into big grins and the room filled with happy chatter.

Outside the front window, Maggie could see parents waiting in small groups for the class to finish. It was one of the first pleasant days since winter broke and people took advantage, catching up with neighbors and acquaintances without being wrapped in heavy coats or clinging to hot mugs of coffee.

Standing a little apart from all of them was Staff Detective Jim Dawes. She frowned. He only showed up here like this when there was trouble. The kids collected their gear, pulled on their shoes, and spilled out onto the street, the more enthusiastic ones demonstrating their cool new self-defense moves to their parents. Maggie waited until they were all out of the dojo before stepping out herself and locking the door behind her.

Jim had been a heartbreaker back in his heyday. Tall, broad, and swarthy, he had some of Animachea's lupine looks without their uncanny gold eyes. Years of drunken brawling had kept him in shape and had also broken his nose more than once and left knick scars across his face. In the last few months though, he'd diminished. The lines around his eyes and mouth had deepened, and his hair was significantly grayer. Even his spirit seemed shrunk down, chipped away at the edges, and curled in on itself.

Absently he flipped a sobriety coin over his scarred knuckles.

Maggie had been thrilled when the Chief Inspector had forced him into treatment but as the months passed, Jim had deflated. He didn't even seem able to stand up straight without more alcohol in his system than blood.

"Hey," she said as she came over, keeping her voice even. "What's the call?" As a volunteer detective, she didn't get pulled into the field unless there was a massive disaster. She hadn't heard anything, but that didn't mean nothing had happened.

"A complaint for a bad odor coming from the old well in Temple Park." His voice had once boomed, but that had withered up like the rest of him.

"A bad odor?" Not the disaster that had been building in her mind. She let out the breath she'd been holding. That didn't even require a second person. "That's all?"

"I thought… I mean, I know you have a break after this class." His gaze held an embarrassed quality as he squinted at something down the street in the main square, not quite looking at her.

The Chief had the schedule for all the volunteers, so it wasn't surprising that Jim had it too, she just didn't understand why he'd pull her for something so minor. Then it clicked. She'd been a little girl when Ceres had been destroyed, but she still remembered that day, where she'd been, what she'd been doing and what she'd been wearing when the first announcement came in about what had just happened. Jim Dawes had actually been there. He'd seen the town sink, all those people buried alive in an instant. Even on his best drunken day, he wasn't going to want to check out a deep hole in the ground. Now that he was sober, all his demons had become that much more real.

"I mean, yeah," she went on hastily. "I can go with you. It should be quick. Probably just a raccoon or something fell in and couldn't get out again."

She did her best not to notice the utter relief that overcame him. "Good," he said buoyed up by her response. "It's good to get out into the field periodically. It keeps your mind sharp."

"Let me just grab real shoes," she replied.

Jim nodded and followed her back inside.

She was always barefoot in the dojo, keeping the lightweight slippers near the door in case she needed to dash outside for a moment. Going on a call though, she'd need actual shoes. Also, real clothing. She changed quickly out of her white gi into jeans and a light jacket before grabbing her boots.

Jim had wandered inside and was looking into one of the glass front trophy cases. She winced internally at his outdoor shoes on her reed mats.

"You won all these?" he asked, nodding to the trophies, medals, ribbons and ceremonial sashes.

"Most of them," she answered. The oldest ones had been won by her mentor Callum Newkirk who'd owned this dojo before her, and some of the newer ones by her students who wanted their awards displayed here for their classmates to see rather than taking them home.

"All I ever got for my trouble was a broken nose and scars," he said. He touched his nose as he spoke, maybe reliving one of those past fights in his head.

Several moments passed in silence before she prompted, "Shall we?"

"Yeah." Jim nodded and crossed to the door.

The day was nice enough and the park close enough that they walked over rather than waiting for the trolley, passing through Ashveil's downtown square with its cafés, boutiques, and restaurants.

Jim stiffened as they walked by the square's main pub and his favorite hang-out until he became sober. He kept his eyes straight ahead, every step stiff and controlled. He clenched his hands so tightly his knuckles were white.

"Deep breath in through your nose," she said quietly like she did when one of her students was having a moment out on the mat. "Let it out slowly. Just focus on your breathing."

He didn't acknowledge her but a little of the tension seemed to ease.

Once they were through the two blocks that made up the square, they just had to cross the street to reach Temple Park.

"I used to play here when I was kid," Maggie said as they stepped onto the sprawling green sports fields. "We used to pretend the well was a secret entrance to the Mountain."

Jim snorted. "So you could sneak in and kill all the... Skilled?"

She heard the trip in his voice. He was about to say kurs but had switched at the last second.

"Yeah," she agreed because she didn't want to admit what she and her best friend Li had really played at, internally disgusted that she'd been such a foolish child.

At the far end between the sports fields and the neighboring houses was a strip of land allowed to grow wild. The trees grew more densely and the underbrush wasn't regularly cleared away. It was meant as a light and sound buffer for the houses butting up against the park, though many children found it a cool extension of their play area. Maggie found her way as easily through the trees now as she had when she was little.

The well was supposedly as old as the town, having been dug down before Ashveil was added to the Water Works Eastern Corridor master system. It had been dry since Maggie's earliest memory and then had been boarded over in her teen years when someone had a devastating fall into it after too many close calls. It looked almost as she remembered it, the old stone overgrown in moss and lichen. Rust stains ran down from where the cover had been bolted on. Despite the rust, the bolts were holding, but the wood had rotted away, revealing the gaping maw of the well.

"Something certainly died in there," she said, pulling up when the smell hit her.

Jim nodded. "Want to check and see?" He held out his flashlight.

She'd come to save him from reliving the worst day of his life. That smell though... That certainly had her rethinking her decision. She took the proffered flashlight, took a deep breath, and went over to the well.

She'd made this walk a million times as a kid, pretending she was about to ascend to the Mountain. Not to kill the kurs, as Jim had assumed, but to obtain Skills for herself. How stupid and naïve she'd been. Kurs may have human forms, but there was absolutely nothing human about them, the same way a toxic radial wasn't a real plant, just a traitorous, poisonous weed. She cringed now even to think about how she'd once aspired to be one of them.

The well had shrunk compared to her memory of it, though it was still plenty big. The reek was so unbearable it nearly forced her back physically. With a click, she turned on the flashlight and peered through the gap left by missing planks. The light glinting back off the water was the first thing she saw, then her eyes landed on blonde hair, the slope of a neck and shoulder disappearing into the dark water.

She beat a hasty retreat.

"There's a body," she said, once she was away from the worst of the stench. "A human body."

Jim's face darkened. "A kid?"

She shook her head. "Looked full grown. There's also water."

"Water?"

Maggie could see him groping in his memory if that was normal or not. "It's been dry since I was young," she said.

He nodded, her words syncing with whatever he'd been trying to remember. "I'll call the Enforcers and make a report."

"The Enforcers?" she snapped. "Why get them involved?"

"It's regulation," he answered. "Unless there's someone on the force you hate enough to make them deal with that smell. Or another of the volunteers? Maybe that new boyfriend of Li's? I know you don't like him."

Of all the details for Jim to remember. "I don't not like him," she answered sharply and too quickly. "He's fine." There was just never going to be anyone good enough to date her best friend.

"We have to report the body to the Enforcers anyway. May as well have them come and fish it out for us."

It spoke to Jim's deep hatred of dark, underground spaces that he'd rather deal with kurs than deal with the well and its contents himself.

Maggie struggled for a second with allowing a kur to handle remains but they were typically respectful of the dead. It was the living they treated like garbage.

"Fine," she agreed, though as a volunteer her opinion meant nothing. "Call the Enforcers."

Jim pulled out his meme and began ponderously typing out the message. Maggie looked back at the well as he did, wondering not only about the dead body but also where all that water had suddenly come from.

Chapter Three

SalNavari

Salasi was still asleep when Navari woke up. Shadows hung thickly in their room. Navari let herself drift in Salasi's dream, careful not to interrupt the dazzling whimsy with her real-world logic.

She needn't have worried.

<Enforcer SalNavari,> Eastern Corridor Command's voice had them both wide awake in an instant. <Report for dispatch.>

Salasi blinked owlishly up at the dark ceiling, her dream dissolving like candy floss.

<We have these days off,> Navari replied with all the appropriate respect and honorifics that was due Command. She and Salasi were off all the days leading up to Squaring the Earth.

<True Human has staged a massive protest at Mountain Village,> Command answered, sounding off-put and distracted herself. <All on-duty Enforcers are dealing with that. Everyone off duty is now on-call, and you're being called.> The details of their assignment flowed from her mind, then her attention moved elsewhere to deal with some other problem.

Salasi threw an arm over her eyes. <It's a census job,> she muttered. <It can wait until after Squaring the Earth. The corpse isn't going to suddenly become more dead.>

Agreement from Navari but she rolled out of her bed anyway. <You know the unSkilled, they throw tantrums if their complaints aren't seen to immediately. At least it'll be quick.> She pulled open the curtains and sunlight streamed in. <And a fair sight easier than dealing with whatever True Human did to Mountain Village.>

Salasi groaned and held out for another minute before she also got up and got dressed.

Among the Skilled, all children were raised in communal creches. For the other Houses, this led to lifelong affiliations between creche siblings ranging from unbreakable friendships to alliances and sometimes bitter rivals. For Animachea, growing up in the creche was when they would Bond.

As little children, sometimes even as toddlers, they would seek out others who either complimented or contradicted them, and they would Bond. Their Skills would grow together, their consciousnesses enmesh with one another. There was a spectrum for this. Most were pairs, though there were groups, some as many as five. A handful even sought out animal companions, Bonding instead with the Wolves – or occasionally something else – rather than another human. Some Bonded partners were so entwined that they became a single consciousness with two or more bodies.

Salasi and Navari were the average for Animachea. Their thoughts and emotions were their own. Any knowledge or experience gained by one wasn't instantly known by the other unless it was consciously shared. Unconsciously the information would seep through from one to the other within a day or two. They could also share their senses – Skilled as well as physical – with ease.

In this way, they were both Salasi and Navari, but also SalNavari. Two who are one, one who is two.

This morning Salasi was far more put out by Command's call than Navari, but then Salasi was also the one courting Getch and had been planning to use these days to angle for a more lasting union between the two of them with a possible future child or children.

Salasi's ire was strong enough that by the time they were dressed and stepping out of their barracks, Navari was also deeply irritated. All around them, the Animachea compound prepared for Squaring the Earth. The main courtyard was in the midst of being swept and scrubbed. The center pond and the surrounding plant beds were being lovingly tended after the benign neglect that came with the winter and freezing temperatures.

<This will be quick,> Navari assured Salasi as they walked past the festivities instead of joining them.

Aggravation poured from Salasi that they were going at all, her eyes skipping from group to group of happy, celebrating people.

All unSkilled births and deaths were reported to House Animachea who in turn sent those numbers to the Houses that oversaw the various towns and villages. The unSkilled had proven themselves unreliable in relaying that information on their own, so the duty had been turned over to Animachea and the Enforcers who already dealt with the unSkilled and the day-to-day conflicts that emerged when people lived together in communities.

They left the joyful prepping activity behind them and walked to Animachea's Carriage stop. Almost all of the stronger Skilled – those ranked Six aught or higher – could transport themselves instantly between one place and another. The stronger their Skills, the further they could jump between places. It was a useful Skill that all the high aughts used.

Navari as a Three and Salasi as a Two did not possess that Skill, instead, they took Carriages, relying on a high aught to transport them. The Carriages were shaped like comfortable bungalows with no windows. The stronger the Skills of the Driver, the more other people they could bring along with them when they jumped. Right now that didn't matter, because no one currently wanted to leave the Mountain. The Carriage stop stood empty, the idling on-call Driver the only person present. Her Bonded partners would be preparing for Squaring the Earth along with everyone else and would likely swap out with her later in the day.

<Where to?> she asked, rousing herself as they walked up.

<Ashveil,> Navari answered.

<We have to take a census,> Salasi added sourly.

The Driver ushered them into the Carriage, before climbing in behind them and securing the door. Another day there would have been a crowd and the Driver would have made multiple stops. Today it was only them, and in no time they stepped out into the warmer air of Ashveil. As soon as they stepped clear of the Carriage, the Driver jumped away, returning to Animachea to await the next low aught who needed transport.

The Carriage stop was at the edge of Ashveil's town center. A high block wall and even higher trees encircled it, so the unSkilled wouldn't see the Carriages popping in and out of sight. Open use of Skills alarmed many of the unSkilled, a trend that had become significantly worse in recent years.

SalNavari sight shielded before they stepped out through the gate. Salasi wanted this to be as fast as possible and the fewer unSkilled who saw them the better. It meant fewer chances that they would be drawn into some unrelated unSkilled drama.

SalNavari had been tapped to be an Enforcer pair in late childhood and had spent their teen years apprenticed under other Enforcer pairs. That meant that they'd had more interaction with unSkilled than most, starting from a young age. Despite that, they still experienced the sensation of 'walking in a field of ghosts' whenever the unSkilled surrounded them. From what SalNavari could glean from older Enforcers like Command, that feeling never went away.

The main square of Ashveil was as full of people as Animachea had been when they left – unSkilled laughing, shopping, talking, moving – but the whole picture felt skewed. Their voices were loud, echoing harshly in SalNavari's ears. Simultaneously their thoughts were silent, leaving a gaping soundless void where laughter and chatter should be. Worse though, and what made them ghosts in the eyes of many Skilled, was that the unSkilled lacked a psychic presence and the psychic scent that presence left behind. There was no sense at all of who they were or where they came from, their strengths, their feelings or who they'd spent time with recently. It was like seeing a painting jump to life, the subjects all did what was expected, but there was no substance to them. They weren't actual people, just two-dimensional representations of people acting out a script.

None of the unSkilled had ever seemed bothered by this. They all seemed perfectly happy as husks, floating through the world unconnected to each other or anything else. Attempts to interact with them as if they were Skilled usually went poorly. Thoughtspeak to them was physically painful, and unSkilled could be killed if a high aught used thoughtspeak with them too forcefully or tried to do something as simple as sharing a memory. Even a low aught screaming long enough and loud enough could do them in. They were fragile as well as being empty.

It took SalNavari a moment to adjust, Salasi recovering more quickly. As the lower aught, when they did need to speak to the unSkilled, it was Salasi who did it, but being used to something didn't mean she liked it.

<Come on,> Salasi said, prompting Navari to start moving.

Navari shook off her initial unease and settled into the unSkilled world where the people weren't quite there.

Navari immediately noticed the signs. Some were little stickers in the corner of shop windows, boasting the word KUR and a red X through it. Far more of them however were large, posters and banners proclaiming support for the True Human movement. A few of the unSkilled were even wearing shirts and jackets with True Human emblazoned across them.

Navari's stomach turned

Disgust washed through from Salasi. <There are so many.>

Agreement from Navari.

The True Human movement had gained traction in the last few years and had gained a marked following recently. Most of the Skilled had simply ignored it. The vast majority of them lived and worked on the Mountain and so had no dealings with the unSkilled. Their demonstrations and protests meant nothing. Those who did have to work with the unSkilled like SalNavari could shield and sight shield and escape an attack. They could also choose to just turn on their assailants and put them in the ground. The aughts and Ones were the weakest of the Skilled and some elected to live among the unSkilled, as did the part-bloods who had no choice. Many of them didn't have the Skilled strength to hide or escape. To them, True Human had become a real threat.

<We'll report them to Command when we get back,> Navari said, looking at as many of the different posters, stickers, patches, and t-shirts that she could put her eyes on.

Ashveil's downtown butted up against a large park. A huge grassy area for running around made up most of it, with a good deal of play equipment on the close end. The park itself was separated from the neighboring homes by a long strip of tall trees and undergrowth matching the forest that surrounded Ashveil.

Command had pinned this park as the place to meet the unSkilled detectives. It didn't take long to spot them, two unSkilled adults attached to no children and performing none of the unSkilled activities associated with parks. They both just stood there, waiting. Salasi dropped her sight shield and approached them directly while Navari circled them, looking for the body they'd reported. With barely a thought their differing views layered over each other, allowing Navari to watch through Salasi's eyes and vice versa.

<Ask them why we're meeting them in the field and not in the morgue,> Navari said, not that she was complaining. The chemicals the unSkilled used for body preservation and cleaning up the morgue itself, burned their noses and throats and made it hard to smell anything for a week after.

The detectives straightened and turned to face Salasi as she approached. The man was physically large and could have been intimidating, but he had a guarded stance, hunched a bit as if protecting an injury. The woman was compact strength, and although she looked small, she could probably hold her own in a fight against another unSkilled. Her hair was a bright, shining blonde, a color that hadn't been seen among the Skilled since House of Wind died out, her eyes though were unSkilled brown.

Salasi greeted them, and the three of them exchanged names while Navari walked into the wooded strip of the park. She picked up the smell of death almost immediately and zeroed in on the source; an old well, long since boarded up and recently ripped back open again. While the Skilled could dial back their vision and hearing when dealing with bright lights or loud noises, the same trick didn't exist for their sense of smell. Times like this made Navari wish she could be as nose dumb as the unSkilled.

She peered into the well, sharpening her sight to see the details in the darkness. Her eyes confirmed what her nose had already told her, very dead human. This close she also picked up the remnants of a psychic scent. Salasi stopped speaking to the detectives mid-word, her attention shifting completely to Navari, watching through her eyes and feeling with her senses.

Navari reached out with her Skills, honing in on the psychic scent that would still be impressed in the bones long after the mind turned to sludge and blood to dust.

SalNavari swore as Navari physically recoiled.

The dead body was not only Skilled but Carnage.

Their simple census assignment suddenly became markedly more complicated.

Chapter Four

Maggie Reeves

The small talk died off while Maggie and Jim waited, and now they both stood in silence. Mostly. Beside her Jim had his hand white-knuckled around the sobriety coin, muttering sobriety chants under his breath and occasionally, "Start digging, they only have one breath."

She guessed he was mired in the past, staring at the ground and not seeing Temple Park, but the day Ceres had been buried. Maggie focused on him to avoid thinking about her own kur-infested past and the damage that they had dealt her.

"Here they come," she said out loud, seeing the kur the moment it stepped out of thin air.

Jim jerked his eyes up, reorienting himself of the present.

Even from this distance, Maggie could see the difference in how the kur moved, and as it came closer Maggie could see the same inhuman qualities in that face. This kur was female. Her black hair had been braided in a cable down her back. Her skin was several shades darker than Jim's, but her cheekbones were too sharp, her eyes too large. It didn't help that they were gold rather than a human shade of brown or black.

"Enforcer Salasi," she said politely when she reached them. "Are you the detectives who called for a census count?"

"Staff Detective Dawes," Jim replied, trying for a courteous tone but it was coming out cold and surly. "Volunteer Detective Reeves." He jerked his head at Maggie.

"Is there a reason you left this body in the field?" the kur asked.

"The well is full of water," he answered sharply. "We thought you'd want to investigate that."

She tilted her head like a dog that couldn't comprehend human words. "A well's purpose is to be filled with water," she said carefully as if he was the one who didn't understand.

"Yeah, well this one isn't. It's been empty for decades."

"It's been dry for as long as I've been alive," Maggie added.

The kur nodded and said, "Your concerns will be brought to the Water Controller."

"They aren't concerns," he snapped.

The Enforcer frowned. "If they're not concerns, then why did you mention—" She cut off mid-sentence.

Maggie had seen that happen before. The kur was talking to someone using thoughtspeak. There was another one here somewhere. Of course there was. Enforcers always traveled in pairs. Maggie tensed up, waiting for one to spring out at her, tonfa in hand.

Without another word, the kur turned and walked away from them.

Maggie glanced at Jim. She didn't want the kur to wander off unsupervised – there were kids in this park – but she also didn't want to leave Jim standing here with a tick in his jaw and a semi-wild look in his eyes.

"Should we follow?" she asked.

He nodded curtly and strode off after the kur who was headed for the well.

As Maggie had suspected, another kur was already there dressed identically to the first in a uniform made from heavy-weight cloth in various shades of brown. She even had the same braid down her back. In front of her floated the sodden, smelly, bloated mess of what had once been a man, dredged up out of the water by her Skills. Very gently she laid him out.

"He is Skilled," the first Enforcer announced. "We will take him back to the Mountain. May we borrow your vehicle to return to the Carriage stop?"

"No," Jim said coldly.

The two kurs stared at him with their unnaturally matching gold eyes.

He glared back without blinking and said, "You're not putting a rotting corpse in the station vehicle."

"We shall carry him through the middle of Ashveil's main plaza then," the kur replied without missing a beat.

The body once more began to float up into the air as the kur lifted it with her Skills.

"Jim…" Maggie muttered. That smell alone would cause a stir among the people of Ashveil not to mention the presence of two Enforcers with a bloated corpse.

"He's a kur too," he hissed back. "Let them carry it."

"Goodbye," the kur said, and with that, they and the corpse vanished from sight.

Jim recoiled from where they had been, body reacting to a blow that didn't fall.

Silence wrapped around them, and bit by bit the smell began to fade. Maggie felt herself letting out the breath she hadn't realized she'd been holding.

"What was that about?" Jim growled, turning on her. "You wanted to lend them a company vehicle?"

"They're going to have to carry it through the square to get back to their Carriage stop. It's the weekend. Do you know how many people are out shopping right now?" Even invisible that smell…

Jim flushed in what might have been shame but it didn't cut through his anger. "I'm not going to help a damn kur do its job!"

Maggie had seen him like this before, he was spoiling for a fight. He used his anger and the ensuing arguments and brawls as a shield against his fear. She wouldn't be dragged into it. "I know Ceres—"

"You know nothing!" he snapped, getting in her face. "You. Know. Nothing," he spat the words at her as if daring her to hit him.

She caught herself sizing him up as she would an opponent on the mat, looking for different ways to immobilize or hurt him. She took a step back. "Call your sponsor," she said coolly. "I have a class to teach." She walked off without giving him the benefit of a fight. He needed to learn how to control his feelings without taking it out on the nearest person or drinking himself under the table.

She was about twenty feet away when she remembered the

meeting. Jim had never come before, preferring his associates at the bar and then later sitting at home alone watching whatever media drivel was on. She turned back, "There's a True Human meeting at the rec center tonight. Doctor Adrian Longcross is coming. *The* Longcross. It might do you some good to be around people instead of just sulking by yourself at home." She turned away before he could answer.

She had her own demons, she wasn't going to take on his too, but that didn't mean he couldn't find camaraderie among those of them who'd decided it was time to fight back.

Chapter Five

SalNavari

It was a smelly, slimy walk back to the Carriage stop. Navari kept the corpse balanced on a shield and floating out in front of her while Salasi held the sight shield around them. Some shields could be used for smells, both physical and psychic, but Navari was not penning the rotting stink in with her. More than a few of the unSkilled gagged at their passing, turning offended gazes on their neighbors or the coffee cups in their hands as if they were the cause of the ungodly stench. As soon as they reached the Carriage stop, Salasi pinged for a pickup as well as a casket

Navari tried to speak to Command to inform them what had happened, but the distance was too great. As a Three, her thoughtspeak range could only reach so far, and she couldn't reach the Mountain from Ashveil. It didn't stop her from trying, because the more she thought about it, the worse the situation became.

The dead man was Carnage, there was no denying his psychic scent, but he didn't at all look like Carnage. His hair was blonde, his clothing unSkilled in cut and style. Hair could be dyed easily, though changing one's appearance like that was seen as frivolous at best and usually severely frowned upon. Tattoos and piercings were unheard of. For a Carnage to be disguised in such a way, he had been on a mission. Dressed as unSkilled, and with the amount of True Human garbage she was seeing, he had probably come to infiltrate them. Even if they hadn't killed him, his death here among them did not bode well for their group. At least she would not be the one to deliver news of his passing. That duty would fall to Command.

The unSkilleds' comments about the well suddenly being full of water was something that would also need to be dealt with. The news would need to be delivered to Controller Ataku of the Water Works, but that matter was of far less importance than the dead Carnage.

The sight and smell of the body had the Carriage Driver aghast. She handed over the casket Salasi had requested before retreating as far away as possible.

Viridae artisans had specially carved and reinforced the casket with the intent of transporting remains. Using her Skills, Navari placed the corpse inside and closed the lid. Special shields built into the wood immediately enclosed the stink and would stop any leaking.

The Driver came back to ensure the shields were sealed and holding before letting them board and taking them back to the Mountain. As soon as the door opened, Navari pinged Command, demanding urgent attention.

Even still, Command was slow to respond, and the minutes dragged by heavily.

<Speak,> they finally said, a different member of the Bonded Eastern Corridor Command partnership than who had dispatched them this morning.

Navari didn't bother with words, just passed over the information. A dry well that was now filled with water, and also contained the body of a disguised and very dead Carnage.

Command gathered his frayed attention to focus more closely. As he did, SalNavari caught a glimpse of what had swamped the Enforcers this morning. What had started as a True Human protest outside the resort town of Mountain Village had dissolved into a riot.

Despite its name, Mountain Village had been built along one of the northern beaches of Iocaste Proper and was home to dozens of aughts and part-bloods. As such, Mountain Village had become a tourist destination where unSkilled could fulfill their fantasies and sate their curiosity about the Skilled. Most of the Skilled who lived in Mountain Village wore costumes and played parts analogous to what could be found on the Mountain. It was a safe and lucrative way to allow the unSkilled to interact with the Skilled without them coming into contact with anyone stronger than a One.

Now all that fantasy had been shredded. People were dead and wounded, and buildings had been broken into and vandalized; the only reason nothing was burning was because Shapash who owned and ran it was a Four of Fire and had put out any blazes. Every Enforcer on duty had gone to deal with that disaster.

Command finished parsing through SalNavari's experience this morning. <Return the body to Carnage and learn what you can. Inform Controller Ataku about the well. Water can decide what they want to do with it.> His attention then turned fully away from them and his presence and voice disappeared.

Navari and Salasi looked at each other, their faces mirror images of alarm.

Navari pinged Command urgently again and didn't wait for a response, <Command, he is dead,> she said, in case that glaring detail had slipped Command's attention.

Command's attention flickered back to them <Many are dead,> he replied. <Advise Carnage of the situation. If they have questions, they can follow up themselves or wait until after Mountain Village has been dealt with.>

SalNavari's hearts sank. They did not want to be the one to bring a message of death to Carnage. As a Three and a Two, they were terrifically outclassed by who they were being sent to speak with. Delaying a message to Carnage, however, may provoke an even more dangerous response. Not to mention ignoring a direct order from Command had serious consequences.

<Split up,> they agreed simultaneously.

Against a high aught, the two of them together were little better than one of them alone. Split up, one of them could observe from a distance while the other saw everything in close detail. Oftentimes in the long run it gave them a fuller picture. As she'd already been carrying the body, Navari would take that back to Carnage while Salasi went to see the Water Controller. The Driver didn't comment as they both boarded the Carriage again.

Calling the home of the Skilled 'the Mountain' was a misnomer. The name encompassed an entire mountain range that hemmed in Iocaste Proper from the north. The House compounds were scattered throughout its peaks, and while all of it could be reached by walking – crossing impressive bridges and taking winding paths – it was faster to travel by Carriage.

Navari was dropped off well beyond the territory marker for Carnage. The Carriage then jumped away, taking Salasi to the Controller Ataku's compound.

Swallowing back her concerns, Navari made her way towards House of Carnage. The trees around her grew tall and wild but the smell of the sun-drenched pine forest wasn't enough to obscure the scent of Carnage. Even the unSkilled with their numb noses would have noticed the difference.

The territory marker itself was an ancient stone wall, no higher than Navari's thigh. On its other side spread the rose garden. All kinds of roses grew here from the natural human roses that had come with the Ancestors from the Moon to the radial roses that were hybrids with Oceanea's Native plants, and somewhere in there, growing in perfusion would be the black roses.

A perfect physical mimic for Carnage's psychic scent, black roses were radial hybrids. Their petals were black except for right at the base where they were a brilliant blood red, the same color as Carnage eyes. The smallest scratch from their poisonous thorns could kill a person in minutes. Legend claimed that their Native ancestors were venomous, a creeping plant that would draw prey in with its beguiling scent before biting and devouring them. Navari believed it. Even the most benign Native plants were terrifying, and the black roses of Carnage did their best to live up to their Native heritage.

She stopped at a gap in the stone wall. A path of safety led in, cutting through the rose garden to the compound itself. Neither suicidal nor a fool, Navari pinged the House to alert Carnage that she was here and requesting an audience. She let her attention shift more heavily to Salasi as she waited.

The Carriage had dropped Salasi off at the Water Works. Controller Ataku was one of the few high aughts not living on the Mountain, her compound residing instead in the neighboring Ice White mountain range to the east, where it presided over the Feyar River.

Built by Earth Skilled on huge rock pylons, the complex spanned the broad, swift-moving river. Multiple smaller rivers and streams throughout the range joined the main body before splitting off again, their new paths formed by Controller Ataku. They would go on to water farmland and supply the towns of the Eastern Corridor. They would keep ponds and lakes fresh and fed. Controller Ataku's management kept water flowing where it was needed, even during dry seasons. She ensured everyone received the water they needed to thrive.

Turbines forged of metal spun in the cold rapids and created power that augmented the Fires in their nearby power plant. Some Fires had an affinity for lightning, and they used the power from the river to supply electricity to the unSkilled towns. Much like Controller Ataku, the Fires sent steady power to where it was needed and stored what wasn't in batteries and generators.

An aerial tram station stood nearby. A special line had been built at the request of the unSkilled so they could visit the Water Works and not have to hike in on foot or request Skilled Carriages. A superstition had taken hold among the unSkilled that they would disappear during the jump, lost forever between places, never to be heard from again. At the moment the station was deserted, the unSkilled needing special permission to use it.

Well-tended footpaths led from both the Carriage stop and the tram station to the front doors. Two Water Skilled stood guard. They both wore immaculate blue uniforms, the symbol of House of Water neatly stitched over their right lapels with the Water Works logo stitched over the left. Their psychic scents showed that they were both Threes, their presence formality and tradition rather than to serve any protective purpose. Controller Ataku herself wielded Nine aught Skills and could defend herself against almost anyone who came to cause her or her complex harm. The day-to-day deterring of pests, however, was beneath her.

Salasi bowed at the hips, her hands curled over her chest.

<We are Salasi of Enforcer SalNavari. We seek an audience with Controller Ataku regarding a well and a dead body from the town of Ashveil.> As she spoke, she sent the two guards images of the well and the unSkilleds' insistence that it had been dry for decades. She also sent them images of the dead Carnage that had been found in that

well.

One of the guards reached out to their superiors regarding the request. For several minutes Salasi stood silently, holding her bow and listening to the unintelligible murmur of a shielded conversation.

<The Controller has elected to see you,> one of the guards finally spoke. <You may enter.> The two guards stepped back, and the stone door swung open smoothly.

The Water Works had been built to look and feel as much like a cave as possible, reflecting Controller Ataku's preferences. Rivulets of water snaked through shallow channels that had been carved in the floor for them. Tiny, sightless fish darted in puddles Salasi carefully stepped over. High slit windows allowed in some light which augmented the small gleams set in recesses over the doors. The air was cool and moist and the whole place was stamped with the psychic sent of Water.

Water had once been the largest House and its Skilled varied widely. Some preferred the still contemplation of small ponds. Some wanted the depth and complexity of lakes. Some rode the river rapids and some rode the waves. Recently the schism between the Mariners of the ocean, most of whom had never set foot on even seen dry land, and those who protected the land-locked waterways, had grown. House of Water had fractured once before with those of Ice creating their own House many centuries ago. Talk had started that such a thing might happen again.

Controller Ataku's preference for underground water systems was clear in the design of the Water Works. Her Skillset also made her well suited as the Controller for the Eastern Corridor waterways. Salasi followed guiding pings that led her down into the heart of the building. Small creatures slithered along the rough-cut walls and disappeared down secret cracks. Not only did the Water Works look and feel like a cave, but Controller Ataku had done her best to recreate a cave ecology.

The control room maintained the cave theme. At the center was a deep, clear, freshwater pool filled with more of the tiny darting fish and a few larger, slow-moving fish that appeared as little more than shadows at the bottom. Water beaded along the stones that made the ceiling and gathered thickly on the floor, splashing with every footstep. Controller Ataku sat at the deep center of the pool as the large shadows curved slow circles around the bubble of air that surrounded her. Salasi knelt at the edge of the pool, water soaking her knees, and waited for the Controller to acknowledge her.

Controller Ataku's Nine aught powers thrummed here in her domain. Her senses would be far away, flowing with the river and all the hundreds of smaller streams and eddies that branched off from it. She could feel the changes in the water and adjust them accordingly. If something had suddenly flooded the well, she would know why and if there was any cause for alarm. Salasi's attention wandered to the bats that clung to the ceiling and the tiny pale cave frogs that dotted the walls.

Back on the Mountain, Navari watched bees flit among the flowers, unconcerned by the toxic nature of the hybrid radials. No one had so far answered her ping. She let her awareness flow cautiously into the garden. Skilled wards laid down over centuries bared their teeth at her, a glimpse of power and hostility in purely Skilled form. She hastily retreated before she accidentally triggered any traps.

Controller Ataku unfolded from where she sat cross-legged.

Navari withdrew almost all of her attention from Carnage and focused again through Salasi's eyes. The Controller rose slowly through the water. The bubble of air breached the surface and didn't collapse until all but her knees were still in the pool. Wavelets sloshed around her calves, swirling the loose ends of her long white shift around her ankles.

She was a tall woman, her skin a deep, shining Water black. Her head was shaved bald, and designs had been dotted with paint on her face and scalp in white. Her long, lean hands rested at her sides.

Salasi bowed, touching her forehead to the floor.

On the Mountain, Navari mimicked the motion, so immersed she was with Salasi.

<Controller Ataku,> Salasi said.

The woman's Skills slid over Salasi and acknowledged that Navari was there. Salasi willingly offered up the memories of the day, opening her mind. Controller Ataku was strong enough that she could have easily ripped through their inner shields and taken what she wanted, leaving Salasi a gibbering pile of useless flesh for the frogs to nibble on and Navari as compost for the roses. Gentle as a babbling brook, the Controller reviewed what was offered. Her Skills then dropped into the pool where she focused for a moment before spreading out down the veins of the river.

<This well is unknown,> she answered at length. <Its water is not part of this river.> And so not part of her domain. <The entrance to an old aquifer perhaps,> she went on thoughtfully. <Another will be sent to review it and tend it as needed.>

SalNavari could feel the orders being sent, even as Controller Ataku spoke to them. Within the next day, perhaps even the next few hours, another Water would be standing over the well and getting a feel for the natural waters that flowed through it.

<And the body?> Salasi asked tentatively.

<Unknown to Water. Carnage will have your answers about him.>

That was the most Navari had expected to hear. If Water had been involved in the death of a Carnage, Controller Ataku would not so openly admit it.

<Thank you, Controller.>

With that the tall woman began to sink back into the pool, the bubble of air reforming around her. Salasi didn't move until the surface of the water had gone still again and Controller Ataku was once again at the bottom, her legs folded beneath her, her hands resting on her knees. Once her Skills curled outward, through the river, Salasi lifted her face from the floor and stood. On the Mountain Navari did the same, brushing the dirt and leaves off her legs as she did.

<No one told you to rise,> a velvety voice purred.

SalNavari's focus shifted in an eye blink, the cave of Controller Ataku replaced by the Mountain and the rose garden, and the Inquisitor now standing in front of Navari.

She wore a uniform the color of blood at midnight – a red so dark it appeared black. She looked like a porcelain doll, with a pale heart-shaped face and glossy black hair that hung unbound past her shoulders. The delicacy and beauty of her features did nothing to hide the fact that she was exceptionally dangerous.

Navari dropped back to her knees, pressing her palms and forehead to the ground in supplication.

<We are Navari of Enforcer SalNavari. We have been tasked with returning a body to you.>

For a long moment, the Inquisitor didn't move. Navari didn't dare glance up and meet the blood-red gaze, she barely even breathed.

Protocol established by the first Matriarchs and taught to all children in creche, decreed the Skilled weren't to kill one another without due cause and without first seeking other, appropriate forms of redress. Knowing that and that the Inquisitor shouldn't kill her because of some perceived slight did not reassure Navari as she knelt at the Inquisitor's feet.

The Inquisitor huffed a laugh, amused by Navari's submission. <Get up.>

Navari rose.

In the Water Works, Salasi stood as well, quietly withdrawing from the control room. She moved carefully, afraid to draw the Inquisitor's attention even from miles and miles away.

With a flick of Skills, the Inquisitor opened the casket. The smell of decay wafted over them. The Inquisitor's bow mouth twisted into a smirk as she recognized the dead man. The coffin closed with a snap before she vanished it.

<Come. Give your report,> the Inquisitor said as she turned on her heel.

Navari hurried after her, hesitating a fraction of a second before she crossed the territory marker and into the rose garden. Now in the company of the Inquisitor, the wards just gave her a hard look as she followed, disgruntled by her passage.

A neatly manicured path of steppingstones curved through the plants, curling around and back on itself. While it wasn't a maze, it wouldn't take much for the wards to misdirect someone unwelcome and walk them straight into the thorny embrace of a radial rose.

They rounded a bend and the House suddenly loomed in front of them. The forbidding outer wall was made from dark stone. The blocks were huge, individual, and fit together so tightly that no light passed between them even with no mortar to hold them together. A pair of Hippoi statues flanked the door, necks arched, manes flying, hooves ready to stave in skulls. Their eyes had been set with large rubies that glittered malevolently at Navari as she passed between them. No door barred the way through the outer wall. Even if someone managed to make it through the rose garden unscathed, the wards here were so old and hung so thickly that Navari could feel them brushing against her skin like spiderwebs as she walked under the arch.

<Wait here,> the Inquisitor said and vanished behind a sight shield.

Navari stopped where she was.

The floor of the entry courtyard had been paved in an interlocking, flowing, serpentine mosaic of red and black, punctuated here and there with white or gold. Like the wall of the House, each tile fit perfectly with those around it, requiring no mortar. It felt smooth under her feet, and her eyes were drawn into the coiling, curling pattern, not all that different from staring into the center of a radial flower.

<You have news Enforcer?>

Navari jumped at the sound of the voice.

Back in the Water Works Salasi also jumped, having drifted to a stop in one of the quiet cave-like halls.

Navari gave a fleeting thought to the pattern that had so easily mesmerized both of them before focusing on the people before her. The others all faded away as she recognized the old woman at the front, staring her down.

Well over a hundred years old, Matriarch Katio stood straight and strong. Her red eyes were as bright as they had always been even though her hair was now completely white and her face heavily lined and deeply wrinkled. Her black robes were embroidered with shining red roses.

Navari's heart skipped a beat just as Salasi's stomach plummeted.

<Matriarch,> Navari said, once again dropping to her knees, forehead and palms to the ground. <We are Navari of Enforcer

SalNavari. We have been tasked with returning a body to you.>

The casket thudded to the ground as the Inquisitor called it in.

Navari offered up the memories.

Matriarch Katio plucked them sharply, her Skills digging in to examine them from every angle for every nuance. Navari winced at the brutal inspection, fighting the instinctive urge to slam her inner shields closed and run.

The Matriarch withdrew abruptly, tossing Navari's memories back at her. Navari shivered and snapped her inner shields back into place. Any one of the Carnages who now surrounded her could rip straight through them, but the meager defense made her feel slightly safer.

<Open it,> Matriarch Katio said.

A moment later the coffin lid opened. The smell cascaded around Navari once again.

There was a sharp inhale of recognition.

Navari dared to lift her head enough to see, expecting the Carnages to be focused on the corpse.

With the Matriarch were three Inquisitors. The woman with the heart-shaped face who had greeted Navari at the territory boundary, a man Navari didn't recognize, and the High Inquisitor Bester herself.

Cold dread flooded through Navari at the presence of both the Matriarch and High Inquisitor. Though Protocol dictated that they should not maim or kill her for simply delivering bad news, if she was slaughtered here, very little would happen beyond a formal complaint sent by the Matriarch of Animachea to the Matriarch of Carnage.

<It's just the throwback,> the Matriarch said dismissively. <Dispose of him.> With that she sight shielded and was gone.

Her tone caught Navari off guard. Even if the Matriarchs didn't know all their people personally, they still cared for them. That was their duty, to protect and defend their Houses. SalNavari had expected at least the formal show of grief if not something of connection and substance. The High Inquisitor appeared resigned and maybe sorrowful. The woman with the heart-shaped face seemed positively gleeful. Only the man looked truly stricken.

<What happened?> he asked. Grief laced his voice, but it was

beaten out by fury.

<There was a report of a foul odor coming from a local well in Ashveil,> Navari replied unwilling to offer up her memories after the Matriarch's callous treatment. Navari could already feel the edges of a migraine crackling across her senses that often followed such an experience. <The unSkilled—>

<No one cares what happened to him but you Mordred,> the heart-faced woman said contemptuously, cutting off Navari.

<He isn't the only one who cares Adira,> the High Inquisitor replied with sharp censure.

Adira realized her overstep and sobered immediately, all emotion wiped from her pretty face. <Of course High Inquisitor.>

<Rise Enforcer,> the High Inquisitor said.

Carefully Navari did. They dressed and acted civilly, but all Carnage were still predators under that veneer. Adira with her fine, exquisite looks exemplified that.

<He was found in Ashveil?> High Inquisitor Bester prompted. <Not Daal?>

<Yes, High Inquisitor, he was found in Ashveil,> Navari answered, and when she wasn't interrupted again, she continued. <The foul odor was reported, and the local unSkilled detectives responded. They found the body floating in the well and reported it to Animachea Command for the census count. We were dispatched to respond.>

<What an excellent use of your time and Skills with what's happening at Mountain Village,> the High Inquisitor said dryly.

Navari hesitated, unsure if she should reply to the sarcastic comment.

<Go home,> the High Inquisitor said before Navari decided how to respond. <Your task has been completed successfully.>

<Yes High Inquisitor. Thank you.> She bowed over her hands and hastily retreated.

The words of the High Inquisitor were enough for her to pass. None of the wards or roses tried to stop her as she scrambled back the way she'd come. She still didn't breathe easily until she was on the far side of the territory boundary and hurrying towards the Carriage stop with Carnage falling away behind her.

A memory drifted up from Salasi's mind, catching Navari's attention. The rumor several months ago that Matriarch Katio had slaughtered her entire creche. Maybe it truly didn't matter to her that one of her people was dead. Maybe she'd only come to view the body to ensure it wasn't one of the few she did care about. Not Navari's concern. She'd completed her assignment. Carnage could now deal with Carnage.

□

Chapter Six

Raid

After six months, Raid had spent enough time in unSkilled clothing that he didn't fiddle with it anymore. He barely ever noticed it. That in itself was concerning. It was one thing to blend in with the unSkilled, it was something else to start thinking like them. He rolled his shoulders, feeling the knife in its hidden sheath between his shoulder blades. Two more were in wrist sheaths on either arm, partially hidden by the long sleeves of the black shirt he wore. He also had an unSkilled style switchblade in his pocket. He had more knives he could call in at any time he needed them but among the unSkilled, it never hurt to have blades they caught sight of from time to time. It was much easier to explain away a knife that seemed to appear out of thin air when they always saw him carrying at least one.

His leather jacket had been styled to look unSkilled but had been crafted by a Carnage armorer. The shields crafted into it could turn a blade or a bullet, useful for situations when he couldn't use his own shields without raising awkward questions. He'd been assigned to blend in with the unSkilled and report back on the True Human movement here in Ashveil, the last thing he needed was to accidentally shield-burn someone.

Around his neck, he wore a shield charm. It was a minor thing he had to recharge from time to time, that blurred his features to anyone looking at him. It muted the color of his eyes and softened the contrast between his skin and hair by bringing everything towards an unSkilled average. Skin a few shades darker, hair a few shades lighter. It shifted the angle of his eyes and cheekbones and heightened the bridge of his nose so he didn't look so intensely Carnage. In crowds as large as this one, it was best to be unremarkable in looks.

Despite arriving early, he'd remained at the back of the rec center's main auditorium, watching the seats fill until it was standing room only. A huge banner hung over the main stage proclaiming TRUE HUMAN in big block letters.

The seated crowd in front of him reeked of excitement and agitation. Their voices a little too gleeful and angry, their eyes a little too wide, and shining a little too brightly. From habit he tried to sense their psychic presence and get a better read on the feelings of the crowd as a whole, but as always came up empty. For all their fervor and physicality, psychically they read like nothing. If he closed his eyes, plugged his ears and nose, and relied on only Skills, he'd think he was standing alone in an empty room.

The vast majority of the crowd was sporting the True Human logo in the form of a patch or printed t-shirt. Some even had tattoos. It made no sense to indelibly mark oneself as a target, but if any of these people had sense, they wouldn't be here.

All of them would turn on him if they found out he was Skilled. Singly none of them could match him but as a mob, they could inflict damage, even against a Five aught Carnage. That's why he was standing at the back near the door. He would have time to run while they were still tangled up in their chairs.

"Hey." Lianan Uncaria slid up beside him.

He looped an arm over her shoulders, turned his face into her hair, and drew a long breath. After a day penned in with unSkilled, her psychic scent was a breath of fresh air. The smell of a garden after the rain. Sunshine on corn. The bountiful harvest.

She leaned into him, tucking herself neatly against his side.

"That kind of day?" she murmured, and he could hear her taking her own deep breath.

"When is it not?" he answered back.

Li was a part-blood Viridae, born and raised among the unSkilled.

Over the centuries, there had been by-blows from Skilled-unSkilled unions. Too weak to live on the Mountain and be raised in their House creche, they were raised among the unSkilled, and their Skills diluted away with each next generation. Occasionally those latent bloodlines would find each other and produce a child significantly stronger than the parents. Though 'significantly stronger' was a relative term. Li had a psychic presence and could coax plants to grow in a way that would be seen as miraculous to the unSkilled, but basic Skills were beyond her. She couldn't shield or use thoughtspeak. Among the Skilled, she wouldn't even rank as an aught.

Had he still been living on the Mountain she would have been far beneath his notice. Even when he'd first come to Ashveil for this assignment he hadn't paid her the least attention. Then the days of living among only unSkilled began to grind on him. It wasn't just the True Human zealots either, though listening to them spew hate and reinvent both history and current events to suit themselves was wearing. The worst part by far was their lack of a psychic presence. They wore the facsimile of emotions and personality, but there was no depth to any of them at all, no texture or vibrancy. It was like living with paper cutouts.

After less than a week of dealing with only unSkilled, Raid had sought out the handful of part-bloods that lived in Ashveil. Initially, he'd planned just to be near them, to reassure himself that real people did exist beyond the flat and vapid world of the unSkilled. That plan had swiftly fallen apart. The relaxation and reassurance that came with being near someone who was present and real in every sense had been too great to resist. Almost as soon as he'd sought out Li, he'd started talking to her.

She'd been wary at first, recognizing him right off the bat as Carnage despite the shield charm, but that had changed over the following weeks as he kept coming around, buying the different flavors of tea she made and asking how she made them. Now…

She slipped her arms under his jacket and just held onto him.

In that moment he wanted more than anything to wrap them in his shields and abandon this assembly. Abandon this assignment altogether. Someone else could tease apart the machinations of the unSkilled extremists and he could go live with Li in her cottage.

That daydream evaporated before it could even fully form. His relationship with her would last as long as this assignment did. Once it was done he would be ordered back to the Mountain, and if he didn't go, the Inquisitors would come to find out why, and that wouldn't end well for Li. Raid pushed that shitty thought away and focused on what was here in front of him.

"A lot of people came tonight," he murmured.

"They're all excited about what happened in Iocaste Proper," she answered darkly.

"What happened in Iocaste Proper?"

She pulled away enough to give him a look. "You still don't use your meme?"

"No." He'd never had any interest in the hand-sized tablet device. The unSkilled used it to communicate and exchange news over distances, something that could easily be done with thoughtspeak. The only reason he had one was because it would look strange among the unSkilled for him not to have one.

"It's more than just a paperweight you know," she said mildly exasperated. She pulled her meme out of her pocket and in a second pulled up the reports.

Raid scrolled through them, his stomach dropping before the slow burn of anger started.

He was no fan of Mountain Village; it gave the unSkilled the wrong impression about who the Skilled were and just what they were capable of, especially the high aughts. That said, that didn't give the unSkilled the right to run roughshod over them.

"This is all accurate?" he asked, looking through the pictures and skimming over the words.

"As far as I know," Li answered with a nod.

Mountain Village hadn't burned because Shapash hadn't let the fires spread. Despite that, the unSkilled had still bashed in windows, bashed in skulls, and stolen everything they could get their hands on. The unSkilled police had been called in only to join on the side of the rioters. Animachea Command had in turn dispatched all of their on-duty Enforcers. Only now, almost twelve hours after the protests had first started, were the rioters finally dissipating. There wasn't a death count yet but the unSkilled were calling the riots a success.

"I thought I'd find you here," a new voice said, coming to them over the room's chatter.

Raid handed back Li's meme, as her best friend Maggie Reeves came sauntering up.

At a distance, Maggie could have passed for a Wind if that House still existed with her pale blonde hair and pale skin. Only her eyes gave her away, being unSkilled brown instead of sky blue.

Like Li, Maggie had grown up in Ashveil. She had a dojo she'd inherited from her sensei when he died and was invested deeply in her community. Despite her young age and not having any children of her own, she was on the board of education and there were a lot of people who listened to her. It was unfortunate that she in turn listened to the True Human rhetoric.

"Maggie," Li said, hugging her friend. "How was your day?"

"Jim came by," she answered flatly.

Li lifted an eyebrow. "Yeah? How'd that go?"

"I don't know. I worry about him. Like today he came by… You remember that well we used to play around in Temple Park?"

Li nodded and Maggie went on.

"So. There was a dead body in it. Jim insists on calling the Enforcers about it for the census count."

"That's Protocol," Li said, echoing what Raid was thinking.

"But then the Enforcers come, and he absolutely loses his shit. Screaming at me, screaming at the Enforcers. Sobriety is supposed to be helping right?" she said, sounding a little at a loss. "But sometimes it seems like it's making him worse."

"He was at Ceres," Li pointed out.

"And some days it seems like he's still there. Like today he came to get me because he didn't want to look down the well…"

Raid tuned out the conversation. Maggie had never taken a liking to him and he hadn't seen the need to remedy that. Even if she wasn't as zealous as some, she still strongly supported the True Human movement. She'd said more than once and in a multitude of different ways that the only way for unSkilled children to grow up safe was if all Skilled were 'gone.' She didn't say 'dead' like so many others but that's certainly what she meant.

"…turns out the floater was a kur," she finished with a vicious grin.

Raid's attention snapped back to the conversation.

Li twitched at the slur, and Raid could feel her Skills fold protectively inward.

Raid shifted closer to her, curling his fingers and ready to call in a knife.

Maggie's satisfaction over the dead Skilled faded when it was met with stony silence and stony looks. Before any of them could say more, the lights began to dim. Maggie deliberately turned away from them to face the stage, her jaw set.

"What would she do if she knew who you really were?" Raid whispered the words directly into Li's ear so Maggie standing beside them couldn't hear.

"It wouldn't matter," Li said quietly but firmly.

"You sure?"

She didn't answer but the warmth of her Skills drew back even further into herself. She had grown up among the unSkilled. She had passed for one of them her entire life and had spent that life enduring their casual hate.

"Your silence speaks for itself," he finally said.

Li pulled away from him physically this time. "She just doesn't understand." Li's own words were barely more than breath, but she knew that with Skilled senses, he would still hear her.

"She understands just fine," he replied, watching Maggie who stared at the stage, watching as Ashveil's True Human board members took care of last-minute details. The murmuring of the crowd grew again as the lights came back up. "And so do you, or you would have told her why your garden grows so remarkably well the first time she dragged you to one of these meetings."

Li crossed her arms and stared unspeaking at the stage.

Raid wanted to pull her close again, to both take comfort from and offer it to the only other real person in this room so full of hate.

Maggie may have been the reason Li had first come to a True Human meeting, but she'd kept coming so she could keep track of them. There were hundreds of part-bloods out there, unprotected by the Mountain and easy pickings for angry unSkilled, as the murders at Mountain Village today attested.

A last-minute arrival came slouching through the doors behind them with leaden footsteps.

"Hey Reeves," he muttered shortly.

Maggie glanced over and did a double take. "Jim," she said surprised. "I didn't think you were going to come."

"Neither did I," he replied. He looked at the packed auditorium. "Quite a crowd."

"Doctor Adrian Longcross is going to be speaking tonight," she said, color coming to her cheeks. Raid could also hear her heartbeat uptick and caught the scent of her excitement. She'd never actually met the founder of True Human in person, but that didn't stop her from having a crush on him.

"Yeah."

There was a pause where Jim glanced over at Raid and Li, looked all over the auditorium, and pretty much everywhere but at Maggie. Finally, he gathered her courage and said, "Sorry Reeves. About earlier. I shouldn't have shouted at you. I was upset. But that's not an excuse. You were a lot of help at the well."

"You're welcome," Maggie said, looking and sounding stiff.

"I came," he said after another awkward pause, gesturing at the auditorium.

Maggie finally seemed to relent. She nodded and said, "I think you'll like these people, Jim. They're here to put an end to the kurs, so what happened at Ceres will never happen again."

Li crossed her arms more tightly around herself.

The main lights flicked off again, this time for real. The crowd hushed, everyone looking expectantly at the still illuminated stage and Ava Biner who stood there. She was broad and sturdy, a working mother who carried the weight of her community on her shoulders. Careworn and weather-worn, she was the heart of Ashveil's True Human chapter.

"Welcome!" she said, her booming voice carrying without the need for a microphone. "So glad you could all make it! I'm sure you've all heard the news from Iocaste Proper?"

A cheer went up, the smell of excitement getting thicker.

"It is a good day for humanity. Always a good day when we

strike back against the kurs."

Human and kur. It was a divisive distinction that the True Humans had come up with, bringing that old slur back into everyday use. Skilled and unSkilled were all human, and really, if anyone was less human it was the unSkilled with their paper doll existence.

"Last I heard the body count was twelve."

Whistles and clapping followed that announcement. Ava smiled congenially at the crowd, as if she'd just announced who'd won the log rolling contest and not the slaughter of twelve part-bloods and low aughts.

"If anyone here has friends or loved ones in the Iocaste Proper Police Department, send them our love. We owe them a big thanks."

Another big whoop of exuberance.

Raid wrapped his arms around Li. She leaned back against him, her whole body rigid with tension, her Skills a coiled ball tight within herself.

"While I'm sure everyone here would love to celebrate, our triumph at Iocaste Proper is not why we're here. Let's give a warm welcome to the man who's done more for humanity in the last few years than anyone else has done in their lifetime. Everyone, Doctor Adrian Longcross!"

The entire crowd jumped to their feet. Stomping, clapping, arms flailing.

Maggie lifted her hands to her mouth and cheered.

After an awkward moment of standing silently, Jim pulled his hands out of his pockets and started clapping.

Raid held onto Li and wrapped them both in a Five aught shield.

Li felt it come up. She unfolded her arms and wrapped her hands around his, gripping him tightly, the only source of safety in this hate-filled place.

Longcross smiled at the crowd. Tall and thin to the point of being gaunt, his neatly trimmed hair and beard liberally silver, he looked like a caricature rather than a real person. Raid reached out with his senses and came up blank. Longcross could be a projection on the stage for all that Raid could tell he was there.

Longcross let the cheering go on a little bit longer before holding up his hands. With a last few shouts, everyone quieted and sat back down.

"The cleansing of the kur town Mountain Village was a triumph today," he started, picking up where Ava had left off. "But it was just a first step. We all know why we're here. The kurs are a threat to humanity. For years, for decades, for centuries, we have abided by their laws. We follow mines only they approve. We log only the trees that they allow us, when they allow us."

Most of the crowd nodded along at that last sentence. Ashveil's main income was logging, but they could only fell the trees that House of Viridae sanctioned.

"Our towns are built or abandoned or restructured at their discretion. There are even places where they limit our very numbers, demanding we prove our ability to care for our own children before they allow us to have any."

Jim shuffled his feet and grunted, a stubborn, faraway look in his eyes. Raid wondered if he'd been denied a child license. If he'd been an alcoholic when he applied, the answer was yes.

"We live within the Border that they built, that they guard, that they refuse to let anyone pass beyond."

Raid wanted to point out that before Soth had given the world to the Skilled, the unSkilled had damn near destroyed it. They were the ones who caused the Cataclysm after all, and it was the Skilled who had put things back together afterward. Besides, despite all their bravado, no one here actually wanted to be on the far side of the Border.

"But the tides of time are changing. The events in Iocaste Proper today prove that. The world was ours once. It will be again."

As he spoke, a light presentation popped up on the screen behind him. It was the familiar map of Iocaste. The rocky Badlands of the north. The huge green swatch that was the Eastern Corridor made up a solid three-quarters of the territory within the Border. Ashveil was one of hundreds of tiny towns that dotted the arable land. The estuaries and salt marshes to the south. The beaches to the west with its handful of barrier islands. A thick black line representing the

Border wrapped around it all, guarded on the land sides by House of Carnage, and in the ocean by House of Water. Two-thirds of the way up the coast, cradled in a deep valley made up of two converging mountain ranges was the city of Iocaste Proper. Fully half the unSkilled population of Iocaste lived within that city.

To the direct north of Iocaste Proper was the mountain range that was the Mountain where the Skilled Houses and all but a handful of the Skilled resided.

The Ice White range to the east served as a rain shield, keeping all the water in the Eastern Corridor where it fed the land and kept everything growing, and keeping it out of the Iocaste Proper valley where everything would flood.

"I'm sure every single one of you recognizes this from primary geography class," Longcross said.

Quiet laughter and gentle smiles from the crowd, completely at odds with the previous murderous cheering.

"Recent surveys have shown more than fifty million humans are living in Iocaste." Longcross pushed a button in his hand and red dots popped up across the map. The biggest was over Iocaste Proper, but there was a thick smattering through the southern hills and into the salt marshes where the unSkilled did their salt mining. There were also dots throughout the Eastern Corridor, though not as concentrated.

"Here's our population. Fifty million people. Fifty million people live in an area of about a hundred thousand square miles. Doesn't seem too crowded right?"

There were a few shouts of agreement, but far more pursed lips and narrowed eyes. The audience suspected a trick question and waited for him to go on.

He clicked the button again, and the map of Iocaste was replaced by a map of the world.

The Badlands of the north continued until they became icy tundra before spiking into the unknowably high northern mountains called the Roof of the World. The salt marshes continued south turning into desert as it neared the equator and then lush jungle eventually becoming forests of different kinds before giving way to the ice of the south. To the east was the huge inland sea, the Grass Ocean, and the sprawling toxic jungle. Even before the Cataclysm that place had been a nightmare. No one who set foot under those trees ever returned.

Iocaste was a small little blip on the single giant continent that spanned the globe from pole to pole. That thin black line of the Border was all that separated Iocaste from the Wilds.

"This is the world," Longcross said quietly. "This is Oceanea."

He let everyone soak in the map before quietly asking, "How crowded do you feel now?"

Raid could feel the tension rising in the room. Fingers dug into armrests, people turned to neighbors and whispered or pointed furiously. Memes were held up as people took pictures of the map to send to friends who weren't present.

"When our Ancestors first came to Oceanea from the Moon, they spread across the globe. They built great cities."

The map faded away to reveal a series of pictures, one shifting into the next. Some were old, some were new. All of them were photographs of the Ancestor ruins that dotted the world. Architecture that could never be duplicated today.

"There are fifty million of us. Our Ancestors numbered fifty *billion*."

That number was a total and complete exaggeration, but it affected the crowd that Longcross had wanted.

Looks of wonder at what the Ancestors had built. Looks of hatred about what the Skilled had supposedly 'stolen' from them. People shaking their heads. People pointing at the screen. Jutting chins. Furrowed brows. The scent of excitement shifted more towards anger.

The series ended with an irritatingly well-known shot. A twisting spire of glass and metal that looked as new as the day it had been built rose from the coast of the inland sea. Trees grew thickly around its base, while vines made inroads up its length, but even after a thousand years, they hadn't even made it a quarter of the way up. Poking up out of the surrounding trees, and out of the placid, bright blue water of the sea, were more ruins, every building defying time, some even defying gravity with their bizarre shapes and architecture.

That picture had been taken by an adventure photographer nicknamed the Madman. unSkilled and yet somehow managing to slip back and forth across the Border without the Witch Angels ever knowing he was there. Worse, the asshole had survived multiple forays into the Wilds and wasn't dead yet. His remarkable survivability made the idiots in the crowd believe that they too could not only live beyond the Border but thrive there with their current lifestyles intact.

"Whichess Down. Dassi Cloud City. Arakator on the Waves." Longcross listed off some of the better-known pre-Cataclysmic metropolises. "Those were the days when humans ruled the world. These are the days of the kurs."

The spectacular ruins were replaced with a picture of a rundown apartment block with a large tent city beside it.

"That's not even our fault," Raid muttered sharply, unable to hold in his own anger.

Grants for new neighborhoods were constantly being approved. Resources were allocated to keep buildings like that from falling into disrepair and to keep unSkilled from living on the street. It was the unSkilled themselves who withheld it, sending lumber and ore off to some other rich high-rise rather than what it was meant for. As Longcross had so eloquently pointed out, there were a lot of unSkilled and the Houses couldn't micromanage every single one of them.

"They don't care," Li answered softly. He could feel the sadness in her.

He held her tightly, wishing he could do more. His Carnage Skills could defend and protect her, but comforting wasn't something that came naturally.

"I know I'm not the only one who sees the difference," Longcross murmured in response to the angry words and looks flickering through the crowd. "I've been where you are," he went on, looking out over the crowd, connecting with everyone sitting there. "This made me sad. This made me angry."

Heads were bobbing as he spoke.

"But then I learned something that gave me hope."

He paused.

Raid could feel the crowd hanging on Longcross's next words. Damn if he wasn't also hanging on Longcross's next words.

"Now I know you've all heard the story the kurs tell, that a thousand years ago the All-God of the Ancestors 'blessed' a human couple by becoming the third parent to their child. That that child was Soth, the first of the Skilled, and that he gave those Skills to his apostles, his 'Cohort.'"

The crowd nodded in agreement. Even the unSkilled knew the story of Soth.

"What would you think if I told you all that was a lie?"

Raid's eyes narrowed as he wondered where this was going.

"Discoveries are showing that the kurs were created by humans from the cellular level up. Grown in vats like livestock." He spoke those words so clearly they almost rang in the air. "I know, hard to believe. I didn't even believe it at first either but I've seen the proof, and soon you all will too. What you need to know is that the kurs were supposed to be our weapons, to help defend humanity from the Natives of Oceanea, but Soth led them astray. They've lost their way. They've forgotten who they serve and that their place is at our feet."

The truth of that story was so twisted up that Raid didn't know where to start.

When the Ancestors first came from the Moon, they'd found themselves utterly outmatched by the Natives that already lived here. Even Native plants wielded Skills, some of them rather terrifying. The All-God that had accompanied the Ancestors from the Moon had seen that they wouldn't last long, and so had given humanity their own set of Skills in the only way It knew how. Once Soth was grown, it became clear to him that a single person couldn't hold the line against the Natives, and so he'd gifted the Skills to his closest friends, the First Cohort who had then gone on to found the Houses.

The Skilled had always been weapons to defend humanity but not because they'd been built like some unSkilled device or bred and grown like camelids.

"A weapon will always be a weapon. It can't be turned into a plowshare. After Soth defeated the Natives, there was nothing more for the Skilled to fight, so they turned on the only people left, the people they served."

"What does he mean, 'defeat the Natives'? They're all still out there. That's the whole point of the Border." Raid's words were loud enough to draw not only Maggie and Jim's attention but also some of the people sitting in the back row. They glanced at him suspiciously, wondering who would dare to contradict Longcross.

Longcross himself hadn't heard and continued. "They'll tell you the Cataclysm was our fault. They'll tell you about plastics and pollution. Water kurs will talk your ear off about the great Panthalassa garbage patch and sea birds choking to death on bottle caps if you let them."

Dark chuckling from the crowd.

"Don't believe it. The Cataclysm was them. The kurs turned on our Ancestors and butchered them all. They decided that if they couldn't have the world, no one could."

"That doesn't even make sense," Raid said, this time only to Li.

But the audience lapped it up.

"Soth felt guilty afterward and brought the handful of survivors to Iocaste and tasked the surviving kurs with caring for them. It was meant to be a gentle stewardship until humanity regained its feet. An apology for their reckless arrogance. Guess what? That didn't happen. Humanity has been self-governing and ready to expand for hundreds of years. But kurs are kurs. Even with the mandates of Soth, they will not willingly give us the world. They will only allow us this tiny piece of it."

The Border darkened as he spoke, making Iocaste stand out more starkly.

"Since they will not give us the world, we must take it back ourselves. Are you ready to stand beside me and fight?"

Those words were met with such a resounding cheer that Raid's ears rang. Beside him Jim was shouting louder than anyone, his face lit up by some inner fire. Maggie gave him an approving look while she clapped hard for Longcross.

"Let's go," Li said. "Let's leave. Now."

Raid knew he should stay, listen to every last lie that Longcross spoke, and then follow him under a sight shield to see what else he might say or who else he would meet with, but Raid could also feel Li's anguish, a hurt so deep it could cut to the bone.

He stepped back toward the door, drawing her with him.

Maggie and Jim were so engrossed in the speech that neither saw them leave.

Behind him, Raid heard Longcross announce that the unSkilled outnumbered the Skilled five hundred to one. Raid wanted to spit back that there was a difference between being outnumbered and being outmatched. Having higher numbers just meant that many more body bags when it came to a fight. Then they stepped out into the warm spring air, leaving behind the crowd of unSkilled watching Longcross with their avid eyes.

□

Chapter Seven

Maggie Reeves

Doctor Longcross spoke for almost two hours. Maggie didn't notice the time pass. Everything he said resonated deeply with her. Born the daughter of a logger, she had grown up under the injustice of the kurs. Her father had taken her into the forests many times and shown her the huge old-growth trees that would create much needed lumber. Instead, the kurs let people go homeless or restricted birth numbers to protect their precious trees.

Li's mother, the botanist, had also taken her into the forest. She had talked about the interconnectedness of nature and how those great trees had served as protectors and nurturers of the small shade plants and sapling trees whose roots were too shallow for them to survive alone without nutrients being passed to them through the roots of those old mother trees. Maggie's memory of the woman's soothing voice tempered her anger. More needed to be taken into consideration than just what Longcross was saying.

Maggie turned to Li to comment about it and found her best friend gone, along with Raid. Maggie's memory of the nature walks with Li and Li's mother instantly soured.

Maggie tried hard to like Raid for Li's sake but just couldn't. A mutual friend had recently said Maggie didn't like him because he took Li's time away from her, but that wasn't true. Maggie wasn't jealous of Raid, there was just something off about him. He wasn't good enough for Li.

She stewed on that until Longcross finished speaking. He promised hope. He hinted at big changes coming.

"The kurs will tell you that Soth 'Squared the Earth' and

remade the world in their favor. Now's the time for us to square it in ours."

The whole auditorium was on their feet clapping and cheering. Maggie would have leaped up if she hadn't already been standing. She clapped until her palms hurt.

Beside her Jim did the same.

Maggie glanced at him and almost did a double take. He stood straighter and taller than she'd seen in a long time. The chronic cringe in his face was gone. Here was the Jim Dawes she remembered from before he'd been told to get sober or be fired.

"I'm going to talk to him," Jim said, starting for the stage.

Maggie followed in his wake as he easily cut through the thronging crowd. He didn't even pause when reaching the stage, just vaulted up it as if stepping up a curb.

"Staff Detective Jim Dawes, Ashveil PD," he said, holding out his hand.

Longcross shook it, barely phased by Jim's sudden appearance. His assistant, a woman in a sharp charcoal gray suit wearing rainbow reflective ski goggles, seemed more put out. She took a step forward to intervene before Longcross waved her back.

"It's fine Bunny," he said.

She stepped back but Maggie recognized her stance. The woman knew how to fight. She was a bodyguard as much as a personal assistant.

"Detective," Longcross went on approvingly with a glance also at Maggie. "Both of you?"

"Volunteer Detective Maggie Reeves," she said quickly, holding out her hand. "I own and teach at the Black Dragonfly Dojo. I think it's important that people know how to defend themselves."

Longcross nodded along as she spoke, and said, "I do too," when she finished.

Warmth spread through her chest at his approval.

"I was at Ceres," Jim said abruptly.

The confession startled Maggie. It was an open secret that he'd been there, but she'd never heard him talk about it before even when someone else brought it up. Not drunk and certainly not sober.

Longcross's face went grim. "That was one of the greatest tragedies of our time."

"It wouldn't have happened if you'd been there," Jim went on. "If True Human had existed back then."

"We can't change the past but we can build a better future. Come with me, I have some ideas about what you can do for Ashveil."

Maggie's heart leapt with the chance to keep talking to Longcross, that he'd singled her out for his ideas. She wanted to see Ashveil safe. She didn't want any of her students to be terrorized the way she had been when she was young. She glanced at Jim. He seemed just as set not to see Ashveil become another Ceres.

Longcross wrapped up a few last things, then the three of them along with Ava Biner and the rest of the True Human board members headed out together. They ended up at Ava's neatly kept two-story house in Ashveil's newer neighborhood over towards the edge of town. Her youngest child had left for university this year, leaving Ava as the sole occupant. She pulled out water cartons and sodas for everyone and passed them around while everyone settled on couches and chairs.

Longcross's assistant Bunny disappeared down the hall, sweeping through every room before heading upstairs.

Ava made brief introductions all around for Longcross's benefit. The rest of them already knew each other.

Rory Kendrik at seventeen was the youngest, a senior in high school and determined to help build a better world before heading off to university in the fall.

Max Riddell was the president of the logger's union and had been a long-time friend of Maggie's dad before he'd passed away. Max had been outspoken against the kurs in general and Viridae in particular long before True Human had entered the scene. He'd joined up thinking the two groups could help each other out.

Maggie knew Cari Cooper from the board of education. She had six kids ranging in age from four to fifteen, all of whom were signed up in Maggie's classes. The two of them were in agreement that the kids needed a better future, and that the best way to secure that was to get rid of the kurs.

"Thank you all for having me," Longcross said when Ava

finished. "And thank you all for being invested in the cause of True Human."

"True Human offers the future our kids deserve," Cari answered firmly.

Maggie nodded in agreement.

Longcross smiled. "I'm glad you think so. People tell me how fantastic I am for founding True Human, but all I do is talk. What really matters are the people like you, the ones who listen, because there is a great deal that still needs to be done, and it's not something that I can do alone."

Maggie listened avidly – they all did – as he expanded on some of the things he'd hinted at in the larger meeting. Historic records had been uncovered proving beyond a doubt that the kurs had been genetically engineered as weapons to fight the Natives. The Ancestors' plan had always been to spread across the face of Oceanea. When the kurs rebelled, the Natives took advantage of the discord. The ensuing Cataclysm resulted in humanity being set back thousands of years. Even now with all the modern advancements, humans still hadn't reclaimed the level of technology that had been lost.

"What good is a weapon if it doesn't have a safety? Or a kill-switch?" Jim complained darkly, for once not anxiously flipping his sobriety coin between his knuckles.

Longcross leaned forward at that comment, eyes intense but a growing smile on his face. "That's the thing," he said. "They do."

Maggie could have heard a pin drop the room became so silent, everyone holding their breath for what Longcross would say next.

"There is a way to stop them, to turn them back from the rabid wolves they've become to the obedient guard dogs they're meant to be."

That was an outcome Maggie had never thought about. Kurs that were tractable. Kurs that were trustworthy. Maybe not trustworthy – even the best dogs could still bite – but obedient, respectful and law-abiding. Actual laws, not the vaguely sketched-out Protocol they cared so much about.

No child would suffer the fate of the children at Ceres.

No child would see what she had seen that day in the dojo all those years ago.

They would be safe. Everyone would be safe. For the first time in a long time, Maggie felt like the world could be a better place.

□

Chapter Eight

Raid

Ashveil was by no means a large town, but twenty thousand residents was large enough. Li bicycled everywhere she needed to go, but tonight she left the bike chained to the rack, and Raid gave her a ride home with his motorcycle. That was one thing the unSkilled had figured out that the Skilled couldn't copy with Skills alone, driving at speed with the wind in his face.

When he'd first moved to Ashveil he'd taken the trolley like any good unSkilled, but it had been too much. Standing in a crowded moving box being physically jostled by the unSkilled while his psychic sense told him they didn't exist had been too disorienting. As soon as he'd discovered motorcycles with their battery-operated engines, he'd bought one, escaping the torture of the daily commute.

Li lived on the outskirts of Ashveil, right against the carefully tended forest that belonged to House Viridae. They oversaw the licensing of individual unSkilled who wanted to go into the forest and practice their own harvesting, as well as supervising what could be harvested where and when for the big companies that didn't want to bother with the training Viridae demanded.

Li's house was a neat little cottage with both its front and back porchs filled with potted plants that couldn't go into the massive garden out back. Branches from the old-growth trees stretched over the fence, offering shade to the plants that needed it. Closer to the house was all sun, perfect for the plants that didn't.

Li wasn't strong enough to shield her house, so instead she had friendly little charms at the doors and windows that would cheerfully alert her if something was amiss. They wouldn't stop even the weakest Skilled and gave Li only the briefest heads up. Raid had started putting up his shields as soon as he'd started visiting her and had put up wards as well until she asked him to take them down. Defensive shields she didn't mind, but she didn't want the offensive wards harming someone accidentally.

Her arm around his waist tightened as they walked to the porch, and she murmured, "Will you stay tonight?"

"Yes." He wanted nothing more.

Inside her house smelled like plants and growing things. More importantly, it smelled like her. Her scent filled this place, sank into crevices in the hardwood, and filled every nook and cranny. He took a deep breath, and the feeling of love and goodwill suffused him. He wanted his scent to mingle with hers, so anyone who came here would know she wasn't alone.

Li didn't bother with the electric lights and lit a handful of candles instead before putting the kettle on to boil. She'd left her shoes in the entryway and now tucked her feet up on a kitchen chair, her chin resting on her knees. Candlelight flickered over her features. Her eyes were miles away.

He stretched out in one of the other chairs and tried to let go of some of the tension this night had brought. He hesitated for a second before unclasping the concealing shield charm. She told him before that she preferred to see him as he was and not toned down for unSkilled sensibilities, but after that meeting, maybe she didn't want to be reminded that he was Carnage, born and bred. He finally pulled it off anyway, slipping it into his pocket.

"Is there any truth to what they're saying?" she finally asked softly.

"No," he answered flatly.

"They're good people…" she faltered

"They would kill you if they knew you were Viridae," he said more harshly than he meant. "They would kill us all if they could."

She flinched and the unhappiness in her eyes deepened. These were people she had grown up with, people she saw every day. She sold soothing teas for their colicky children and tinctures for their grandmothers' aching joints. They were friends, neighbors, cordial strangers, all of them pleasant to her only because they didn't know she was Skilled.

"Longcross was right about some things, the world was theirs up until the Cataclysm, and look what they did to it," Raid went on. In creche, he'd learned about the Ancestors. They'd built their wondrous cities, but it had come with a price. Thousand-year-old plastic was still washing up on beaches and poisoning sea life. The wrecks of deep-sea oil rigs constantly leaked toxins into the ocean. House of Water managed them as best they could because no Earth was willing to dive so deep to permanently rearrange the seafloor where the unSkilled had damaged it. Scouts from all the Houses traveled out into the Wilds to keep track of the ruined cities to make sure nothing was about to collapse and explode, or secretly leeching toxins into the ground as ancient containment systems broke down.

"But do the unSkilled need to be licensed?" she asked quietly. "Do they need to be culled? Carnage..." She trailed off and looked away from him.

"Carnage doesn't cull anyone unSkilled." Despite the current pop culture trends. The Skilled – Carnage especially – were always the villains in the media dramas.

She looked back at him, and he could see the doubt in her eyes.

"You know the nature of Carnage Skills," he said, a little stung by her look. "Untrained part-bloods are dangerous." Born with the predatory instincts of Carnage, but without the training that came with growing up in the creche. Eventually, they all turned on their neighbors or their family.

"The unSkilled can deal with the unSkilled, but Carnage deals with Carnage," he said. Anyone they culled was a member of their House, even if it didn't seem so from the outside. "The part-bloods can't be left to run amok."

"Like me?" she asked unhappily. "Would you cull me?"

"You aren't Carnage," he answered.

Her look was still unhappy.

The kettle started to sing.

She stood up and poured the boiling water into mugs. Immediately the room filled with the aroma of loose-leaf tea of her own devising.

"Viridae cares for its part-bloods. So does Bone and Animachea," he pointed out. They were the Houses whose instincts weren't as lethal. The Enforcers had turned out in force to defend Mountain Village and the part-bloods and low aughts who chose to live there. "They won't cull you."

She handed him his mug but didn't sit back down. "There's just… no place for us," she said quietly. "The people tonight…" From the stricken look in her eyes, he guessed she was thinking about Maggie specifically. "They would kill me if they knew."

He'd said that exact thing a few moments ago but it killed him a little now to hear her say it.

"But the Houses don't want us either," she went on. "We're not strong enough. We'd be a liability on the Mountain."

She spoke true, not that it made him like it any better.

He set his tea aside, and hers, and pulled her into his arms. "You're fine here. This place loves you, even if the people don't."

A short, watery laugh escaped her lips, and she pressed her face into his chest. "This place…"

"Go outside and say that your garden doesn't love you. That those trees beyond your fence don't love you." He could practically hear the plants singing every time she went out into her garden. Her teas and tinctures worked so well because her plants loved her and always produced their best.

They sat there and he listened to their heartbeats. He could taste and feel her thoughts, but she was too weak for him to share them. If he tried, he'd burn out her mind which happened whenever Skilled tried to connect with unSkilled using more than spoken words or just the lightest thoughtspeak. He didn't need to hear her thoughts though, he could feel her body relaxing against him, her breath evening, her scent calming.

"Will you Square the Earth with me?" she asked quietly.

'Yes' was on the tip of his tongue but he bit it back.

Squaring the Earth took place on the spring equinox, starting with the dawn and lasting through to the following morning. It was the time when all the Skilled came together as one. No matter their aught rank or House affiliation they were all there, from the youngest infants on the hips of the creche nannies to the eldest of the elders, their Skills often holding up their frail bodies. It was a day they all remembered Soth and his sacrifice to the world. It was also the reminder that despite their differences, the Skilled were all still the children of Soth. Crippling injury or illness was the only excuse the Matriarchs would accept for missing the day that commemorated when Soth remade the world.

"Tomorrow," she added quickly when he didn't answer.

"Tomorrow? The equinox isn't for two more days."

"And you'll be on the Mountain for it." Her dark eyes searched his. "Soth remade the world, and you remade mine. Please?"

His heart skipped a beat at her words. He kissed her. "Yes."

He would celebrate with her, just the two of them. They would Square the Earth together and remake their corner of the world into something better and brighter.

"Yes," he said again. For Li, it would always be yes.

Her arms curled around him. One slid under his shirt and jacket, her fingers coming to rest just beneath the knife sheath on his back.

She nipped his bottom lip and whispered, "Remind me that I'm not alone tonight."

"You will never be alone." Not if he could help it. Then together they moved to the bedroom, and he proved it to her.

—

<Where the fuck are you?>

The angry demand had Raid bolt awake in a second. Shit. Beside him Li was asleep and content, the worry of earlier smoothed from her face. Careful not to wake her, he slipped out from between the sheets and jumped in the shower, scouring himself raw with the most floral-smelling soap she had. It made his eyes water it smelled so strong.

<Coming,> Raid answered.

<The High Inquisitor is paying for this apartment for you.

Why aren't you in it?>

<Something came up.>

He could feel Mordred dripping with scorn.

Raid toweled off and pulled on his scattered clothing. He could still smell Li on him, but he could explain that away as just spending time in her general vicinity.

Thank Soth Ashveil was small. This time of night it only took a few minutes to cut across town to his apartment.

It was a small place, good for one person. He hadn't spent much time decorating because he'd been told the assignment wasn't long-term. By the time he realized he was going to be in Ashveil a lot longer than expected, he'd already met Li and wasn't spending enough time in the apartment to care about the décor, much less put in the time and effort to decorate in a way that would be acceptable to the unSkilled. It had come furnished, and the only part of it that was personal to him were the shields and wards he'd wrapped around the apartment itself, the building, and the grounds. They were set to alert him to strangers who didn't normally pass through them. They should have told him Mordred was coming before Mordred was there, standing in Raid's living room, looking pissed.

Raid pulled up short when he saw him.

Even the unSkilled who couldn't have used the psychic scent as a marker would have known a predator as soon as they laid eyes on him. Mordred was every inch the nightmare they thought of when they thought of Carnage. He was all lean muscle and lethal grace with the blood-red eyes of Carnage the unSkilled found so disconcerting.

Tonight he dressed as an Inquisitor. The high-collared jacket and pants looked black, only highlights from the sun would show it was dark, dark red. No knives were visible on him because Mordred would call his blades in with his Skills if he needed them.

As weird as it was to think of Mordred as an Inquisitor, that wasn't what had Raid wary. Mordred had always been the strongest of the four of them, but not by a lot. He was still a Five, just a few shades stronger than Raid. He shouldn't have been able to get in without tripping the wards, but a quick review of them showed they were all content and had nothing to report. That was different, and wrong-footed Raid enough that he fell back into the safety of formality.

<Welcome. Your visit is unexpected.>

Mordred scowled at him at the use of formal grammar and speech patterns. <Where were you?>

<Away.>

<Cut the shit. You reek of her. Are you even doing your damn assignment?>

Shit. <Yes,> Raid answered shortly. <There was a meeting a few hours ago. Longcross was involved. You were going to get a report about it later today.>

<After a romp in the garden with a Viridae?> Mordred sneered.

Shit! Shit shit shit. <She has nothing to do with this,> he said tensely.

<She has everything to do with this! You're off task and distracted! She's going to get you killed!>

Mordred didn't move but was suddenly looming. Raid took a half step back, knives in hand without a second thought. Not that they would do him any good, Mordred had always been the better fighter as well as being the stronger rank, but the weight of them in Raid's hands made him feel better.

Mordred's eyes narrowed as he took in Raid's shifted weight and knives.

<Fuck you. You're not going to be harmed,> Mordred snapped.

At the moment, Raid wasn't that sure, and he certainly wasn't going to trust Li's wellbeing to Mordred. To this Mordred. When had he become an Inquisitor? Inquisitors had to be Seven aughts at least.

<Have you talked to Cain?> Mordred said sullenly when Raid didn't answer,

<Not recently. He's too far away to reach by thoughtspeak.> There were limits to how far they could speak to each other. The stronger the rank, the farther the reach, but Cain was in Daal, a ski resort town tucked up into the high valleys of the Ice Whites, a good long way from the temperate forest surrounding Ashveil. <Why?>

<Because he's dead.>

The air sucked from the room and Raid's heart felt like it had been banded with iron. He couldn't form words, he couldn't even breathe. The horror and the question of what had happened swirled around him in a mild psychic storm.

<Don't know what happened,> Mordred answered, his façade cracking enough that Raid could tell his creche brother was barely holding it together. His scorn and anger masked his fear. He'd come to deliver terrible news only to find Raid gone also.

<How do you know he's dead then?> Raid asked, the words only finding traction because he wanted another explanation.

<The Enforcers brought his body back to the Mountain. They found him in a well a block from here.>

<Here?> That sent a jolt through Raid. <Why was he in Ashveil?>

<Looking for you,> Mordred answered sharply. <Why else would he come?>

<He never said anything.> Raid dredged through his memory. Their last conversation hadn't been any different than others. Complaints about how awful it was to live among the unSkilled. Wondering what they'd done to offend Mordred enough that he'd landed them these shit assignments. <He never mentioned coming. He never said anything to you?>

While Raid and Cain hadn't been talking much to each other, Mordred had been in touch with both of them, collecting their reports and giving back specific orders when he had them.

Mordred shook his head. He looked lost. <No. Nothing.>

The silence stretched as Raid tried to remember anything Cain might have said that could have meant something. He'd talked about his weekend backpacking trips. Cain had dealt with the unSkilled by getting as far away from them as much as possible while still carrying out reconnaissance.

<And you don't know what happened,> Raid repeated.

Mordred shook his head. <The Enforcers pulled him out of a well. He'd been in there awhile.>

Raid grimaced, trying not to think about what state Cain had been in when he was found. <Did you check the well yourself?>

<Thought we could together,> Mordred said carefully as if

bracing himself for Raid to reject the notion out of hand.

Raid nodded woodenly in response.

He felt frozen inside as they walked silently down the street. He'd walked or ridden past this park a hundred times. It was more than close enough that Raid would have heard him if Cain had called out. So why hadn't he?

The park was in shadows, both moons having already set for the night. Raid sharpened his vision to see through the gloom. The psychic scent left by the Animachea Enforcers had faded but was still fresh enough. They'd just been here this morning while he'd been out doing road work, part of a construction crew helping improve the tracks of the rail line that snaked through the Eastern Corridor, connecting all its small towns. Still, even that far away he would have been close enough to hear Cain.

The scent of the Enforcers led straight to the well Mordred had mentioned. The smell of decay hung heavy on it. Raid felt sick. That was Cain. That rot was all that was left of him. Raid opened his senses and took a better feel for the well and the area surrounding it.

The Animachea had been here. Below their scent, older and faded to almost nothing, was Cain's. Raid could sense no details other than that. If he hadn't known Cain as well as he did, he wouldn't have known even that much.

<Can you sense anything?> Raid asked.

Mordred shook his head, likewise coming up empty.

Without speaking they circled out from the well, looking for any clue about what had happened to Cain and why he'd ended up here.

The smells they found were all expected, sunscreen and snacks, excitement and play. There were no footprints to find or trail to follow, everything had been crossed and recrossed too many times. That didn't stop them from looking, hoping that something important would suddenly leap out at them. They found nothing. Whatever had happened to Cain had been obliterated by the mundane activities of the unSkilled.

<Will he be sung back to the land?> Raid asked, his voice too loud in the long and heavy silence.

<He already has been,> Mordred answered.

Raid felt hurt. <Already?>

<There wasn't time to get you.>

<The Carriage ride is what, twenty minutes?> Raid snapped. <Bullshit you didn't have time.>

<You weren't there,> Mordred snarled. <And if you'd been paying attention at all, none of this would have happened! Cain came here for you! How did you miss him?>

<And if you hadn't thrown us both off the Mountain, this wouldn't have happened either!> Raid shot back. <You dropped us out here with the unSkilled and just left us to figure it out! Which we did. Without your help.>

And just like that his creche brother was gone and he was facing down a pissed-off Inquisitor again. <If you can't stay on task, the Viridae distraction will be removed so you can focus.> Then in the blink of an eye, Mordred was gone with a shift of displaced air.

Raid made a half-strangled noise.

Mordred had just jumped between places. That terrified Raid far more than the threat. Mordred had never been strong enough to make a jump. Strong Sixes could sometimes do it, but it was a Skill only found in higher aughts.

Children were born with their Skills and their Skillsets continued to grow and develop until their late teens when they settled. The rank a man had at that point was the rank he stayed at. Women increased their rank again after menopause, their bodies shifting from childbearing to defense and leadership in their Houses, often gaining another rank or two in their fifties and sixties.

Mordred had settled as a strong Five. He had been settled for years. Where in the Inkwell was this now coming from?

Raid ran his hands through his hair.

Mordred couldn't be getting stronger. That just… didn't happen.

Something had been going on though. Mordred snuck up on him tonight, and he'd done it before just not so blatantly. Even way back when this assignment first started Mordred had managed to get the drop on him in the Toxic Garden at the Arboretum.

<Shit.>

His first instinct was to go to Cain and pour out all his concerns but that couldn't happen. That would never happen again.

Raid turned his back on the well, feeling sick.

He had no one. Not one of these thousands of unSkilled paper dolls that surrounded him would give even the first shit about Cain. They would all just cheer, the way they'd been cheering for the deaths at Mountain Village.

Raid pinched his eyes closed as he realized just how incredibly stupid he was. Hadn't he just told Li that she would never be alone? That sentiment went both ways. She would care that Cain was dead. She would care that Raid hadn't been there for him. She would… probably have no idea about Mordred, but Li had the patience of the ancient trees. She would listen and she would understand.

No matter what happened with Mordred and Cain, Raid would always have Li. He would never be alone.

Chapter Nine

Raid

Raid made it back before Li ever knew he was gone but when she woke up the next morning, she could still tell something was wrong.

She propped herself up on an elbow and studied him. "Do you want to talk about it?" she asked softly.

"Cain's dead," he said, speaking the words that had been rattling around in his mind since Mordred told him.

She sucked in a sharp breath, her eyes going wide with surprise before crumpling with concern. "I'm so sorry. What happened?" As she spoke her Skills unfurled, reaching for him like a friendly cloud, present and reassuring.

He pulled her close and she curled up against him. She felt warm and vibrant and alive. He listened to her steady heartbeat for a moment before telling her about the night before.

Mordred's unexpected visit and even less expected news. Neither of them had any idea what had happened or why. How there was no useful information around the well that would tell them even where they could start looking.

"The well in Temple Park?" Li asked after he finished.

He made a sound of agreement. "The one down the street from the apartment."

"That well has been dry my entire life," she murmured. "Maggie and I used to pretend it was an entrance to the Mountain. One time we secretly borrowed Callum's ladder from the dojo so we could climb down to the bottom."

"How'd that turn out?" he asked because he'd rather hear stories about Li's life than dwell on what had happened to Cain.

"We lost the ladder. The well was a lot deeper than we thought and the ladder went crashing all the way to the bottom," she answered lightly. "We never did tell Callum what happened, though I think he suspected."

A peaceful quiet descended between them. Li traced random patterns across his bare chest with her fingertips, her Skill trailing behind her touch, gentle as the caress of a new blossom.

"Do you know why Cain was here?" she asked softly.

"No idea," he said, but several scenarios had churned through his head last night when he couldn't sleep. Cain could have been killed somewhere else and his body dumped, but who had killed him and why the well? If someone Skilled had wanted to hide the body, there would have been no body to be found; Cain simply would have disappeared. If the unSkilled were doing it, even they had better methods of disposal than tossing him into a well.

If Cain's death was meant to send a message, again, why the well? Why not dump him at the apartment or one of Raid's work sites? That would have certainly grabbed his attention. It was too haphazard to leave him in the well and hope the body was found and identified.

More likely Cain had come to Ashveil himself, but why not tell Raid? They may not have been able to reach each other with thought-speak between Ashveil and Daal, but Cain certainly would have been able to reach Raid once he was on the bullet train and heading east. He could have even used one of those stupid unSkilled memes to make a call.

Raid had had a paralyzing moment of dread last night when he realized Cain might have reached out and Raid had simply missed it. The relief was so sharp it hurt once he saw he had no missed calls or messages. Cain hadn't died because Raid had been too disdainful to answer his meme.

"Cain probably came here on his own," Raid said, giving his thoughts a voice. "But he never said he was coming."

"He has friends in Daal, right?" Li asked. "Maybe he said something to them before he left."

"Not sure if they're friends," Raid answered.

Cain's assignment had been the same as Raid's in that he was supposed to learn what he could about True Human, but Daal was a resort town, its population increasing by tenfold through the winter months. Cain was supposed to tag the names of anyone with strong True Human leanings and gather statistics about those who came to the True Human events that the Daal chapter hosted.

"Most of them he knew through True Human." Just like most of the people Raid knew were True Human members, and those that weren't – like the other men on his work crew – he wouldn't count as friends. They would talk, and share drinks occasionally, but Raid would never trust them the same way he trusted Li.

"What about Mordred?" she asked. "He came last night to tell you. He'll want to know what happened too, won't he?"

"He'll want to know…" Raid agreed. But wanting to know wasn't the issue. Mordred was now an Inquisitor. Mordred had gained aught ranks somehow. Mordred was changing and Raid wasn't sure it was for the better.

"But?" Li prompted softly when he trailed off.

"Mordred's not that approachable." He used to be, but then Nico had died and Mordred had become both far more protective of Raid and Cain, and far more distant. Last night he'd been downright frightening. "What did you and Maggie plan to do once you made it to the Mountain?" he asked, wanting to think about something softer than Cain being dead and Mordred being… whatever was going on with him.

"Gain Skills," Li answered, letting him change the subject.

"You have Skills," Raid pointed out.

"Real Skills. To be able to grow a plant with a gesture." She stopped tracing his skin and flicked her fingers elegantly in example. "Maggie wanted to be a Fire."

"That fits." He could picture her conjuring flames and slinging lightning.

"We had these old necklaces of her mom's, costume jewelry. We would pretend they were talismans that we retrieved from the Mountain in a grand adventure and that they gave us all sorts of Skills."

Raid caught her hand while she spoke and kissed her palm,

then her wrist. "Do you wish you were stronger?" he asked.

She stilled at the question, and he felt her Skills withdraw from him. "It was a game back then, with Maggie. As we got older though… I wished the Skills would go away. I didn't like the way the plants called to me. I just wanted to be normal, not the kid who came to school every day with dirt under her nails, getting snagged on every passing branch because the leaves wanted to say hi."

"You never said that before," Raid murmured, his heart hurting for young Li.

She shrugged. "That was years ago. Now? Now I do wish I was stronger. Strong enough to live on the Mountain, strong enough for Viridae to intervene on my behalf."

"They would anyway," he protested.

"They wouldn't," she answered with a sigh. "To them, I'm just a cute kid growing a tomato in a bucket."

"Carnage would," Raid said fiercely. More to the point, he would. Carnage would then either have to back his actions or cut him loose. Regardless, he would still be with Li.

She gave him a soft smile with a wicked edge that soothed his heart and sent pleasurable shivers down his skin. He traced her cheek with the back of his hand before lacing his fingers through her hair and pulling her close.

She kissed him chastely and said, "Are we still going to Square the Earth this morning?"

"We have time," he answered, kissing her back more thoroughly. His work shift didn't start until this afternoon and Li's job with the co-op involved checking and assessing the community gardens, something that could be done any time of the day so long as it got done.

He could feel her smile against his skin. Her Skills like a balm flowed over him, building connection while easing heartache and loneliness.

Cain was dead, and the path that led from that would be dark and bloody. Raid chose to enjoy this moment of unconditional warmth and attachment, and not think about the fact that it may be the last such moment for a while.

"I think your right," she said, shifting her body to straddle him. "Soth would understand."

Li deepened the kiss and Raid focused on nothing but her.

—

It was late morning by the time they finally made it out of bed. A late start for Li who was often up with the dawn, but still early for Raid who was nocturnal by nature.

On the Mountain, Squaring the Earth started within each House, honoring their individual founder. For Carnage, that was Rejo. The Skills Soth gifted her augmented her innate abilities. She had already been fierce and strong and proficient in combat. Her new Skills turned her knives into an extension of herself. She became faster, stronger, and stealthier. She defended Soth against all comers and had argued adamantly to accompany him when he went to confront the unNamed that dwelled within the Devil's Inkwell. She had been rebuffed. All of the First Cohort had been. Soth had insisted on facing the unNamed alone so that the rest of the Skilled would survive. As long as they lived, they would be able to protect the unSkilled and help rebuild the civilization that had been lost.

When the official Squaring the Earth took place, Raid would be within Carnage, running a gauntlet of combat matches and tests to recreate the trials Rejo had faced so long ago. He would meditate on her strength and sacrifice while being left bruised and bloody by other members of the House.

Once the sun set, they would go down to the Grand Plaza where all the Skilled from every House would gather and celebrate Soth himself and the full story of his life until the sun came up the next morning. Here in Li's garden, she recreated Viridae's tribute to their founder Undomiel.

She walked barefoot out into the sunlight and danced.

It reminded Raid of a new shoot breaking through the crust of soil to stretch to the sun, of the great mother trees that anchored the forest with their roots and protected the smaller shade plants with their boughs. There were the sharp edges of poisons and thorns and strangling vines, but there was also the harvest. Viridae didn't have the flashy awe-inspiring Skills as some of the other Houses, but they were the roots and the boughs that kept everyone else from starving.

Undomiel hadn't argued to stand beside Soth as he fought the unNamed. Instead, Undomiel had promised to offer aid to Skilled and unSkilled alike, whenever they would need it. Soth's sacrifice to defeat the unNamed would not be in vain. The people he died for would be protected.

Her dance then shifted from tribute to Undomiel to reverence for Soth. This part of the dance Raid had seen before, performed by the best dancers within Viridae in the Grand Plaza for everyone to admire.

Soth fought the unNamed and won but the cost was his own life. Before he died though, he Squared the Earth, lining up the edges and snipping away the ragged tails. When he finished, this small piece of the world that he carved out for the humans was stable and safe. As long as the Houses stood, Iocaste would be protected.

Squaring the Earth, when the world was remade for the third time.

The third time when Soth remade it to be whole again.

The second time when the Cataclysm remade it in anger.

The first time when the Ancestors came from the Moon and remade it in their image.

Li finished her dance, arms raised to embrace Oceanea's moons and heavens. She didn't have the poise and precision of Viridae's professional dancers, but to Raid, she was far more interesting and lovely.

"That was beautiful," he said.

She turned to him, pleased and smiling. "Come scatter the seeds with me," she said.

She had a basket full of seeds, a portion of everything she had harvested throughout the year before. Raid followed her through her garden and out the back fence into the forest beyond. He scattered the seeds where she told him, listening to her stories about what each plant was and what it could do once it grew.

In Viridae after Squaring the Earth, they scattered seeds for the following harvest. In Carnage he would be nursing the lacerations and maybe broken bones he'd received while running the gauntlet.

"Do you ever think the world will be remade for a fourth time?" she asked as they reached a glade and the end of their seed scattering.

"Yes," Raid answered.

She lifted her eyebrows at his immediate reply.

"We say that Soth remade the world to be whole, but he didn't. Only Iocaste was Squared. House of Water is still out at sea, undoing the damage caused by the Ancestors. When they finish in their tasks, they'll have remade the world for the fourth time."

"I like that idea," she said, climbing up onto a fallen tree trunk and using it as a path to walk out into the glade.

"What do you think will happen?" he asked, catching the smallest edge in her voice as he followed her.

"The unSkilled want to remake the world." The tall grass around them grew directly out of knee-deep water. This glade had been a pond once and was now slowly filling in as the forest crept in at the edges. "You saw the map last night. What would happen if Longcross Squared the Earth so it only lined up for unSkilled?"

"Oceanea would quickly be remade for a fifth time as the Natives came over the Border and reclaimed all the human land," Raid answered.

Li's eyes were shadowed even though she stood in the bright sun. "There isn't a way this ends well," she said softly.

"Longcross will never be able to remake the world," Raid replied bluntly. "He can make as many maps as he wants, spew whatever hate he wants. He'll never be able to take down the Mountain no matter what he says about us being 'built.'"

Even if Animachea's Enforcers completely dropped the ball on Skilled-unSkilled relations, the Inquisitors were there, the high aughts, the Matriarchs. The unSkilled couldn't get anywhere near the Houses without setting off alarms and wards. They'd be dead before they could take two steps into any offensive campaign.

Their so-called triumph at Mountain Village was proof of that. The unSkilled congratulated themselves on the twelve part-bloods they'd killed without thinking about the high aughts that were now hunting them down. There would be consequences for what had happened to Mountain Village.

Just like there would be consequences for what had happened to Cain. Whoever had killed him was already dead, Raid just hadn't caught up with them yet.

The shadow he'd been holding back fell heavily across his heart, and he couldn't find any more words to tell Li it was going to be alright. Instead, he took her hand, offering what little reassurance he could through the gesture. She squeezed his fingers back in response but they both stood there in the sun, lost in their own dark thoughts.

Chapter Ten

SalNavari

Not all physical wounds fully declared the extent of their injury until after some time had passed. The same held true for psychic wounds. The morning following Navari's visit to Carnage she couldn't stand. The whole room rocked around her as she lay in bed. Light hurt. Sound hurt. Her memories felt swollen and like they'd been knocked loose from their mooring. Matriarch Katio's carelessness had inflicted more serious damage than either of them had first realized.

Navari could feel Salasi speaking urgently to Command.

Command lodged a complaint with the Bonded Matriarchs of Animachea – the only people who could censure another Matriarch – and sent healers to see to Navari. The healers in turn requested the presence of a Bone Body Walker. All Houses had their own healers, but Bone's Skillsets focused primarily on healing.

Navari could feel the Body Walker Skills slipping through her mind and from Salasi, could feel another Body Walker checking her over as well. They soothed the worst of her symptoms and urged her to rest. What Matriarch Katio had done did not appear permanent, but it would take time before she was on her feet again.

Unfortunately, all Enforcers were needed to aid with the mess that was Mountain Village. Any other time other Houses would have volunteered aid, but they were all busy with their preparations for Squaring the Earth. Navari would be allowed to rest, but Salasi could still stand, and any extra hands would be put to work. Her protests were brushed aside, and she was sent to Mountain Village to help.

Mountain Village was one of Iocaste Proper's many, small neighborhoods. The quaint cottages and villas had been constructed along the beach and extended several blocks inland. An elegant wall surrounded it on three sides with three archways for entrances, one towards the city, and the other two bracketing the boardwalk along the beach. There was no fourth wall, just the town looking out on the beach and the ocean itself.

The most basic wards had been woven into the wall. All they could do was strongly urge those with ill intent to head in a different direction. For one or two people looking to stir up trouble, such simple wards were fine, but they had quickly collapsed under the weight of the protest. Salasi could feel the last tattered remnants of them as she walked past a sizable broken chunk where the wall had been torn down.

Like the wall, the buildings were in ruins. Windows and doors had been smashed with equal abandon. Lovely, decorative fountains were cracked and full of trash. The plants in every garden and window box had been yanked out by the handful, thrown on the ground, and stomped on. Anything that could be spray painted had been. TRUE HUMAN RULES and FUCK KURS glared down at her from all angles. A few more intricate paintings depicting Skilled being shot or strung up by their heels from trees flashed here or there. Those artists had felt safe enough to take their time with the details while Mountain Village was being mutilated around them.

Multiple houses and stores were scorched and blackened where fires had started and failed to take hold. All of Mountain Village from the beach front to the edge of each wall belonged Shapash. As a Four aught Fire, she had stopped the whole place from going up in smoke, but she hadn't been able to stop all the damage.

With Navari as ill as she was, and her injury seeping through to Salasi, Command assigned her to simply catalog the damage. A higher-ranked Enforcer gave her a pen and clipboard, and a meme to take photographic evidence of what she described, before pointing out which buildings she needed to review, and leaving her to work.

Salasi ran her Skills over the walls of the beach house, feeling for weaknesses and instability. All the windows were smashed, and the door had been ripped from its hinges, but the structure itself was stable.

In Navari's dreams, she walked down an endless path surrounded by radial roses. Their fractal symmetry pulled at her, encouraging her to look at them and them only, and pay no attention to what might be slipping up behind her.

Salasi reassured them both that no one was watching them, but Navari had the stronger Skills, and Salasi's reassurance slid off Navari's dream like water on oil. It didn't help that these nightmares were driven by psychic injury. Salasi couldn't just wake her up like she would have for any other bad dream. These dreams wouldn't fade until Navari's mind healed the damage inflicted by Matriarch Katio.

Even knowing it was just Navari's dream, Salasi glanced around, double-checking that there was no one else on the street. The unSkilled had all either fled or been detained last night, but some of them may have hidden. If they didn't make any noise and hadn't washed themselves in floral detergents and shampoos, they could disappear from unSkilled senses. She took a deep breath and reminded herself that even the quietest unSkilled couldn't stop their hearts from beating. If she sharpened her hearing and listened carefully, she would know that she was alone.

Salasi did just that. The ocean surf washed rhythmically against the beach. Gulls cried and wheeled overhead, looking for snacks in the chaos and destruction of Mountain Village. The wind blew gently, bringing with it the scent of salt. She could sense other Enforcers nearby. They moved through ruins in Bonded pairs or groups, performing the same task together that she did alone. She touched Navari's mind, but Navari still walked through the endless maze of toxic radial flowers and didn't notice.

Salasi sighed and went to work.

She photographed the broken door and windows, the pots on the front porch overlooking the beach that had been smashed. If there had been any deck furniture, it was gone. The bonfire pit in the back was filled with half-burned paintings, books, and photographs that had been dragged out and lit up.

Inside the beach house was destruction for destruction's sake.

Salasi let her senses roam. This cottage had been owned by an elderly part-blood Earth who had lived alone. The space had been tidy, the woman surrounding herself with fond memories and routine. Salasi moved slowly through the main room, documenting the wreckage. Shelves upended and smashed. Sofas and armchairs that had been slashed to pieces. All the lovingly tended knickknacks were shattered on the floor. The kitchen was awash in broken dishes. The wave cooker had been stolen. The cold box had been emptied and all the food now thawed on the floor. The smell of raw meat, wilted vegetables and spilled milk wafted around her.

Dutifully she wrote it all down, clicking pictures to accompany her notes.

None of this was urgent, she didn't need to be here now. She wanted to be with Navari, but orders were orders and Command had been in no mood to argue. They wanted this dealt with before Squaring the Earth so they wouldn't still be fielding complaints when they should be off for the holy day.

Shouts drew her ear. Salasi turned her head and listened, reaching for Navari's hearing to help triangulate the sound better. For a confusing moment she heard the gentle murmur of a fountain before remembering that Navari was asleep in their room, her head full of nightmares. Salasi was here on her own, with only one set of eyes and ears. Salasi let go of Navari's perception and followed the shouting outside.

A large group of unSkilled had dragged one of the shallow-bottom sailing canoes out of storage and were happily struggling to get it into the water. The canoe itself belonged to Shapash – just like everything else in Mountain Village – the waves, however, were the domain of House of Water. Any sailing or swimming between the beach and the barrier islands was because Shapash had struck a deal with Water. These unSkilled here didn't have such a deal.

<There's a situation,> Salasi said, reaching for the nearest Enforcers.

<We see it,> came the grim response.

Salasi stepped down from the front deck of the house and onto the boardwalk. Several other Enforcers had come out as well. Part of their job as Enforcers was to smooth interactions between Skilled and unSkilled. They took the census, they dealt with complaints. They were also some of the only Skilled to speak out loud for any length of time. SalNavari had been the translator in many meetings between Skilled and unSkilled where the high aughts refused to speak aloud and the unSkilled minds couldn't hear high aught thoughtspeak without pain. Even Navari hated it, detesting how her voice sounded when she spoke, leaving it to Salasi to translate out loud.

One of the other Enforcer pairs whistled. The sharp sound caught the attention of the unSkilled.

"We're going sailing you fucking kurs!" one of them shouted back, making a rude gesture. "And you can't fucking stop us!"

Salasi reached for Navari before being forcibly reminded that she wasn't here. "House of Water will not take kindly to your trespassing," Salasi said, trying to think like Navari or SalNavari instead of just Salasi alone.

"You can suck my dick!" he shouted back.

Several of the other unSkilled hooted and jeered.

"True Human rules!" another one shouted.

Exasperation and disgust rolled from the other Enforcers.

Salasi reached for Navari again. Regular dreams could be easy to break into, all she had to do was use real-world logic to point out the bizarre flights of fancy and the dream collapsed. Triggered by an injury and under the influence of Bone tinctures, this dream was not so easily swayed. Salasi tried to shake Navari loose anyway, but the gaze of the blood-red roses held her tight. Salasi gave up.

When she focused again on the unSkilled, they had their boat in the water.

"Don't!" Salasi said, taking a step towards them.

A gunshot cracked through the air. The bullet sent up a blast of sand near her feet.

They were shooting at her.

The next shot hit her square in the chest.

Her heart and lungs seized for a second, the force of the bullet hitting her shields like a camelid kick to the chest. Several more shots split the air before she finally drew a deep breath which immediately dissolved into coughing and spluttering.

A warm pair of hands pulled her to a sitting position and patted her on the back until she could breathe without coughing.

<Are you alright?> the other Enforcer asked.

<They shot at us!> Salasi said indignantly. Her whole chest radiated pain.

<They'll be regretting that soon.> the other Enforcer replied with a nod toward the water.

Salasi glanced down the beach, then out over the waves to where the canoe was now well out into the water.

<This will end badly,> Salasi said grimly.

The other woman – Four aught Devi of DevAriella who typically oversaw the ranches and homesteads of the northern Badlands – nodded once in agreement and helped Salasi stand up.

Her partner Ariella had walked down to the water line and waited. There was nothing for them to do now but see what Water's response to the interlopers would be. If the Water Guardians out today were in a generous mood, they would just send the boat and all its passengers back unharmed. If they were feeling less charitable, only the boat could come back in one piece.

The group was whooping and high-fiving each other. One fired his gun into the air for the fun of it. They were well-pleased with themselves and enjoying their success right up to the moment one of them noticed and pointed out the wave. It came from beyond the barrier islands, so huge and so sudden there was no way it was natural.

The laughter turned to calls of alarm. There was a flurry of activity as they tried to turn the canoe back. One of them, still long-limbed and gangly with youth, waved frantically at the shore as if there was something the Enforcers could do to help. Maybe if one of them had worked the boardwalk territory of Iocaste Proper and knew the Water Guardians they could have asked for clemency, but every Enforcer present was a stranger here, doing the scut work so those familiar with the territory could deal with more pressing matters of deaths, injuries and arrests.

<Can anyone help?> Salasi asked anyway, shouting her thoughtspeak at anyone in range to hear.

There was no answer.

On the boat, a girl who looked no older than the gangly youth took shelter in his arms. They cowered together as the massive wave engulfed them.

Salasi grimaced and let out her breath.

The Animachea Enforcers existed to keep incidents like this from happening, but there was only so much they could do when the unSkilled so willfully broke the rules.

The canoe popped back up to the surface, its mast snapped off at the base but was otherwise intact. There was no sign of the unSkilled in the swirling water. The canoe jetted back towards them, a wave lifting it clear of the beach and depositing it back in the boathouse from where the unSkilled had dragged it. House of Water wasn't going to punish Shapash for the unSkilled stealing her property.

All the Enforcers continued to wait. The water calmed and smoothed over, the waves returning to normal. Nothing further popped up, not even bodies. Water had made its will known, there would be no leniency for trespassers.

Salasi pressed a hand to her chest, and the deep, radiating ache there. They had shot her without pause or concern. If she hadn't been shielded, she would be dead. House of Water had answered those actions in kind.

<Will you be alright?> Devi asked as Ariella made her way up the beach to them.

Salasi nodded. <Yes. The shields held.>

<Good.>

Ariella clapped Salasi on her shoulder, <We're here if you need us.>

<Thank you,> she said with another nod.

DevAriella went back to the house they'd been surveying and Salasi returned to the cottage. She wondered if that young man with his young girlfriend had been part of the riots here last night, smashing and looting people's homes, or if he was just riding along in the excitement, enjoying True Human's so-called 'success.'

Back in Animachea, Navari's dreams shifted, the garden of radial symmetry filled with ocean wrecks while the now blue flowers bobbed all around her like waves.

Chapter Eleven

Maggie Reeves

Jim popped into Maggie's dojo just as she finished cleaning up after her last adult morning class. She now had some time until the kids started coming in for the afternoon classes. There was a definite pep to his step and jauntiness to his voice when he greeted her. The last several times she had seen him like this, he was already several grave diggers deep at the bar.

"Have you been drinking again?" she demanded alarmed.

"What? No," he answered, offended by her question. "Why would you even ask that?"

"You're..." she trailed off for a moment before just answering. "Well, you're happy."

"Is that bad?"

"No! I just... I haven't seen you happy like this in a while. Usually when you're like this you have a grave digger in hand and several under the belt and are looking to start a fight."

"Wrong on the first two."

"But right about the third? You're going to start a fight?" she asked dubiously.

"*We* are," he corrected with a grin. "Come on."

Maggie had misgivings about what Jim had in mind, but she was more afraid of what he might do if she wasn't with him as a voice of reason.

She followed him out front, locking the door behind her. The sun sat in a brilliant blue sky as they walked through Ashveil's square, an almost identical walk to the one they'd made yesterday. Only now Jim strode along beside her, nearly bouncing on the balls of his feet.

It gladdened her heart to see him so upbeat. He must have

finally made a breakthrough with his sobriety.

She opened her mouth to ask if the Chief Inspector needed them to check on the well, but fell silent as she saw the crowd gathered loosely around it. She recognized several as the moms of her students. Maggie lengthened her stride, worried for a second that one of the kids might be hurt, before she saw what had earned their angry and distrustful looks. A kur stood on the edge of the well.

He was bare from the waist up. His Water black skin was carefully painted in red and white dots and lines, and his black hair twisted in elegant knots all over his head. His full lips were pursed, and blue eyes narrowed as he gazed down into the well as if not quite sure what to make of it.

"What's going on?" Maggie demanded.

"He's 'investigating' it," Jim answered with an edge to his voice.

"Investigating it or poisoning it?" she answered back acidly.

"Poisoning?" one of the moms' gasped, giving Maggie a wide-eyed look.

Maggie waved the comment off. House of Water wouldn't poison the well, they'd be too worried about hurting whatever plants and animals might get into it. That didn't stop the kur's presence from being an assault on the people of Ashveil. These parents were here trying to enjoy their day with their children, and now this kur was here upsetting everyone.

"Does the Chief Inspector know about this?" Maggie asked.

"Yeah," Jim replied. "This is Zumi, son of Ataku."

Ataku, Water Controller for all of the Eastern Corridor.

Everyone in all of Iocaste had heard the story of Ceres. It stood as a warning, spread from neighbor to neighbor, through families and friends, about the petty vindictiveness of kurs, and about how there could be no reasoning with them. Spoken about far less often was what Ataku could do – and had done.

She had dried out entire towns on a whim, cutting off not only drinking water and all indoor plumbing but also disappearing streams and ponds. She'd even cut off single houses or businesses, forcing the owners to rely on the community for showers and fresh running water.

Some people and places could pay the fearsome water taxes that were levied against them and get their water back, but not everyone could afford that.

Regardless of what Zumi found, the kurs would decide what to do about the well without any input from the people of Ashveil. That could mean anything from permanently capping the well – no different really from how things were now – to removing everyone from town and installing a new Water Works and sub-Controller if the kurs considered the new water source valuable enough. The thought of everyone she knew dispersing through the Eastern Corridor, her entire community gone, filled Maggie with dread.

<Is there something you need help with?> The voice almost brought her to her knees. The words hot-wired themselves straight to her brain and left her reeling. All at once she was twelve years old again, hearing thoughtspeak for the first time. The horror of that moment engulfed her. Her decades of training in the dojo deserted her and she wanted to bolt.

"You're fine," Jim said catching her arm, to either keep her from falling over or stop her from running away, she wasn't sure. "Deep breath, just like you're always telling me."

Maggie nodded and steadied her breathing. That didn't stop her heart from hammering. Around her, she saw similar looks of alarm. Several people clutched their ears, and several parents had run, dragging their children after them.

"I'm Staff Detective Jim Dawes with the Ashveil PD," Jim answered, his voice carrying easily to the kur as well as the growing crowd. More people were coming over to see what was going on. "This well belongs to Ashveil."

<All water in the Eastern Corridor belongs to Controller Ataku.>

Maggie's stomach turned both from the sound of his voice and what he was saying.

<It was reported that the water present now is a new development. This evaluation is to assure you that your town is not about to fall into a sinkhole.>

Beside her, Jim drew in a sharp breath, no doubt thinking of

Ceres, but his voice was steady when he replied, "Shouldn't Earth evaluate that?"

<House of Earth will be contacted should they be needed.>

"And what about the people who live here?"

<The evaluation will be reported to the Water Controller. You will await and abide by her decision.>

Jim sucked on his teeth for a moment before saying, "Thank you for your time."

It was the most polite Maggie had ever seen him. "I thought you said there was going to be a fight," she muttered, keeping her voice low. For a moment she wanted the brawling Jim Dawes back, tackling that kur off the edge of the well and beating in his face.

"In a minute," he answered her. "We're going to need you to back up," he announced to the crowd. "Back to the sidewalk."

"But he's poisoning the well! You should do something!" the woman who'd first overheard Maggie shouted.

"Something will be done," Jim assured them. "For now, you just need to be patient."

The crowd allowed him to shoo them back to the sidewalk and the play park. Most of the little kids promptly lost interest in what the adults were saying and went back to the slides and climbing gyms. A few clung to their parents' hands or legs, looking wide-eyed.

"Stay back where it's safe," he added. "And leave the kur to the professionals."

The parents came together in a tight cluster, whispering and worrying and shooting dark glances over at Zumi.

"This wasn't what I came to show you. Come on," Jim said, then caught Maggie's arm and pulled her along when she didn't immediately respond. After a minute or two of walking in silence, he added, "I hate when those things speak."

Maggie nodded. Zumi's words felt as if they'd been branded across the inside of her skull. She could feel the pain start to build up behind her eyes.

"Izoklakeite just laughed," Jim said after a long pause, so quiet that Maggie could barely hear him. "I can still hear that laugh."

Maggie didn't answer, not wanting to break whatever moment

was drawing this out of him.

Izoklakeite had been the Earth kur who oversaw the town of Ceres. His job had been to shore up the mine and keep the human miners safe. Instead, he'd destroyed the entire town.

Maggie had been to Ceres once as part of a high school field trip. After what Izoklakeite had done, the mine had closed. Less than a third of the population had survived and most, like Jim, had left. Those that had stayed had turned Ceres into a town-sized museum and monument.

It had been eerie and horrifying to walk down the street and then down the stairs to below street level and see all the houses that had been interred. She couldn't imagine what it had been like for Jim to be there that day, to watch the ground turn to liquid and swallow every house, every person, that had been standing on it. To know, even as he frantically dug at the now solid earth, that he would never be able to reach anyone in time to save them from smothering.

They all had their own demons. She'd been twelve when she met hers. "I remember Callum telling me to run," she offered quietly when Jim didn't say anything further. "Run and don't look back."

"They're all monsters," Jim said. "Every single one of them. And we're going to fight back."

They'd been walking the entire time they'd been talking and were now a few blocks down from the park in one of Ashveil's older neighborhoods. Maggie's morning runs often took her through here, especially in the spring and summer when Grandma Suri's garden would be in full bloom.

The wizened old woman had been the town librarian for decades and had outlived not only her husband and all her children but all her grandchildren as well. One of her great-grandchildren had just moved back from Iocaste Proper to help around that house. Despite her age, Grandma Suri was still out in her garden when the weather was nice and inside at the library when it wasn't.

Not thinking, just wanting to see and be near something reassuring, Maggie started towards Suri's house.

Jim cleared his throat and called her attention to a different house. She knew this one too. It was worn down and neglected. The leaves looked like they hadn't been raked in years and were a thick mat where there should be a lawn. Bushes were overgrown, hiding the porch and front windows from sight. Moss grew in geometric shapes following the pattern of the roof tiles and the green paint had faded and chipped to a dingy off-gray. On her runs, she'd periodically wondered who would pay for a house like this one just to let it get so run-down.

"This is your house?" she said surprised as Jim pulled the keys out of his pocket.

"Yeah."

"How did you afford this?" she couldn't stop herself from asking.

As a police officer, he made a better salary than she did, but she hadn't expected him to live in this neighborhood. She'd always pictured him in one of the utilitarian apartment blocks like the one Raid stayed in. Houses like this one came on the market rarely and Viridae had to approve any tenants. Even with approval, the leases were expensive.

"It was part of the compensation for Ceres," he answered quietly. "Never had to pay a dime."

Maggie winced at his reply. He swung the door open and stepped inside before she could apologize.

The inside matched the outside.

An intensely flowery scent hung in the air but that didn't mask the mustiness underneath. The stains and grime rings on the hardwood floors suggested there had been a huge mess present until recently. The sparse furniture was ratty. Cracks and stains laced the bare walls and spiderwebs still hung in the corners.

The solid wood dining room table had been scrubbed clean and some mismatched chairs hastily gathered around it. Through the partially closed curtains, she could see a wildly overgrown backyard. Li would have a heart attack if she saw it.

Maggie guessed that Jim had started cleaning when he'd been forced into sobriety. The fact that he'd invited her in struck her as another big step in the right direction. She stopped next to one of the seats at the dining room table. Jim watched her a little anxiously, expecting her to pass judgement on the state of his house.

"So," she said instead. "You said we're going to start a fight?"

"We are," he replied, seeming relieved she hadn't mentioned that decades of neglect had turned a perfectly nice house in an excellent neighborhood into a craphole. "We're waiting for a few others. Can I get you anything to drink?"

"I'm alright," she answered, not quite trusting anything that might come out of that kitchen. What little she could see from here wasn't appealing.

A knock on the door broke the awkward silence. Jim hurried to answer it. Murmured voices came from the front hall. A moment later Ava walked into the living room. Her hair had been scraped back into a ponytail but wisps and flyaways circled her ruddy, good-natured face.

"Maggie," she said warmly. "It's good to see you."

"I didn't expect to see you again so soon," Maggie replied caught off guard. "Was there a meeting notification I missed?"

"No. This is off the books—"

The door knocked again, cutting her off momentarily.

"I'm glad you're here," Ava went on while Jim went back to answer the door. "It's time that we made a difference."

Those firmly stated words gave Maggie a vaguely uneasy feeling that evaporated the moment Doctor Adrian Longcross walked in, trailed by his assistant Bunny still wearing her rainbow reflective ski goggles.

"Doctor Longcross," Maggie blurted, now well and truly floored. "Wow… It's… I didn't expect to see you again." She moved forward to shake his hand, then felt awkward and blushed. She'd last seen him only a few hours ago, she didn't need to shake his hand, but she also had just met him for the first time a few hours ago, so wouldn't a handshake be appropriate?

"Maggie Reeves, right?" he replied, taking her hand and silencing the inane chatter in her mind.

She nodded, pleased that he had remembered her name.

"Let's all sit," Longcross said, gesturing to the table.

The four of them did. Bunny drifted through the rooms,

checking through everything carefully – even the kitchen – before silently starting up the stairs to check the other floors.

Maggie noticed Jim imperceptibly wince at that and wondered just how much of a mess still existed upstairs.

"We talked a great deal last night, and I've asked you all here today because of two things. Everyone here has a story, and everyone here has a dream. Our stories are all different, but our dream is the same; to live in a world without fear."

Maggie nodded. Those words were exactly what she'd been thinking this morning, and last night during his presentation.

"More importantly," he went on. "To live in a world where our children will be safe."

Longcross looked at each of them in turn. Maggie felt her cheeks flame when he met her eyes. It felt like he could see straight to her soul, all her dreams laid bare before him. That didn't stop her from blurting out, "What about the others? Cari, Rory, Max… They all care about kids too." Cari probably most of all.

"They still have a part to play," Longcross agreed. "But theirs is less immediate than what we do here. Max will protect the future, Cari will raise the future and Rory is the future, part of the generation who will grow up in a new world. You three, however, are the ones who will fight for that future."

Maggie found herself smiling in response to what he was saying, elated to be here listening to him.

"As I'm sure you all already know, I am a real medical doctor, not a professor or an academic. I graduated top of my class from the University of Iocaste Proper and completed an internship and residency in emergency and critical care medicine at Grace of Waves Hospital."

Maggie nodded along. She knew all this. Being a criticalist and treating kur inflicted injuries was what had caused Longcross to step away from being a doctor and instead found True Human. He made the decision that rather than simply fix broken bodies and send people back to their now broken lives, he would find a way to keep them from being broken in the first place. No more kur related 'accidents.'

"What I don't often talk about is the case that finally flipped me. Her name was Lila Stiles. She was seven years old. She was the only survivor of a tenement fire. A kur looking to collect on a debt started the fire. When the debt wasn't paid, he burned the building to the ground along with everyone in it. Close to seventy deaths including Lila's entire family. How she survived..." Longcross shook his head. "I'll never know. It was both a blessing and a curse because she was burned over ninety percent of her body. Needless to say, despite our best efforts, she didn't live long."

Maggie's heart broke for that little girl. The pain she must have been in those last few days, not only badly burned but also knowing her entire family was dead and she was alone in the world.

"You three are here with me today because I know you all have similar stories." Longcross fell silent and looked at them all expectantly.

Jim surprised Maggie by speaking first. "I was at Ceres that day with Izoklakeite. I..." His voice thickened and his entire body clenched as if protecting himself from the blow that was coming. "I had the day off and I... I took my son James to the park." It took him a moment to gather himself. Maggie found herself holding her breath. "There was new playground equipment, and he was so excited. He was three feet from me, about to come down the slide... and then he was gone. I watched him disappear. I watched the earth swallow him. He was three feet away and I couldn't grab him in time. And Izoklakeite laughed. He just laughed and laughed and laughed. I can still hear him."

Jim didn't go on but he didn't need to. Maggie had read the first-person accounts of the survivors, tearing into the ground with their fingernails trying to reach the buried. She'd always known Jim Dawes had been at Ceres the day the town was lost, but she hadn't realized he'd lost his son. She hadn't even known he'd had a son.

Ava told the story of her sister who'd been taking the train from the Eastern Corridor into Iocaste Proper for her sixteenth birthday when an Ice iced the tracks and sent the train off the rails for fun. That accident hadn't been the tragedy of Ceres, or even the tenement fire. Ava's sister had survived along with just about everyone else. All of her friends, however, had been among the dead. Driven by the guilt and grief of that day, for her seventeenth birthday, Ava's sister had committed suicide.

Silence fell and the others looked expectantly at Maggie.

"I was twelve," she said softly. "I was training for the Grand Champion tournament in Iocaste Proper. Sensei Callum had been going – and winning – every year since he was sixteen." She had been so excited to go with him. She wanted so badly to impress him, to be just like him. How stupid and trivial it all seemed now.

She'd walked into the dojo and a sound had drawn her attention. The scuff of feet. She'd believed at first that Callum was sparring with someone else, and she'd been so jealous. She was the only one he was supposed to be training with that night.

She saw them then.

In her memory, their eyes glowed red. Alien and inhuman.

"His prowess in martial arts drew the attention of Carnage. A pair came to hunt him. There's nothing more challenging than human prey."

She had just stood there dumbly, staring at them.

They saw her. They smiled. She had never seen anything so terrifying in her life.

"Run Mags."

It wasn't until she heard Callum croak that she saw him, hunched over but still standing, between them.

He was covered in bruises. It looked like his hands had been broken. One eye was swollen completely shut. Blood trickled from his nose and his mouth. From dozens of shallow cuts that covered him, staining his white gi red.

"Run Mags," he said again. His voice was broken. "And don't look back."

<Yes,> one of Carnages whispered, its voice wrapping itself around her like a vice. **<Run. Please.>**

One of them took a step towards her.

There was no fighting the animalistic terror. She ran.

"I walked in on them as they were killing him," she went on. Her voice didn't even sound like her own. "They would have killed me too if Callum hadn't stopped them."

A heavy silence descended, broken only by the creaking floorboards overhead as Bunny continued her survey of the house.

"Children," Longcross finally said quietly. "Our patients. Our sons. Our sisters. Ourselves. This is why we fight. For our children. For the future."

Maggie nodded. When True Human had come to Ashveil, she had immediately enrolled. There was a tightrope line she walked, wanting to teach her students – especially the kids – how to defend themselves and fight back, without them being so good and succeeding so well that they caught the attention of some Carnage looking for a canned hunt.

True Human offered the chance for her students to excel without her needing to warn them about the cost of excellence. She and the other True Human members could build a world where no one needed to fear kurs anymore.

"This is why we fight," Ava echoed softly.

Bunny reappeared. "You're clear," she said, her musical voice catching Maggie with her words.

"Thanks, Bunny," Longcross said.

Bunny nodded and stepped back to where she had the best line of sight for the entire bottom floor.

Maggie shook herself off, refocusing on what Longcross was saying.

"We talked last night about safeties and kill switches, about the real history of humanity that the kurs don't want you to know."

"That they'd been genetically designed by humans and grown in vats to protect humans from Natives," Ava said, summarizing the night before.

"That exactly," he agreed. "They were weapons to protect humanity, but they rebelled and became weapons against humanity. An associate of mine has been working diligently to find a way to even the odds between humans and kurs, to remove the unfair advantage that is the Skills. After decades of work, she was finally able to replicate the methods used by the Ancestors."

Jim leaned forward, an eager gleam in his eyes, no doubt

thinking about the shield penetrating guns or sonic cannons that would reduce Carnage to piles of goo and rubble, as were portrayed in popular media. Instead, Longcross pulled a leather dog collar out of his pocket and set it on the table.

Jim leaned back, confusion and disappointment clear on his face.

Maggie seconded that feeling.

"That's it?" Ava said with a frown.

"That's it exactly," Longcross replied indulgently as if he'd been expecting that response. "Take a look." He handed it first to Maggie.

The inch-thick matte black leather was heavier than she'd expected. The iridescent buckle gleamed in the light. She turned it in her hands. An iridescent strip ran down the inside, with divots and bumps marring its glittering surface.

"A shock collar?" she said, asking the only thing that made sense to her.

"A null collar," he corrected. "What you have in your hands will nullify the Skills of any kur wearing it. No shields. No wards. No thoughtspeak. No Skills. No power at all."

Maggie lit with excitement. If the Carnage kurs had been wearing these the day they'd come for Callum, he would have been able to fight them off. He could have beaten them two to one if they hadn't cheated with their Skills.

"What stops them from just taking it off?" Jim asked, plucking it out of Maggie's hands.

"The same microtech that disrupts their Skills also causes adverse reactions when anyone with Skills tries to touch it. Once it's on, only a human can remove it. The kur wearing it won't be able to touch it without detrimentally harming themselves. Just wearing it causes discomfort."

The initial excitement at seeing the collar began to dim as multiple problems began to present themselves. First and foremost: "How do we put them on?" No kur would just sit by placidly and let themselves be collared. If kurs were that tame the problem humans faced now would never have existed in the first place.

"That's what I'm here to discuss with you all. We have an unexpected opportunity with this situation involving the well. Before we discuss anything further, I need to know your dedication to this. There can't be any backing out once we get started. Where kurs are involved, your human compatriots need to know that they can count on you no matter what."

"I'm in," Jim said almost before Longcross finished speaking.

Ava nodded too, fingering the collar Jim had handed to her. "So am I."

Longcross looked at Maggie.

She'd always had a vague dream about a safe world, a place where kids could play, where their parents didn't need to worry about them. Longcross had filled in the details and was now holding out the map of how they could get there. A world without kurs. A world without Carnage.

Maggie nodded slowly and met Longcross's eyes. "Yes," she agreed. "Let's do this. What do you have in mind?"

Longcross looked at her and smiled.

□

Chapter Twelve

Raid

Raid stood quietly under the trees and listened to the birds. The construction crew was on a meal break, and he used it to get away from them. His crew mates were all unSkilled and all had been talking nonstop about Longcross's presentation. All of them seemed stuck on the statistic that unSkilled outnumbered Skilled five hundred to one and they weren't letting it go.

He'd tried reasoning with them at first. Five hundred people facing an avalanche outnumbered it five hundred to one, but they were still going to end up crushed. They'd laughed and insisted the comparison was ludicrous. A person was a person, not an avalanche. That statement just showed that none of them had ever faced a Ten aught and how powerful their Skills were. Hexaferrum, Matriarch of Earth, had far more in common with the destructive power of an avalanche than she did with these idiots he was crewing with.

At least his request for family leave had been approved. Starting at the end of this shift he had the next two weeks off if he needed them, with full pay and benefits still in place. He would head to Daal tomorrow and see if he could figure out why Cain had come to Ashveil, and more importantly, why he was dead.

<What are you doing?> Mordred demanded.

Raid recoiled with a hiss, knives in hand, before realizing it was Mordred. Mordred in an Inquisitor's uniform. Mordred who now could jump between places.

<Working,> Raid answered, straightening out of the defensive crouch.

<Why aren't you trying to learn what happened to Cain?>

<Why aren't you?> Raid shot back.

Mordred suddenly seemed to tower, all his Skills and all his anger focused directly on Raid.

Raid fell back a step, knives raised.

As quickly as it flared to life, the towering menace dissolved and Modred was no more than the pain-in-ass strongest brother he'd always been.

Raid stayed on edge, trying to decide whether he was dealing with his brother and could continue to address Mordred as such, or if switching to a more respectful grammar form would be safer.

<The High Inquisitor. She's tense. She's keeping everyone on a short leash. It's like she's expecting something to happen,> Mordred finally said. He was still speaking in casual-family grammar, so Raid took his cue from that.

<Is something going to happen?> Raid asked, eyeing Mordred's uniform.

<Fuck if anyone knows,> Mordred muttered, running his hands through his hair. <Would Cain have come here for anyone but you?> he asked changing the subject.

<Don't think he knew anyone here.>

<What about the part-bloods?>

Raid tensed, waiting for Mordred to start in about Li but he said nothing, so Raid replied, <Don't think he knew them. Never mentioned them.> Although Raid had never told Cain about Li, so it was possible Cain was seeing someone he'd never brought up.

<Let's go see them.>

<Right now?>

<Why not? The High Inquisitor is busy with other things. She won't notice.>

<Working,> Raid answered, hooking a thumb back towards where the rest of the crew was still talking about True Human.

<Tell them you're leaving.>

Raid wanted to argue just because of Mordred's bossy tone, but he stopped himself. He sure as shit didn't want to finish this shift listening to the unSkilled piss and moan about the Mountain. It only took a few minutes to tell the shift supervisor that the family emergency he was leaving for had suddenly become much more urgent and he needed to leave right now.

The shift supervisor gave him the rest of the day, telling him nothing was more important than family. In a few minutes, he was off the work site and walking back up the maintenance road that ran along the tracks.

<Can you vanish this?> Raid asked, nodding to his motorcycle when they reached the spot where the vehicles had been parked for the day.

Mordred did so without pausing.

Raid shouldn't have been surprised. Mordred could jump now. His Skills were getting stronger, and his psychic scent had that wispy around the edges feeling that kids and young adults had when their Skills were growing but their scent hadn't caught up yet.

Anyone with an aught rank could vanish things – psychically carry things with them without feeling the physical strain – how much they could carry varied. The higher their rank, the more they could vanish. Raid couldn't vanish a motorcycle and would hurt himself if he tried.

Mordred must have known Raid wanted to ask about it, because he grabbed Raid's arm before he could and jumped.

When he wasn't passing as unSkilled, Raid traveled by Carriage. It had been a long time since he jumped tandem with someone like this. He'd forgotten that freezing black moment of being between one place and another.

<A little warning next time,> he said with a jagged breath after they arrived.

Mordred didn't answer. He was already taking a sense of the building in front of them.

Angels Landing was Ashveil's big claim to fame. Without the hospital, the town would be just one more dinky logging town managed by Viridae. Angels Landing was equipped with state-of-the-art unSkilled tech and staffed with the best doctors and support staff outside of Iocaste Proper. All of the critical injuries and hospitalized cases were shipped to Angels Landing for treatment. It didn't hurt that one of the emergency doctors was a part-blood Bone. Mordred wrapped them both in sight shields and went to find her.

When Raid had seen her the first time, her blue smock had been splattered with blood and she'd been calling out orders to her team to stabilize someone who'd fallen off a ladder with a running chainsaw in hand. Today they found her between crises, propped up at one of the nurses' stations, typing up her records.

Her scent was unmistakably Bone, and Raid could see the Bone in her facial features, but her color was all wrong. She had butter-yellow eyes, and her light skin was spattered liberally with freckles. She'd securely tucked her hair under a scrub cap which meant she was dressed in ceil blue from head to toe. Her keycard badge labeled her as Doctor Lightfoot.

<Have you ever spoken with her?> Mordred asked.

<No.> Raid had found her intimidating. She was several years older than he was, confident and competent. Here she was saving lives, and he'd shown up because he felt lonely and unnerved being around so many unSkilled. He'd crept out without speaking to her. <Do you want to talk to her?>

For a second it looked like Mordred was going to say 'yes,' and Raid had a flash of how much the unSkilled would panic if an Inquisitor just popped up in the middle of their treatment room.

<No,> Mordred finally said then took Raid's arm and jumped again.

This time they landed at Gemma's farm. Raid knew her. She and Li were friends, Li traded her tinctures and lotions in exchange for yarn, meat, and eggs. As a part-blood Animachea, Gemma had a much tighter bond with her pack of herding dogs than any unSkilled could boast. He'd heard unSkilled comment that Gemma's dogs responded to her as if they could read her mind. On some level, they probably could.

Gray-haired but still spry, Gemma took care of her farm and was congenial and welcoming to everyone who came. Like with Lightfoot, Mordred showed no actual interest in approaching her.

Raid ducked away before Mordred could grab him and jump again.

<What are we doing?> Raid demanded. <None of these part-bloods know anything about Cain.>

<Maybe they do,> Mordred answered stubbornly.

<If you thought that, you'd actually be talking to them. We need to go to Daal. Whatever answers we're going to find are there.>

Mordred didn't reply. He didn't even look at Raid.

<You do want to figure out what happened to Cain, right?> Raid pressed as the silence stretched.

<Of course!> Mordred snapped back.

<Then let's go somewhere useful!>

<This is useful!>

<Like hell it is!> Raid snarled, the shock and pain and grief over losing Cain coalescing into fury. <You dropped us out here in the middle of Soth damned nowhere to live with a bunch of paper dolls and now he's dead and we're chasing around after part-bloods why?>

Mordred actually backed down from the onslaught.

<If it weren't for you, Cain would still be here!> Raid finished, close enough to strike if he felt like it. A small part of him pointed out that this was not a safe place to be given that Mordred could deal far more damage than he could, but he was too angry.

<You think I don't know that?> Mordred raged back, but he directed his anger and blame only at himself. <That this is my fault? This assignment was to keep you both safe! To keep you out of Katio's reach! She's culling everyone she deems 'unfit' and you and Cain were right at the top of her list.>

Raid's anger broke hearing Mordred take such personal accountability for Cain's death. <What about you?> Raid asked quietly. Matriarch Katio had culled Nico years ago, and if Raid and Cain were at the top of her cull list, that still left Mordred right in her line of sight.

<Doesn't matter,> Mordred answered, retreating into himself. <It's fine.>

<Mordred—>

<You're right. The answers we need are in Daal,> he said, shaking off Raid's concern.

<Mordred—>

Mordred grabbed him and jumped, the shock of between cutting off the rest of Raid's sentence, then they were dropping five feet to a road in Daal.

<You need to work on your landings,> Raid muttered.

<Next time you can take a Carriage,> Mordred answered. <Stop being so touchy.>

Mordred flicked him with Skills, the same way he had when they were in creche.

Despite everything, it made Raid relax. This was the Mordred he remembered from before Nico died, the one he saw so painfully rarely now.

Neither of them spoke as they scanned their surroundings.

Daal had been built in one of the glorious alpine valleys of the Ice Whites and had ski slopes the unSkilled fought over. Cain had told him the wait list for staying in Daal's lodges during the winter was several years long. Pine trees towered over everything, giving a bright, crisp smell to the air. The upper two-thirds of the town was mostly the huge ski lodge along with the oversized winter cabins of the wealthy unSkilled. A long, winding road then connected all that to the lower part of town where the residents and year-round employees lived.

Now that it was spring, Daal was a skeletal version of itself with only a tenth of its winter population still here. The slopes and streets had been reduced to mud as the snow melted which gave the whole place a dirty, unkempt appearance.

Raid looked at everything closely, trying to make a connection. What here had sent Cain to Ashveil to find him? What had started here that had ended with Cain dead in a well?

He never would have escaped Daal if a stronger Skilled had been chasing him which made it unlikely the Matriarch had come after him. Though there were some like Adira who enjoyed the chase. She would always give her prey enough of a head start that they always believed they had a chance of escape.

For a horrible few minutes, Raid entertained the possibility that Adira had taken an interest in Cain the same way she'd once been obsessed with Nico. He pushed that thought aside. He remembered what she'd done with Nico and wasn't going to think about what she may have done with Cain until there was proof of it.

More likely it had been someone unSkilled. The unSkilled

could be intensely frightening in their unpredictability. They could be cagey and smart but then would do amazingly stupid things. They were willing to risk their lives on gambles, only to be shocked to discover that they were gambling their lives. True Human was at the top of Raid's list, they were the people he'd start with.

<Cain had a cabin,> Mordred said and started down the street.

Or they could start there.

Raid stayed close enough to stay within the influence of Mordred's sight shield as they walked. No need to draw attention if they didn't need to.

Cain's cabin had a large yard that was wild in a kept way. Alpine trees and bushes had been planted in a pleasing disarray. The walk to the front door was battered concrete broken by tree roots and stained green and black from lichen and years of beating weather. Li would love it.

The cabin itself was made of wood with a stone foundation. The windows were dark. The wards around it were fading. Raid paused, feeling the familiar wards, catching the fading psychic scent that wound its way back through his childhood. None of them had been stronger than Five, but there had been four of them, and together they'd been safer and stronger than any one of them would have been alone. How many times had they braided their power together to make something tougher than just a single shield?

Cain's fading shields and wards recognized the two of them and let them pass, unlocking the door as Mordred reached for it. That was a neat trick. For a split-second Raid wanted Cain to teach him how to do it so he could use it himself back in Ashveil, before the memory that Cain was dead and gone forever reasserted itself.

The cabin was a single sparse and clean room with a loft for a bedroom. The paintings on the walls were all mountain landscapes, though there were some beautiful charcoal sketches of plants and birds that were framed and hung as well. A small bookshelf filled with birds' eggs, pinecones, and other detritus of the wilderness stood against one wall. All part of Cain's cover as a wildlife guide, and yet feeling far more like a home than Raid's apartment back in Ashveil.

There was produce on the counter and food in the fridge,

abandoned long enough for some things to start turning. The counters were wiped clean, the seats all pushed into the table. No scent of fear or pain permeated the air, no sign of trouble. Cain had left here intending to come back.

Raid climbed the steep stairs to the loft. A neatly made bed covered with a faded quilt in dark greens and blues took up most of the space. The rest went to a squashy chair turned to look out one of the windows and down the steep slope this place was built on. Cain's scent was strongest here but it was still fading. It had been days since he had been here last. Raid wracked his mind for when they'd last spoken. They'd talked occasionally on the memes, but it was so awkward and stilted, sending spoken words through a device. That couldn't have been more than a week ago. Two at most. The spot just under his sternum tightened with guilt and dread. How had he missed that his brother was gone? The pinched look on Mordred's face indicated he was thinking the same thing.

The two of them began moving through the cabin more methodically, checking the drawers and the cabinets. *Hidden Trails of the Ice White Mountains* was tucked into the squashy armchair between the cushion and the arm. It was battered and dog-eared and saturated in Cain's scent. Raid took a deep breath and tried to memorize it. A scent that was so important, so familiar, and would soon be gone entirely. Tears pricked his eyes. After losing Nico, Mordred had sworn that it wouldn't happen again. They weren't going to lose each other. Now Cain was dead and gone, and neither of them had noticed it happen.

Soth, damn it all.

He slipped the book into his jacket pocket and kept looking. The wardrobe was filled with warm, sturdy clothes. Cain had a jacket not that different from the one Raid wore, but everything else in his closet was just regular unSkilled clothing. Raid was about to close the wardrobe door when Mordred said, <Do you smell that?>

Raid paused for a moment, parsing the air carefully before he caught the scent. It was just a slip of a thing, there and gone.

Mordred was already moving, seeking it out. The scent came from a pair of gloves that had been stuffed in a jacket pocket.

Aught Earth. A woman.

<Looks like you aren't the only one crossing House lines,> Mordred muttered.

<So you'd let Adira fuck you just to keep Carnage bloodlines strong and pure?> Raid snapped.

Mordred recoiled.

Raid admitted to himself that that had been a low blow, regardless of how raw he was feeling right now. <Sorry. That was uncalled for,> he said softly. <Any Skilled in the area would have caught his attention. A week with the unSkilled and you're tearing your hair out with nothing but paper dolls for company.>

Friendships with the unSkilled happened, but longstanding relationships were rare. Maintaining anything of substance with someone who had such a limited view of the world was difficult at best, which was why he had sought out Li and the other part-bloods. He needed someone. Cain had likely felt the same, and if her gloves were in his pocket, he probably knew the Earth fairly well.

Sex with unSkilled was tolerated, and by-blows happened, each House taking its own measures in dealing with part-bloods. Taking a lover from another House, however, was deeply frowned upon because a child born of two Houses was taboo. Their Skillsets were unpredictable and so were their minds. Such children in the past had wrecked hideous devastation on scales that made Ceres look cute.

Both Raid and Li were on contraceptives because neither of them was selfish or sadistic enough to bring a doomed child into the world. If he looked, Raid knew he'd find contraceptives somewhere in Cain's cabin.

Raid eyed Mordred. Another Inquisitor would have hunted down Li and killed her the second they'd caught her scent on him. Mordred hadn't. Raid considered asking him about it, but decided against it. The less Mordred knew about Li, the better. The less he thought about her the better. Protecting the aught Earth, however, wasn't going to help them find out what had happened to Cain.

<Your nose is stronger,> Raid said, holding out the gloves. <Think you can find her?>

Mordred nodded curtly, still looking hurt by the Adira

comment. Without a word, he led the way back outside.

Chapter Thirteen

SalNavari

Salasi stood in front of her second assigned cottage and couldn't bring herself to step inside. FUCK ALL KURS!!! Had been painted along the outside and the wall was riddled with bullet holes. There had to be hundreds. She would need to go through and count, label, and photograph each one. She would then need to go inside and catalog the damage all those bullets had done. She already knew part of what she would find, enough blood had been shed inside she could smell it from out here.

<Navari,> she said, reaching for her partner, trying to shake her out of her nightmares. <Navari, wake up.> She knew Navari needed to rest but Salasi felt so alone. At least one of the twelve people who had died last night had died here, shot to death in their own home.

On the beach, a high aught Animachea Enforcer pair now bargained with House of Water to return the bodies of the fools who'd tried to go sailing. Beyond the broken walls of Mountain Village, police cruised by, menacingly blipping their sirens, and it wasn't a warning to the unSkilled rioters who were starting to gather again. The story of Water drowning the unSkilled on the stolen boat had already reached them.

<Navari, please,> Salasi whispered.

They had both suffered incapacitating injuries in the past, but the other had never been expected to work through it.

Navari's dreams shifted back and forth between the radial roses and the rippling ocean. Sometimes it was both at once, making Salasi's conscious mind curdle. She knew she needed to calm down, her panic was influencing Navari and making it harder for her to heal, but at this time and in this situation, calming down was hopelessly beyond Salasi. She breathed slowly, counting her heartbeats and desperately ignoring the smell of blood. She steeled herself to walk into this next house when Command jumped in beside her.

He looked bad. His gold eyes had the sheen and dark circles of someone who'd been awake and focusing for too many hours. His skin had a distinct ashy cast and pulled taut over his cheekbones and his clothes hung loose from his frame. He'd lost a significant amount of weight in a short amount of time, the sign of someone drawing too deeply on their Skills for too extended a period. If he kept that up much longer, his body would move into auto-dissolution.

<Command,> she said respectfully, not commenting on his dreadful appearance or dissolving into relieved tears at his presence. He would direct her duty, and reassure her about the tension growing outside of Mountain Village. If luck was with her, he'd send her back to Animachea to be with Navari.

<Enforcer Salasi,> he answered. The strain of the past day weighed heavily in his voice. Her name alone and not twinned with Navari's sounded strange to her. <You're being reassigned.>

Her heart soared – she wouldn't have to set foot in the bullet-ridden house – then plummeted. Reassigned meant another assignment, not returning to aid with festive decorating with Getch; that would have given Navari something much sweeter to dream about.

Command passed over the details from his mind to hers, then jumped them. He jumped again as soon as they arrived, leaving her alone at Ashveil's Carriage station with all of her questions unanswered. She stood for a moment in the familiar setting, letting the breeze and the trees blow away some of the stress of the last few hours. She then parsed through the information he'd passed her.

A situation had developed in Ashveil since she and Navari had been here yesterday. Controller Ataku had dispatched her son Zumi to assess the well. He'd reported the well more complicated than expected and the evaluation which should have only taken a few hours, looked like it would take longer. The unSkilled, agitated by the events at Mountain Village, were behaving in a threatening manner. Since Salasi was already aware of the situation, she was to monitor any developments and aid Zumi in any way he needed.

Zumi was sixteen and already around a Five in strength. He was destined to be as strong as his mother and was already three aught ranks stronger than Salasi. It wouldn't be her watching his back so much as him watching hers. Orders were orders though, and she preferred these to cataloging the destruction of Mountain Village.

She barely set foot in the plaza when she realized this situation was far more volatile than Command had presented. A milling crowd held handmade signs and posters boasting foul True Human slogans. Everyone was wearing a TRUE HUMAN shirt, jacket, or armband. Despite her sight shield, Salasi fell back from the wall of hostility and immediately pinged Command.

Command waved her off. She had her orders, and they were too busy for handholding, she would be fine.

Shielded and sight shielded, she slipped into the crowd. She tried to keep to the edges, hugging the buildings so tightly her shoulder brushed the wall. It wasn't enough though, there were just too many unSkilled.

A man walked directly into her and yelped when the shields burned him.

"What was that?" one of his friends demanded.

"I think I was stung by a bee," he answered, rubbing his shoulder where his bare skin had touched the shield. Salasi could see the red welt already starting to form. She rushed away before they realized that a bee wouldn't leave a mark like that.

Several more people clipped her shields as she hurried by, all of them crying out in pain or alarm at bumping into something unseen. She didn't wait around long enough for any of them to realize someone Skilled was in their midst. She'd hoped for a reprieve when she reached the park and all that open space, but here the crowd merely thickened. It seemed like all of Ashveil was here. She finally managed to make her way through to Zumi. He'd erected a shield that extended ten feet out from him and held the crowd at bay.

Salasi politely tapped on the shield and introduced herself. Zumi was younger than her by quite a bit, but he was also much stronger, so she used grammar forms that would respect his rank and not reflect his age.

The shield parted enough for her to slip through. Being within his shield didn't make her feel safer like she'd hoped. Instead, she felt like she was in a fishbowl with all these angry, distorted unSkilled faces glowering in at her.

<Animachea Command sent assistance,> she whispered but with the rancor that surrounded them, she didn't think that there was anything she could do to help.

<Your company is appreciated,> Zumi said, sounding relieved and also using casual-respectful language, deferring to her age and experience. <These people make it difficult.> He glanced up from where he was balancing on the edge of the well.

They noticed his attention and roared to life. The individual screams of protest almost immediately morphed into a chant.

OUR WATER! OUR WELL!

FIVE HUNDRED TO ONE!

The words rolled over the shield. Salasi shuddered.

<Perhaps it would be better to come back and finish another day,> Salasi murmured. Even under the protection of Zumi's shields, she hadn't dropped her own. It was incredibly rude not to do so. As a higher-ranked Skilled, Zumi could see her clearly through her sight shield and would know she was actively trying to hide. Given these circumstances, she could only hope he would understand and not take offense.

<There's something here,> he answered, his gaze dropping back to the water at his feet.

The way he said it had Salasi creeping over next to him.

She could still smell the dead Carnage but it had faded to a tolerable level now that his body had been removed. The water came up to a few feet shy of ground level and was dark and placid. To her, it looked just like a well should, but she didn't have Water Skills and knew there were many nuances she was missing.

<What do you sense?> she asked.

His eyes narrowed as he peered down into the depths of the well. <Not sure.>

The clattering thud of something hitting the shield drew both their attention.

That first projectile proved to be a catalyst, and suddenly all the unSkilled were throwing whatever was in their hands. Reusable food containers and utensils, rocks, sticks, and glass bottles still filled with drink, all of rained against Zumi's shields.

Salasi called in her tonfas, the feel of steel-tipped hardwood familiar and reassuring. Without Navari, Salasi could only see what was directly in front of her which left her half-blind. She kept darting looks over her shoulder, trying to keep track of anyone sneaking up behind her.

A dirty diaper landed with a disgusting splat against the shield. The crowd roared approval. The chant FIVE HUNDRED TO ONE picked up strength and volume.

All at once the water of the well came rushing upward in a twisting column. It moved with Zumi's will, spiraling around the inside of the shield before slashing outward.

He could have turned the water into a fine-edged blade and cut them all down where they stood. Instead, the water hit bluntly with bruising force bowling over the nearest rioters. Those in front would have retreated if they could have, but the crowd in the back was still chanting and surging forward, oblivious to Zumi's response.

Zumi drew more water up out of the well, creating a smothering wall that inched forward, forcing the crowd back. A few people tried to push their way through it, only to find themselves caught halfway and unable to escape. The chant finally stuttered to a halt as even those in the back realized something was happening.

Salasi watched dispassionately as one part of the mob was caught between Zumi's wall of water and the block wall that divided the park from neighboring houses. He could have easily crushed or smothered them all, but he left enough leeway for them to struggle up over the fence and escape into the yards. The rest he pushed back until he'd cleared the entire park, the mob now mashed together on the plaza and narrow street and spilling down the rails used by Ashveil's trolley.

As soon as the last person stepped off the grass, the water wall collapsed and began rolling back towards Zumi like an eager puppy. He directed it back into the well with a negligent wave of his hand while his attention stayed on the crowd.

Their expressions showed everything from terror and surprise to anger and humiliation. Several of them were already picking themselves up and getting ready to storm back into the park. Did they not realize how easy it would be for Zumi to kill them? And with such threatening behavior from the unSkilled, any tribunal would uphold his actions as just. Maybe they just didn’t care.

A familiar blonde woman had appeared and was shouting at people, ordering them back off the grass and onto the street.

<She’s a volunteer detective,> Salasi said to Zumi. <Maggie Reeves.>

He nodded, watching for a few more minutes until he was satisfied that no one was going to come rushing towards them again. With his shield securely in place, he turned his attention back to the well.

Salasi kept her shields up and her eyes on the crowd. She sharpened her hearing but couldn’t hear Maggie’s words over the rumble of the mob. Salasi let go of trying to overhear them and settled in to watch, hoping desperately that they’d all learned their lesson and wouldn’t rush the well a second time.

□

Chapter Fourteen

Maggie Reeves

Maggie left Jim's house before the others because she had classes to teach. Longcross had said he'd be in touch with more specific details when the time came. He'd assured her that everything that mattered was in place, the specific timing however would be determined by the shape of the day. Based on what he said, he and his other associates had contingency plans for all manner of events. He'd waved off Maggie when she'd asked for more details, telling her she didn't need to worry about any of it until they were necessary.

Maggie liked having things scheduled so she could consider them well in advance, but she also understood Longcross's caution. His plans were revolutionary and if the kurs caught wind of them, that would mean trouble for everyone involved. The less any one individual knew, the safer they all would be.

That was all blown right out of her mind as she turned a corner and found herself face-to-face with a mob of people. She saw a lot of angry and worried faces. Harsh whispers. Sharp gestures.

"What's going on?" Maggie said to the closest person.

"A kur is poisoning all our water!" he answered furiously.

"What?"

He jabbed his finger towards the heart of the crowd. "Some kur is filling up the well with water and is going to poison all the groundwater! They're planning to kill everyone in Ashveil!"

"The well already had water in it," she said, but the man wasn't listening, he'd gone back to his conversation about how they needed to take back the well by force before the kurs killed anyone else.

"Anyone else?" she asked horrified, who had died? When? How?

A chant of OUR WATER OUR WELL had started somewhere nearby and they ignored her.

Stomping insoles and throwing elbows, Maggie put her martial arts training to good use and cut her way into the crowd. The further in she got, the wetter everyone became until she was standing at the edge of the grass with people who were so thoroughly drenched their teeth chattered. A few started towards Zumi.

"Stop!" she ordered. She'd just spent an hour being briefed about just how dangerous Zumi could be despite his young age, and that utmost caution should be taken around him.

"He's poisoning our well!" the woman beside her shouted.

"He's not poisoning the well!" Maggie shouted back.

They didn't listen to that.

"HE'S BEING DEALT WITH!" she shouted louder, using her sensei voice. "You're putting people in danger by acting recklessly!"

That stopped most of them.

"Professionals are dealing with this and you're going to get them – and yourselves – killed if you keep this up."

"State agents are useless," someone muttered.

"It isn't the staties," Maggie answered. She paused for just a moment before dropping her voice and murmuring, "True Human has something in the works and they're the ones you're going to get killed. *Our* people. The ones who are fighting to make a difference."

The name True Human shifted the feelings of the crowd. Those who'd been ready to run heedlessly into danger, held back now. They were ready to spend their lives saving Ashveil from the kur trying to poison it, but they also trusted Ava and the other True Human members.

"Stop. For now, just stop. The more you keep this up, the more dangerous you'll make it for us."

Her words filtered out through the crowd. Slowly, grudgingly, everyone dispersed. Maggie caught more than a few comments about the uselessness of state agents and how staties were just toadies to the kurs. She also heard others correcting them. Staties weren't the ones dealing with the well, it was True Human and True Human knew how to take care of business.

Maggie felt some of the tension unknot from her shoulders. Longcross had plans for Zumi and his getting killed in a mob attack wasn't part of it.

By the time the crowd had completely dissolved, Maggie had already missed her entire first afternoon class and it was more than halfway through the next. The few people who remained at the park seemed more intent on constant vigilance than starting another fight, though she was sure they had a posse on call should Zumi step even one toe out of line.

She left them to their own devices and hurried to her dojo picturing all the kids slumped around outside waiting for her and thinking about all the calls she'd have to make tonight apologizing for canceling the earlier class without notice. Only it wasn't her students waiting for her. As if talking about them had summoned them, a quartet of state agents were standing outside her dojo doors.

State agents were the human counterpart to Animachea's Enforcers. State agents dealt with any kur-related incidents, and almost always came down in favor of the kurs. They also weren't always the quickest to act, carefully collecting and collating all the facts before they did anything. It certainly surprised her to see them here already, news about the mob at the well had certainly spread fast.

"Volunteer Detective Maggie Reeves?" the only woman in the group asked as she walked up.

"I am," Maggie answered cautiously.

"State Agent Kasia Laren," she said, offering a hand. Her dark hair had been slicked back so tight in a bun it had to give her a headache. "These are my trainees, Ogwo, Smith, and Park. We're here to discuss the body in the well."

Maggie shook her hand.

"May we come in?"

"I only have floor seating," Maggie warned.

"That's acceptable."

All four of them were wearing matching black suits with crisp white shirts and gleaming patent leather shoes. Such formal attire made the three men look gangly and awkward as they sat down on the reed tumbling mats with her. Laren however folded her legs and sat at her ease.

"It was brought to our attention that a body was discovered yesterday in a well in Temple Park," Laren said, enunciating everything very clearly.

"Yes," Maggie agreed.

"Please elaborate."

A vague and yet all-encompassing statement. Maggie started at the beginning with Jim coming to her between morning classes and asking for her help. She discussed the discovery of the body, contacting Animachea Enforcers for a census count, them announcing the dead man was a kur, and then taking the body with them.

Laren listened attentively without comment, her back ramrod straight, her hands resting on her knees. When Maggie finished, the questions started. The first was for clarity, confirming that Jim was a Staff Detective with Ashveil PD, and that Maggie was a volunteer Detective who typically only worked large-scale assignments that needed extra hands.

"It is understood that the original complaint was just for a foul odor, no body was expected at that time, correct?"

"Yes."

"Why did Detective Dawes ask for your help for something so straightforward?" Laren's tone remained pleasant but Maggie felt her back going up. It suddenly seemed like Laren was looking to pin something on him. Fury rose in Maggie. After hearing Jim's story, and learning about his son, it was amazing that he even got up every morning. Now here he was, opening up about Ceres, starting to live life again – without needing to drink – and the staties showed up to take it all away.

"Was it wrong for him to ask for help?" Maggie asked sharply.

"No. Simply curious as to why he asked for help. You're a volunteer Detective. You work full-time elsewhere. You do in fact, own and run your own business. As a volunteer, you should not be expected to close your business and lose revenue over such a trivial matter as an odor in a well."

"Jim is one of the survivors of Ceres," Maggie replied coldly. "Peering down into a dark hole in the ground is hardly trivial."

"Apologies. His reason for requesting your help was personal then?"

"Yes."

"When you checked the well, you discovered the odor was from a human corpse."

"Yes." Maggie half expected Laren to ask why she and Jim hadn't pulled the body out themselves to immediately start CPR.

Laren proved not to be so dumb or officious. "You then contacted the Enforcers and not the Medical Examiner of Angels Landing. Why?"

"The Enforcers would need to be contacted anyway to take a census count and they would have an easier time raising the body from the well than we would."

"They informed you that he was Carnage?"

"No," she answered, caught off guard. "Only that he was a kur."

"You will refrain from using derogatory slurs," Laren said reproachfully.

Shame washed through Maggie that Laren had called her out for the use of 'kur' and then also angry that she felt ashamed. Ashveil was her town, after all, she should be able to protect it. Before she could snap anything back at Laren, or ask about the Carnage, the statie had moved on.

"Are there any incidents you've been aware of in the last week?"

"Incidents?" Maggie asked, thrown by the change in subject.

"Anything that seemed unusual to you? Anything that struck you as abnormal?"

"No. Why?"

"Carnage is not a House that dies easily, nor are they ones to leave bodies simply lying around. The circumstances themselves are quite unusual. Perhaps something that appears unrelated may be connected."

"No," Maggie said again.

"Can you explain the tumultuous nature of the gathering at the well now?"

"The Water Controller sent Zumi to evaluate the well. The people are upset with his presence."

"For what reason?"

"He's poisoning it." The words slipped from her lips easily. She knew they weren't true, but a small piece of her wondered. What if Zumi had come here to poison the well? Izoklakeite sank Ceres because he could. Some unknown Ice had been pissy and whipped up a snowstorm that sent a train off the rails, killing dozens. House of Carnage had hunted down Sensei Callum simply for the challenge of it. Why wouldn't Zumi be just as bad as them? Why not poison an entire town just for fun? He'd never be punished for it.

One of Laren's sharp eyebrows lifted. "Poisoning it?" she asked.

"That well has been here for centuries. There's no reason for a— for a Skilled to suddenly need to 'evaluate' it."

"Then it stands to reason that Controller Ataku would want to know where the water is coming from. Would the people of Ashveil not also wish to know this?"

Personally, Maggie did want to know that. When she was a child, her grandmother had learned that she and Li played around the well, pretending it was a secret entrance to adventure, the old woman had told them her own stories of when she was a little girl, pretending that there was a great lost treasure buried at the bottom of the well, because why else would it be dry?

"Maybe," Maggie allowed. "But the... Skilled... won't offer any details." She tripped over the word, having to remind herself not to say kur.

"Perhaps he does not know them yet. Do you report to your students' parents every single move they make as they make them, or do you give them an overall report at the end of your class?"

"I give them reports when they're upset and demanding them," Maggie answered sharply. "I open a dialogue to learn what the problem is and address it, I don't just ignore them because they're inconvenient."

Laren nodded thoughtfully, accepting Maggie's response. "That matter will be discussed with Zumi. Is there anything else?"

She made it sound as if Maggie had requested that they come. "No."

"Very well. We will be in touch." Laren stood easily. The three men clambered awkwardly to their feet after her. She offered a small bow to Maggie and then walked out, the three men filing after her through the door.

Maggie kept an eye on them through the front window. They walked through the square, off to whatever other state agent business they had to attend to when Laren froze. Her mouth dropped into an O of horror, and she sprinted out of sight, absurdly fast in her formal shoes.

Maggie bolted out the door after her, heart pounding over what could upset the state agent so suddenly.

From here she could see to the end of the square, across the street, and into the park. The park where a delivery vehicle was now flooring towards Zumi at top speed.

She sprinted after Laren, already knowing that no matter how fleet foot the statie was, she wouldn't reach Zumi before the vehicle did. Maggie watched the van careen into the well with the shriek of breaking stone and sheering metal. It flew through the air and came down with a crunching thud on its side.

Maggie reached the wreck as the staties started speaking to the driver, asking him clearly if he was okay. He was shouting back at them, "Our well! Our water!" His words were slurred though, and blood trickled down his forehead from where it had smashed into the airbag. Maggie didn't recognize him, though he wore a True Human shirt and jacket. There were too many people in the chapter for Maggie to know them all.

She spared him just that glance before leaving him to the staties and turning her attention to the well.

A sizable chunk had been taken out of it and she was surprised to see that under all the moss and lichen, the stone had once been bright, shining white. The broken edges nearly glowed even in the shade of the trees.

Around the broken well, there was no sign of Zumi at all. Instead of feeling elation that the kur had gone, her heart sank. All of

Longcross's carefully curated plans, everything he had laid out for her and Jim and Ava this afternoon, had just been destroyed.

□

Chapter Fifteen

Raid

It didn't take long for Mordred to track the scent. He took them to Daal Mountain Nature Center. The building stood at the end of the aesthetically pleasing Main Street. Tourists must have loved Main Street with all its little boutiques selling art and clothing, and cafes with a bougie take on 'rustic' food and drinks. A few places rented out climbing, camping, and hiking gear, and a general store meant to look like a ski lodge stood tall and proud to one side. Raid caught no scent of Cain. In public places like this, the footsteps of all the unSkilled along with the weather would have wiped it away.

That wasn't the case when they walked into the Nature Center. Cain's scent was still here but fading. Raid also caught the scent of the aught Earth. This was where she spent most of her time. Cain must have worked with her. He'd been hired by the unSkilled forestry department to work in conjunction with House Viridae to do things like bird surveys and hike trails to make sure they remained passable.

Raid and Mordred walked past the exhibits of taxidermied animals, examples of different kinds of pinecones, and warnings about toxic radials. Mordred ignored the sign that said, 'Employees Only' and walked into the back, Raid a step behind.

The large room had several desks stacked so high with papers, pictures, and various paraphernalia that they were unusable. Hats. Binoculars. Nets. Traps. It all had the air of a temporary placement that had become permanent in the overcrowded space. His eyes swept over all of it before settling on the woman.

She was too thin, her wrists, chin, and cheekbones jutting. Her clothes hung off her like they would a wire coat hanger. Her eyes were sunken and shadowed. Her brown skin had a sickly yellow-gray undertone. Her hair was lank, pulled back into a thin, lackluster braid. Raid couldn't smell sickness on her but he could smell all the medications she was taking. Something was seriously wrong with her.

Currently, she was cleaning the cage of a small snake. Her long, spidery fingers carefully scrubbed out its water bowl.

<Drop the sight shield,> Raid said, knowing and hating when the high aughts spoke to him as disembodied voices, refusing to let him see them.

Mordred did.

The woman froze, her eyes locked on the Inquisitor's uniform.

"You knew Cain," Raid said, speaking out loud. Some low aughts preferred it to thoughtspeak. He held out the gloves, drawing her attention away from Mordred. There was a flash of recognition when she saw the gloves. She nodded slowly. "Is he missing?" she asked tentatively.

"He's dead."

Genuine shock ripped through her. She had enough presence of mind to set down the water dish and close the tiny snake's enclosure before sinking into the nearest chair. "You're certain?"

Raid nodded curtly. "What do you know about him?"

"He started working here before tourist season, maybe six months ago?"

Which was when Mordred had dispatched them on this awful assignment.

"Fast learner. Excellent trail guide. People started requesting him specifically. Especially for the High Saddle Trail."

<What made you think he was missing?> Mordred asked.

She flinched.

<Speak out loud,> Raid hissed to just Mordred.

"He always shows up. Always on time," she answered. "He's not someone who just up and vanishes. He and Mad had a back-packing trip planned. He didn't show."

"That didn't concern you?" Mordred asked.

She flinched again.

<It's not the thoughtspeak,> Mordred said to Raid.

<Yeah, it's just you she finds painful.>

Mordred flicked his shields.

"It did," she answered carefully and eyed them both. "The two of us checked all the trails in case he went off alone and was injured. We didn't find anything. We just…"

"You just?" Raid prompted.

"We just hoped he'd gone back to Carnage. He talked about having brothers, we thought he'd gone to see one of them." She looked at them both, realized who they were, and amended the statement. "One of you."

Cain had, only Raid hadn't realized it. Cain had been in Ashveil and Raid had been completely oblivious.

"You didn't report it," Raid accused, but then why would she? A sick aught, with no allies or she wouldn't be here alone smelling of unSkilled medications, wouldn't have wanted to bring any attention to herself. She would have left Carnage to deal with Carnage.

She shook her head. "No."

"Where's Mad?" It sounded like they'd been friends with Cain also.

She rattled off an address.

Easy enough to get to. "And you are?"

"Kaolin. You?"

"Raid and Mordred."

That brought a slight smile to her face. "He talked a lot about you."

Raid wished he could say the same. He hadn't heard the names Kaolin or Mad before now.

"Do you know how he died?" she asked.

"No."

She clenched her hands tightly.

"Is there someone you suspect?" Raid asked.

A bitter laugh escaped her lips. "True Human. Who else? They were here all winter, gangs from all over Iocaste spewing their garbage."

"Any one of them stand out to you?"

She shook her head. "They were all obnoxious but no one was overtly hostile. Mad might know more. He spent more time around them, working the slopes and the trails. Not many of them would come in here to learn about wildlife."

"We'll look. Thank you."

"Whoever killed him, make them pay," she said, her voice hard.

<Without question,> Mordred answered before dropping them both behind a sight shield again.

—

While almost everyone lived in town, even Cain, there were a few scattered cabins beyond the main road. While Kaolin had given them the address, it took trial and error to finally find it, tucked up in its own valley, built along a small creek. Unlike so many unSkilled roads that allowed for vehicle access, the path to Mad's cabin looked more like the start of a trailhead. If Mordred hadn't finally caught a scrap of Cain's scent heading down it, they would have kept walking right past it.

The path curved through the trees and ferns, narrow but well-maintained. Gravel had been laid down to help with traction in the snow and mud, but it was dry now, sunlight dappling the ground around them. After a final curve through the bracken, he spotted the cabin up ahead. Raid sharpened his vision and hearing as they approached but nothing appeared out of the ordinary. The windows were open to let in the light and the breeze. Away from the main road, Cain's scent grew stronger, stronger even than it had been at the Nature Center because there was less foot traffic to wear it away, though wind and rain and time would blow it all away eventually.

Unlike at the Nature Center, Mordred didn't just walk straight up to the front door and let himself in, instead, he prowled around the cabin.

<What is it?> Raid asked.

Modred shook his head. <Don't know. Something.>

<Unhelpful.>

Mordred didn't elaborate.

Raid waited and tried to get a sense of the place while Mordred circled twice more. Raid picked up nothing more than Cain, and the ghostly footprints of the unSkilled who lived here, most likely Mad.

Mordred finally came back to him.

<What?> Raid asked again.

<It feels like there was a high aught here,> Mordred finally answered. <Can't get a read on the scent, it keeps slipping away.>

<Then they weren't here recently,> Raid answered.

Mordred still looked uneasy.

<We're going to learn nothing just standing out here.> Raid went to the door. The lock was simple and easy enough to pick with Skills. He let himself in.

This cabin was smaller than Cain's and crammed full of everything. For all that it was filled to the brim, it was neat and orderly. One wall was covered with coiled ropes and hanging clips meant for rock climbing. High shelves held backpacking frames, and tents and sleeping bags that had been carefully rolled up and stored. There was a wall that was nothing but bookshelves completely packed with books. Some were wildlife guides like what Cain had, but most of them weren't. History, anthropology, archeology, art, photography… Mad read anything and everything. There was a 'kitchen' along the third wall, mostly a hot plate and half-sized fridge, and the last wall was covered in charcoal sketches not that different from the ones Cain had hung. Probably made by the same artist.

Suddenly the door to the bedroom opened and Mad was standing there. Raid didn't know what he'd been expecting, but it wasn't this.

Mad was all sinew and wire, lean and weathered from a lifetime spent climbing rocks and hiking the back bowls. He was shorter than Raid, his black hair looked like it had been cut with a knife and kicked up in all directions. He hadn't shaved in a couple of days.

What caught Raid off guard was that Mad could see him, even through Mordred's sight shield. They stared at each other, Mad's black eyes full of fire. Raid called in his knives, ready to meet to onslaught because Mad looked ready for a fight. Then that look faded.

Mordred dropped the sight shield and Mad blinked in surprise as if seeing them both for the first time. Maybe he hadn't seen Raid through the sight shield. Raid must have imagined it.

"Raid and Mordred?" Mad guessed cautiously.

"You know us?" Raid asked before silently answering his own question. Of course, Mad knew them. Just as Cain had told Kaolin about them, he'd told Mad too.

"You're either Cain's brother or you're Witch Angels and I'm in deep shit." He regarded Mordred's Inquisitor uniform. "Might be in deep shit either way."

<Cain's dead,> Mordred said.

Mad's body went still, face blank. He shifted his feet, his stance becoming more solid.

Mordred tensed, ready to attack. <He knows something.>

Raid agreed, his fingers tightening on the knives already in his hands. Everything about Mad's body language was braced for a fight, for blows to start falling.

The silence between them stretched to breaking, both sides waiting to see what the other would do.

"What happened?" Mad finally asked, his voice so laden with pain and grief that it nearly knocked Raid off his feet. Mad had locked up not because he was priming for a fight, but because he was barely holding it together. Suddenly Raid realized that he'd made a wrong assumption. Cain hadn't been in a relationship with Kaolin. He'd been in one with Mad.

Mordred realized the same thing and muttered, <What is with you two? You're off the Mountain for a few months and you're sleeping with a Viridae part-blood and Cain's sleeping with the unSkilled.>

<Maybe you shouldn't have kicked us off the Mountain,> Raid snapped back.

<It was for your own safety.>

<Keep telling yourself that,> Raid answered before saying out loud, "We don't know. We were hoping you knew something."

Mad was quiet for a long minute. He didn't so much as twitch, settling even further into a rock-solid steadiness. His breathing didn't even change even though tears started to fall. Mad must have faced some terrible situations in the past to remain so outwardly calm in this moment even though his heart was breaking.

"Arcana," he said, and all the feelings he wasn't showing came pouring out with that word.

"Arcana?" Raid echoed, unfamiliar with the name.

<Arcana Industries,> Mordred supplied. <The High Inquisitor has dealings with them.> He flashed Raid the basic information he knew.

Seeing that made Raid realize he also knew Arcana. He'd seen their advertisements in Ashveil; the smiling doctors with the pretty pills and promises. They were a drug company that Li thought very lowly of. He would have to ask her more about them later.

Mad nodded once as if the physical movement pained him.

"Not True Human?" Raid asked because that's where he was sure this was going.

"Arcana is True Human."

<How?> Mordred demanded sharply.

There was another long pause as Mad gathered his words around his pain. "Arcana is one of True Human's major donors. Maybe their biggest one." His voice caught. He just breathed for a moment before finally going on. "True Human's founder Adrian Longcross went to medical school with Arcana's head of research and development, Reefa Mazuli."

<You know them?> Mordred asked.

"They come here all the time," Mad said, a sharper edge appearing through the grief.

<What else do you know?>

Anger gave Mad something to hold onto, and while his pain was still clear in every word he spoke, it wasn't so much of a struggle. "They're always here. Year round. Seminars. Small groups. Leadership retreats. Industry-wide conferences. There's always an event. They always requested Cain as their trail guide for everything once they knew he was here. Short hour-long meadow walks to multi-day backpacking trips. They always wanted him."

"You didn't like that," Raid observed.

"The only other person they've ever shown that much interest in is Kaolin. She sees one of their doctors every time they have an event in town. They pay for her to go to Iocaste Proper for advanced testing and imaging. They have her convinced that only their medications and interventions can help her."

Raid was about to ask what was wrong with her when Mordred said to only him, <There are only two Skilled in Daal, and Arcana is interested in both of them.>

<How would Arcana even know? Cain doesn't look Carnage.> He had been born blue-eyed and blonde, a surprise to everyone, but his psychic scent and Skills had been Carnage through and through. Adira had always been quick to taunt him that he was a 'throwback.' For this assignment, however, it meant he didn't need to wear or worry about the shield charm the way Raid did. Raid's fingers went to his neck, double checking that he was wearing it.

<How *would* they know?> Mordred echoed darkly, his focus was inward, churning through something.

<What are you thinking?> Raid asked.

<That Bester knows Arcana,> Mordred answered, his use of casual language when discussing the High Inquisitor was a sign of deep disrespect, and a reflection of how angry he was, angrier than Raid had realized.

<Do they have an address?> Mordred demanded of Mad.

"Not here," Mad answered. They'd lost his attention when they'd been speaking to each other, and Raid could feel the struggle as he answered them when he wanted to be left alone and in silence. "Everything was always billed to their corporate office in Iocaste Proper."

Mordred nodded curtly, then took Raid's arm and jumped away before Raid could even ask what Mordred had in mind.

Chapter Sixteen

SalNavari

Salasi watched the vehicle coming. unSkilled most often used individual vehicles to make deliveries too large to transport by bicycle. People with disabilities also utilized private vehicles modified with the appropriate accommodations to easily move through town. The vehicles were all battery-operated with interchangeable parts that could be traded out as things wore down, allowing the vehicle to still be operable while the broken part was refurbished or recycled.

It struck her as odd that this one drove over the grass rather than on a vehicle road, and also drove straight towards her. It didn't occur to her until too late that the driver might be planning to run her down.

<Zumi!> she shouted horrified while her thoughts leapt straight for Navari and the comfort of her partner.

Zumi grabbed Salasi around the waist as she braced for impact and dove into the well. Water closed over her head as Zumi pulled her deep.

Overhead the vehicle hit his Five aught shields with enough power and momentum to shatter them. A moment later the water around her convulsed as the vehicle struck the well. Several stones splashed down, one striking her shoulder as it sank. Silence descended. Salasi held still. The water would be dark to anyone looking down, but she didn't want to aid them in finding her by thrashing about.

She reached out with her Skills. She could sense people walking around the well, but no one stood directly beside it, waiting for them.

<It seems to be over,> Salasi said quietly, trying to hide the growing strain of holding her breath.

<Yes,> Zumi agreed. Still holding her tight to him, the water around them shifted, delivering them in a blink to the surface.

The vehicle lay on its side nearby, black-suited state agents arresting the driver.

<Thank you,> she murmured respectfully to Zumi. <Please let go so this may be dealt with.>

Zumi loosened his grip on her and she could feel how rattled he was. He was strong and would be stronger still as he aged towards adulthood, but for the moment he was a frightened youth.

Salasi stepped off the edge of the well. As she did, she felt Navari's presence fill in behind her eyes. Feeling Navari with her was such a relief she could have cried. Navari was bleary and in pain and exhausted, but she was there.

Salasi immediately shared her memories of the last few minutes. Navari's pain and exhaustion faded marginally as she glared hatefully at the driver.

<What is this?> Salasi demanded, her voice echoed and reinforced by Navari so it came out stronger and more imposing than one alone.

Two of the state agents flinched.

"Unknown Enforcer," another state agent, a woman, said coming directly over. "We were sent to investigate the circumstances of the body in the well and happened to see this crime being committed." She gestured to the driver and the vehicle. "Are you two unharmed?"

Navari ignored the question, her attention on the driver. Salasi followed her lead. <What is this?> she repeated, her words focused solely on him.

He winced and moaned in response then slurred out, "Our well!"

"He appears to have sustained a head injury," one of the other state agent's said.

Blood trickled from the driver's hairline and he didn't seem wholly aware of his surroundings.

"It may be a few hours before he's recovered enough to answer you, Enforcer," the woman said. "We will stay with him to ensure he answers all questions satisfactorily once he is able."

"See that you do," Salasi replied. "Until then, Zumi will return to the Water Works."

<No,> Zumi said politely, only to her.

<No?> Salasi echoed just as privately. <They just tried to kill you.> With everything happening in Iocaste Proper and now here, he needed more protection than she could offer as half of a low aught Enforcer pair.

<There's something here,> he answered. <This water… it's different.>

Volunteer Detective Reeves stepped forward, her blonde hair shining in the sunlight. "Please, if I may," she said politely. "These are turbulent times and the people are scared. They're acting foolishly. It would be better for you to stay here now and finish this survey as quickly as possible than to try and come back and do it later."

<It will be fine,> Zumi said confidently.

Now that the terror of the moment was over, Navari was starting to fade away behind Salasi's eyes as the Bone medicines pulled her back into unconsciousness.

"The Ashveil PD will assign officers to keep the crowds at bay so they can't gather the way they did before," Maggie added, unaware of the thoughtspeak conversation.

<You're sure?> Salasi asked quietly.

<Yes,> Zumi assured her.

"Very well," Salasi replied. "You may assign your officers."

"Smith and Park will remain here," the state agent said. "The rest of us will accompany the suspect to the hospital. Maggie Reeves, do you not have a class to teach?" The last sentence was pointed.

"I do," Maggie answered. "But this is more important."

The state agent studied her for a moment before nodding. "Very well. Please go see to the dispatch of your department."

"Right away," she said and started running back across the grass with a long easy stride.

<Are you sure about this?> Salasi asked again as the two state agents hauled away the driver and the other two began patrolling around the park.

<Yes,> Zumi said, his attention already sliding downward through the water. <There isn't anything the unSkilled can do.>

Salasi thought of the bullet-ridden houses in Mountain Village and wondered if the owners had had similar thoughts. She pressed her hand to her chest, feeling the dull ache from where she'd been shot.

<They almost ran you down with a vehicle,> she pointed out, her discomfort at arguing with a higher aught rank overruled by the fact that she had so nearly almost died for the second time today.

<But they didn't.>

If Navari had been with her, Salasi may have kept arguing but her partner had returned firmly to her dreams, and the garden with its ocean-like flowers now dotted with wells and overturned vehicles. Salasi wanted nothing more than to go back to the Mountain and fill her mind with loving, joyful thoughts that would filter out the horror that filled these last two days. Instead, Salasi wrapped herself in a sight shield and dredged up what happy memories she could think of and tried to feed those to Navari. She then paced the inside of Zumi's shield, determined not to be caught off guard by the unSkilled's bizarre behavior again.

Chapter Seventeen

Raid

Mad's overstuffed cabin was replaced by Raid's empty apartment. The difference was stark. It made Raid never want to come back to this place again. He didn't want a place where he could sleep, he wanted an actual home. He reached for Li, trying to feel her presence at the co-op where she would be selling fresh eggs and produce and the handmade items that Ashveil's various crafters created and sold.

Her psychic presence was minimal compared to a Skilled, but it still felt to him like a sunbeam.

<What are we doing back here?> he asked.

<Going to go talk to Bester,> Mordred answered harshly. <You're staying here.>

The way he said that alarmed Raid. <You're not confronting the High Inquisitor.>

<She knows something.>

<What she knows won't make a difference if you're dead.>

Mordred glared at him; his rage so icy it felt like the temperature around them dropped. <Bester has dealings with Arcana,> Mordred said coldly.

<And? We don't even know what that means.>

Mordred looked absolutely set. Raid could feel his panic growing. Bester was a Nine, second only to Matriarch Katio in power and influence within Carnage and was one of the strongest Skilled on the Mountain period under the Matriarchs. No matter what new Skills and strength Mordred had now, it would not be enough to go after Bester and win. If Mordred died, that would leave Raid alone, the last of his creche brothers. The idea terrified him.

<Look,> Raid went on, scrambling desperately for something to distract Mordred from that self-destructive idea. <Why don't we find Reefa Mazuli or Adrian Longcross? We can find out what they know. If either of them is involved in Cain's death.>

A long moment passed before Modred nodded curtly. <Fine.>

They jumped again, this time to a sprawling neighborhood of sprawling houses with huge, immaculate lawns.

<Where are we now?> Raid asked.

<Overlook,> Mordred answered. <Longcross lives here.>

The gated community belonged to Iocaste Proper's wealthiest and most suicidal citizens. Their back fences butted right up against the boundary marker that divided Iocaste Proper from the Mountain, and the land where no unSkilled could set foot under penalty of death. With what Raid knew of Longcross, it came as no surprise that he would live here.

The Longcross house was excessively large and sprawling for a single-family dwelling. A long driveway with carefully tended trees and manicured beds led up to it. It had a huge arched front door, at least three floors and two wings, and a multitude of big glass windows. Mordred picked the fancy digital lock with Skills and let them in.

Li's whole cottage would have fit in this foyer. Expensive and rare pieces of art hung on the walls or stood on their own personally lit plinths. The polished tile floors glinted and the white carpet on the double set of stairs sweeping up to the next floor had vacuum lines on it.

The sitting room to one side was filled with floor-to-ceiling bookshelves and an impressive fireplace surrounded by leather sofas. The heavy, leather-bound books gave the impression of having never been touched much less read. To the other side of the foyer was a music room with a grand piano, a cello on a stand, and several guitars hanging on the wall. Raid ran his Skills over all of it, looking for hidden compartments or anything else that seemed unusual.

<You're sure Longcross lives here?> Raid asked. Despite the furnishings and decorations, this place reminded him of his apartment; an empty front for show.

<Yes,> Mordred answered.

Unsurprisingly there was no psychic scent to confirm anyone's presence. He also didn't pick up the smells he usually associated with unSkilled. No sweat, no food, no mud tracked in. This house was so clean it almost seemed unlived in.

<Does anyone live here?> he asked rhetorically.

Mordred suddenly pulled up short. His eyes narrowed.

Raid sharpened his senses, trying to feel what Mordred reacted to.

<Bester wants to talk,> Mordred said, a hard and challenging gleam coming into his eyes.

Raid didn't have time to react before Mordred jumped away.

<You better not get yourself killed you asshole!> Raid shouted, spearing the thought at Mordred.

Mordred responded by flicking Raid's shields and sent an image of his motorcycle parked outside on the street. A moment later Mordred's attention turned fully away from him, the thoughtspeak equivalent of hanging up a meme.

<Well shit,> Raid muttered. At least Mordred left the motorcycle so Raid didn't have to walk out on foot, but that was the least of his worries. He could only hope that Mordred wouldn't pick a fight he couldn't win and get flattened.

Raid found a secondary, far less impressive staircase leading from the kitchen and took that upstairs to avoid leaving footprints on the plush carpet. There were Skilled ways to walk without leaving footprints, but this was easier. On the second floor, he found the children's bedrooms as well as the master suite. Who knew Longcross had children? One would think he'd take better care and be more cautious as their lives could be taken as collateral against his. They were as much in the crosshairs Longcross had created for himself as much as he was.

Here at least smelled like the unSkilled and looked lived in. Maybe it was only the downstairs rooms that were just for show. Raid studied the kids' rooms thoroughly enough to know there weren't any hidden doors or cubbies before starting on the master suite.

It took up half of the second floor. There was a bedroom but also a sitting room, reading room, and office, not to mention a bathroom with a tub so large it looked useless. It put him in mind of the suites the high aughts had in the Houses, the space they occupied reflecting their rank rather than what they actually needed or used.

The rooms themselves were austere. Everything was shades of gray and off-white with the occasional blue highlight. The fixtures were all silver. Had Longcross chosen Ice colors on purpose or had all this been accidental? There was nonsense artwork on the walls, probably as expensive and prized as the artwork downstairs. The books in the library were all medical tomes, leather-bound and gilt with gold. None of them looked useful for studying medicine. The whole suite just seemed like a smaller, more intimate version of the downstairs.

The office was the most interesting, and also the most lived in. When Longcross was home, he spent his time here. The locks on the file cabinets and drawers were easy to pick, and he methodically worked his way through all of them, finding nothing he didn't already know. There were reports and testimonials of suspected Skilled on unSkilled violence. Police reports. Medical exam notes. Autopsies. There was a list of towns with restricted populations and the requirements needed to be approved for a child. Animachea's census reports on births and deaths throughout Iocaste. Viridae, Earth, and Water and the resources they allotted, who had received them, when, and why.

A lot of number crunching and data manipulation that would feed the True Human propaganda.

Raid had lived in Ashveil for months now. Those people wanted for nothing. No one was starving. No one was homeless. Everyone had access to clean water. It wasn't a restricted birth town so they could have as many kids as they could produce. What else did they want?

As much information as there was, none of it tied Longcross to Cain, and nothing mentioned Arcana, not even tangentially. There wasn't even mention of the Skilled beyond the long list of grievances that True Human always had.

Something tickled the edges of Raid's perception.

He paused and listened. A car door slammed in the distance.

A moment later the front door opened, and a male voice drifted up through the floor.

Longcross was home.

Quickly and quietly Raid set all the files right and closed all the drawers and cabinets. He double-checked his shields and sight shields before slipping out of the master suite and onto the upstairs landing. From here he could look down over the sprawling great room.

Longcross was dressed in a suit, talking to someone on his meme. Through the window, Raid caught sight of the driver pulling the car around to the garage.

"The staties were coming, it would have been worse if I stayed in Ashveil," Longcross said defensively. "If you want Ataku, this is how we're going to do it."

Whatever the response had his face darkening. Raid sharpened his hearing but couldn't catch the voice of the speaker on the other end of the call.

"Yes," Longcross said sharply. "I was clear on the timing. Yes, I know how important the timing is. I'll be secure on my end. You just make sure that Hayes and his people are ready."

Raid shifted his weight carefully as he made his way down the stairs, using Skills to keep him from making footprints on the carpet. He needed to get close enough to hear the other half of the conversation. Longcross would already be dead and bleeding across his immaculate tile floor if Raid wanted it, but he wanted more to hear what Longcross had to say.

"Hayes is ready to move?" Longcross seemed relieved. "Remember it has to be hard and fast. They can't be given a chance to respond or recover."

The edges of Raid's perception began to prickle again. The not quite itchy, not quite pain of an insect crawling along his skin. The hair on the back of his neck stood on end.

He called in his knives.

It felt like there was a stronger Skilled nearby. One high enough in rank that they could hide themselves from him completely but were choosing to show just enough of themselves to set him on edge.

A white moth fluttered across his vision.

Odd that a moth had escaped the laser intense focus of the housekeepers that kept this place so pristine. Another fluttered in the corner of his eye, keeping up with him as he prowled down. It distracted him enough that he stopped midway on the staircase and batted at it.

It didn't go. Instead, it brought friends. One moth became twenty. Fifty. A hundred. A thousand. So many their round, furry bodies obscured his vision, and he could hear nothing but the soft beating of their wings. The world tipped around him, spiraled and shrank. He had no sense of the Mountain beyond Longcross's backyard, then no sense of the house itself. The stairs he stood on vanished under his feet leaving him with nothing but the moths swirling around him.

He was alone, cut off from everything. Nothing existed besides himself and the moths. Alone. Insignificant. Trapped wholly and solely within his skin. Blind and deaf and dumb.

"Shit! There's one here now!"

Longcross's voice was both too loud and too distant. Muffled but painfully sharp. Echoing in ways it shouldn't. Coming from everywhere and nowhere.

"Carnage I think. It's carrying knives."

He couldn't even feel himself. The only things that felt real were the moths.

"Yes. Fine. I'll bring it to you alive if I can— Well maybe you shouldn't have broken the last one Reefa."

Raid's hands tightened on his knives, muscle memory taking over where conscious thought failed.

A hand closed over his wrist.

He struck, hard and fast. He didn't need to think for that. Years of training with Nico, Cain and Mordred had burned instinct into every muscle fiber. His blade slashed where a neck should be.

Hot blood spattered across the white moths.

The hand let him go.

The blood began to burn the moths away.

Raid rediscovered his feet. He'd collapsed on the stairs. He somehow managed to straighten and started to stagger back up towards the second floor. The moths crisped away completely. His vision cleared. The world slowly bled back in.

A person lay crumpled at the bottom of the staircase wearing a charcoal gray suit and strange rainbow ski goggles. Her throat was slit ear to ear, blood soaking her shirt collar and pooling across the tile floor. Raid couldn't make sense of her or where she'd come from, but hers was the throat he'd slit.

Longcross gaped at her horrified, but recovered faster than Raid. He suddenly had a gun in his hand. Raid tried to throw up a shield but his brain was too scrambled. All he could do was stare as Longcross pulled the trigger.

□

Chapter Eighteen

Raid

The sound of the gunshot ripped through Raid's ears.

The bullet hit him low in the chest, just off midline. It punched him backward, blew the breath from his lungs. The jacket held. For all the seamstress had been pissed about the request, her Skill work held. Raid scrambled to his feet and threw himself up the stairs. Two more bullets bounced off his back. He reached the landing and kept going up.

He could hear Longcross pounding up the stairs behind him, spitting into his meme that Bunny was dead, and he needed backup *NOW*.

Raid reached the third floor and finally managed to pull up a shield. It was flickering and weak but gaining strength now that the moths were gone. He tried for a sight shield and failed. Down the hall into the massive home gym with huge windows looking out over the sprawling backyard. Shit. He'd just run himself into a corner.

Longcross hurtled into the gym behind him.

Raid hurled a twenty-five-pound barbell at him. It crunched into Longcross's shoulder, and he shouted wordlessly in pain, the gun dropping from nerveless fingers.

<What the hell was that?> Raid snarled. Panicked and in pain, he wasn't gentle.

Longcross yipped as the thoughtspeak seared through his mind.

<Where the hell did those moths come from?> It was knee jerk to share the image, so much easier and swifter than stumbling through spoken explanations. Raid sent him the growing terror as the world faded away under the softly beating wings of the white moths.

Longcross's unSkilled, unshielded mind popped and fizzed

under the image. He gurgled bloody foam and began seizing. Shit. "Shit." Raid kicked the gun away and grabbed Longcross by the lapels on his jacket. "What was that? What did you do?"

Longcross's eyes were flickering, unseeing. unSkilled minds were so ridiculously fragile. Raid dropped him, left him twitching on the floor. His meme lay nearby. A tinny voiced hissed from it that they were on their way now, just hunker down and hold tight.

Raid doubled back the way he'd come, picking up his knives that he'd dropped when Longcross shot him the first time. The woman was still dead at the bottom of the stairs. Raid went to her and pulled off her goggles. Her pupils were fully dilated, leaving no color to her eyes but black. No wonder she was wearing ski goggles even inside, normal light had to be blinding. He vaguely remembered seeing her at the True Human meeting helping set things up before the big speech. She was Longcross's personal assistant.

Most alarming was her psychic scent. He hadn't noticed it until he crouched over her because it was faint and more childlike than weak, like she still had some growing to do. She smelled of huge spaces, dark and empty. He'd never scented a Skilled like her before. She didn't belong to any of the Houses.

<Mordred.> He speared the thought directly to his brother. Overlook was directly in the shadow of the Mountain. Mordred had to be able to hear him. <Whatever you're doing, get back here now.>

No answer.

<MORDRED!> He dumped as much strength into the call as he could spare.

He felt Mordred's attention on him. <Hold on,> was the cold answer, and then his attention was gone again.

Raid cursed a bloody streak. He didn't have that kind of time. He left the woman, started towards the front door and escape right as cars came screaming up the driveway. Longcross had called for backup and it was already here. Raid fell back, trying again for a sight shield. It stayed for a second and popped out. His Skills were prickling again. He fell back through a doorway and into a dining room with a table set for twelve.

Running feet. Shouting voices. Someone pounding on the

front door. The door being kicked in when no one answered.

The men came in guns drawn. They were all in body armor and tactical gear. Behind them came in two women dressed in gray coveralls. Both of them wore full reflective black face plates that hid all their features along with protecting their eyes.

The moths began to blur his vision. Oh shit. Not this again.

One of the men was shouting for Longcross.

Other people in tactical gear poured through the door. Two of them flowed upstairs, the other four swept towards him. Raid retreated further, now into the kitchen. Trying again for a sight shield and getting nothing. His regular shield was starting to fail under the beating wings of moths.

Out into the backyard onto a grand patio with a fire pit. The moths followed him. He focused on the far end of the massive green lawn. If he could get there and over the wall, on the other side was the Mountain. The unSkilled were banned from ever setting foot on it.

People were shouting. More running footsteps. More gunshots. He'd been seen.

<What the fuck?> Mordred said, suddenly there.

Raid grabbed him – usually a bad idea for a low aught to grab a high one, shields burned – and shouted, <GO!>

Mordred didn't question. He grabbed Raid back and jumped.

In a second the terrifying moths were gone, replaced by the soothing welcome of House of Carnage. They stood just outside the rose garden. Raid could feel the wards that had been laid down over generations. Safety. He was safe here.

He just about fell over the thigh high wall that ringed the rose garden in his haste to get into it.

<What happened?> Mordred asked, pulling him away from the wall and towards the entrance.

The best Raid could do was send him alarm and jumbled images. And moths. Those hideous white moths.

<Come on,> Mordred said, and led the way into the rose garden.

Radial roses grew in perfusion around regular trees. Skilled gardening as well as the Skills themselves kept them growing healthy and vibrant. Steppingstones swept clean of leaves led from the entrance in the wall through the garden. The smell of the roses and earth and forest, soothed Raid's nerves. He could feel the Skills of the House and the presence of all the Carnages who had come before him and been sung back to the land here in the garden. Cain was here now too.

<What happened?> Mordred asked again.

<You first,> Raid replied, not ready to think about the moths that had somehow stripped him of his Skills. <What happened with the High Inquisitor?>

<Nothing,> Mordred said sullenly.

<What, you didn't demand she give you all the answers?> He'd meant the comment as a light quip, but it came out flat and harsh.

<Fayette and Adira were there.>

As the right hand of the High Inquisitor, Fayette embodied all the worst things the unSkilled believed about House of Carnage. She was in charge of tracking down the part-bloods and eradicating them. It was suspected that she also hunted unSkilled just for fun. With no body or witness, no formal tribunal had every proved it.

Adira had grown up in creche with the four of them and had been fixated on Nico, stalking him relentlessly. Even after she'd split off to be with the high aught children and them with the low, she'd still come after him. She was well on her way to being just like Fayette, worse more than likely.

<What did they want?>

<To talk about the growing unrest among the unSkilled.>

<The attack on Mountain Village?> Raid guessed.

<And the idiots that tried to sail for the barrier islands. Water is apparently holding them hostage.>

<Better than drowning them all.> Probably. Depending on how Water was feeling, those unSkilled may never set foot on dry land again much less return home.

Mordred didn't answer.

<Anything else?> Raid asked after a moment. <Anything about Cain?>

<She said she'd look into it after Squaring the Earth.>

That was something. Raid had been half expecting her to refuse to help at all.

Still feeling off-balance and spooked by the moths, and not wanting to think about them, Raid asked bluntly, <When did you change rank?> Because he had. There was no other way Mordred could do what he'd been doing. Sometime in the last few months, he'd stopped bing a Five. <And how?> Because that didn't just randomly happen.

Mordred stared very intently at the path in front of them as they walked. Raid could feel the tension radiating off him. <We're dying out,> he answered, passing information on to Raid.

The birth records of Carnage. The steadily declining birth rates. The steadily declining Skillsets. High aught parents siring low aught children. All things Raid knew. The reason Cain hadn't been killed in the cradle despite the fact he didn't look a thing like Carnage was the chance his children could be strong.

All of that wasn't happening only to Carnage though. House of Wind and House of Shadow had both died out completely about a hundred years ago, their Skillsets vanishing entirely from Oceanea. Ice was poised to go next with only a few hundred Ice Skilled left. Unfortunately, Carnage wasn't all that far behind.

<Katio sought to make us stronger by killing all the low aughts,> Mordred went on.

Raid thought of Nico, one of the Matriarch's early culls, and the creche she'd wiped out only a few months ago.

<Bester's been looking into other ways to strengthen Carnage.>

<Like Matriarch Attora's plan?> Raid asked.

The previous Matriarch of Ice had instigated a strict breeding program of her own design, meant to create a powerful new generation. It had mostly involved inbreeding and while the children of those couplings were powerful, many of them also suffered debilitating physical or mental disabilities. That hadn't stopped the current Matriarch Thaydra from continuing what her mother Attora had started.

<No,> Mordred answered. He hesitated for a second before

saying, <Bester found pre-Cataclysm technology. Something that can boost Skills.>

<That's not possible,> Raid said automatically. Because it wasn't. Children aged into their Skills and the rank they had at the end of their teens was the rank they stayed at. Women would gain in strength again sometime in their fifties and sixties. That was how aught ranks worked, how they had always worked. Only Raid knew Mordred. He known Mordred since before they could walk, and he could feel the difference. <Why you?>

<She needed a willing volunteer.>

That wouldn't have been hard. There were many people both within Carnage and without who would volunteer if it meant currying favor with the High Inquisitor.

<You always were ambitious,> Raid finally replied.

<That wasn't why,> Mordred said quietly, his uncertainty and fear trickled through to Raid. <Matriarch Katio was going to cull both you and Cain. Bester offered to get you off the Mountain and out of sight in exchange for volunteering.>

Raid felt his blood turn to ice. He had always worried about Cain being culled; there was no disguising the blonde hair and blue eyes or the fact that he trained doubly hard to make up for it. Even though Mordred had mentioned it earlier, Raid hadn't really realized he had also been on the chopping block, or that they'd both been so close to being culled. Suddenly walking through the rose garden didn't feel as safe as it had.

<Cain died anyway,> Raid said quietly.

Bitterness rolled off Mordred like a wave. His words from before echoed through Raid's mind. *You think I don't know that? That this is my fault?* Of course Mordred agreed to volunteer. He would have agreed to anything if it meant keeping them from ending up like Nico.

<How strong are you now?> Raid asked.

<Seven.>

Raid couldn't stop himself from recoiling. <You've gone up *two aught ranks* in less than a year?> Even children didn't get that strong that fast.

Mordred nodded woodenly.

<Shit.> If this worked, if there really was a way to boost the Skills… <Are there any side effects?>

<Not so far.>

<Are you going to get any stronger?>

Mordred shook his head. <No. It boosts two ranks, nothing more.>

<'Nothing more,'> Raid echoed, like two ranks was something minor.

<Your turn,> Mordred said changing the subject. <What happened with Longcross?>

<Something…> Raid said, not entirely sure how to describe it. <There were moths…> He passed Mordred the memory, keenly aware that Mordred could just pry open his inner shields and rifle through whatever he wanted.

<What is that?> Mordred asked appalled.

<Don't know,> Raid replied. <The moths came and the world just… vanished.> Remembering it sent a shiver down his spine. He hadn't been able to think much less shield. He pulled up a shield now, and a sight shield, just to prove to himself that he could. The Skills came as easily to him as they always had. <The moths disappeared as soon as she died,> he added, flashing an image of the dead woman with the hyper dilated eyes. <She had a strange psychic scent.>

Mordred stopped short, just before they rounded the last curve that would lead them to the House.

<What?> Raid asked.

<Something you heard,> he answered.

Raid could barely remember what he'd heard. Longcross had been on the phone talking about the arrival of state agents, everything after that was obscured by the beating of moth wings.

<Longcross was on the phone with Reefa Mazuli,> Mordred said, sending back the snip of memory.

"Maybe you shouldn't have broken the last one Reefa."

<Mad said they knew each other,> Raid replied. The founder of True Human and the head of Arcana's research and development. They had gone to medical school together. They clearly still talked to

each other.

Mordred turned his back on Carnage. <Let’s take you back to Ashveil.>

<Why?> Raid demanded.

<Going to talk to Bester,> he answered. <Without Adira and Feyette there.>

<You’re not doing that by yourself,> Raid growled.

<What good are you going to be?> Mordred snapped. <You’re still a Five.>

<And you’re only a Seven. The High Inquisitor can wipe the floor with both of us as easily as she can just you.>

<You’re not risking your life,> Mordred said sharply.

<And you’re not calling the shots anymore. Not alone.>

Mordred could have just dragged him back to Ashveil and left him there, a Five couldn’t stop a Seven, but he didn’t.

<Fine,> Mordred relented. <Let’s go.>

Together they walked into Carnage.

Chapter Nineteen

Maggie Reeves

Maggie blew on her hands and tried to think warm thoughts. A chilly breeze blew through the night, and she shivered. She'd felt too silly wearing her knee length coat when the weather had been so nice, but now she regretted leaving it in her apartment. She had several more hours on this shift before she could go back and get it because apparently kurs never slept.

In the moment it had made sense to request that Zumi stay. If he remained in Ashveil, then Longcross's plan could continue the way he'd instructed.

The Chief Inspector had been disgruntled when he learned she'd volunteered the department for guard duty and relented only slightly when she offered to take the overnight shift. When she'd made the offer though, she'd assumed the kur would leave at some point and she'd be able to sleep, but no, it looked like he was just going to power straight through the night.

Jim came trudging up to her. "Here." He thrust a beverage at her.

Maggie gratefully wrapped her hands around the warm thermos.

"I didn't think I'd be seeing you tonight," she said, inhaling the lovely scent of chai. His shift watching the park didn't start until tomorrow morning, when his actual work shift started.

"I didn't want to wait to tell you," he answered.

"Tell me?" she paused mid-sip at the ominous tone in his voice.

"Longcross was just ashed."

Maggie felt like she'd been run through with a sword.

"*What?*" the word escaped her as a choking croak.

"He was found unresponsive in his own home this afternoon," Jim said grimly. "He was rushed to Grace of Waves Hospital and he's on life support but it's not looking good."

If Maggie thought she was cold before, it was nothing compared to how she felt now. It felt like everything inside her had frozen solid. All her dreams for a safe and better world shattered to the ground at her feet. She couldn't move, she couldn't speak, she couldn't even breathe.

Jim stood silently beside her, looking bleak. It looked like all the years he'd shed over the last day had piled back on with interest. He hunched in on himself, shabby and worn. There would be no justice for his son, just as there would be no justice for Callum. The world would move on just as it always had, the kurs being kurs and the humans making do.

"No," she whispered to herself. "No. I don't accept that."

Jim barely stirred, glancing at her out of the corner of his eye.

That well had been a part of Ashveil for all of its history. If the kurs cared at all about the water in it, then they should have come looking for it long ago. Zumi's mere presence here was a poison. It was time to get rid of him.

"Can you keep watch?" she asked. "There's something I need to do."

Jim straightened at the tone in her voice. "Sure," he answered. "Anything."

"Thanks." She pulled her meme out of her pocket as she walked away and began to spread to word, starting with Ava. Even this late at night, people responded. Some had heard about Longcross, some hadn't. Everyone was angry or sad about it. Everyone was willing to come out.

Maggie called Li rather than messaging, wanting to hear her friend's voice.

"Hey," Li answered, picking up almost immediately despite the hour. "You're up late."

"Long story. Did you hear about Longcross?"

"No." There was rustling in the background. Maggie pictured

Li sitting at her kitchen table sorting through dried leaves as they spoke.

"He was ashed."

The rustling stopped. "What happened?"

"Some kur broke into his house and ashed him this afternoon."

Li blew out a breath. "Wow."

"Yeah. We're holding a candlelight vigil for him tonight at Temple Park."

"At Temple Park? Who's we?"

"The entire town," Maggie replied.

"Tonight's not really a good night," Li said after a moment.

"You can bring Raid," Maggie added. She didn't think much of Li's boyfriend, but he did care about True Human, he'd come to every meeting. He'd want to know what had happened to Longcross if he hadn't already heard.

"It's not that. It's just…"

"Just what?" Maggie asked when Li fell silent.

"It's nothing," Li replied. "Tonight's just not a great night. Maybe we can get together later in the week?"

For a second Maggie opened her mouth, ready to tell Li exactly what it was she had in mind for tonight but decided otherwise. They would celebrate later once it was all over. "Sure," she said. "That would be great."

"Have a good night, Maggie."

"You too."

Li clicked off and Maggie returned to Temple Park, having walked around the neighboring streets while she messaged and called. When she got back, the first protesters had already gathered. They had candles or flashlights that now filled the air with balls of soft light.

Jim was standing where she'd left him, watching all the people coming. The two state agents dashed about looking alarmed, telling everyone to go home or to at least stay back on the sidewalk. It made Maggie's heart proud to see no one paid much attention to the staties. This was their town, their community, and they weren't going to stand aside and let the kurs take it.

Ava came puffing up a few minutes later, her breath fogging in the cold air.

"You have it?" Maggie said quietly.

"Yep," Ava replied patting her pocket. "You?"

They both looked at Jim.

"No," he answered. "It's all back at my house. Give me a second."

"No rush," Maggie said. They still needed time for the crowd to gather.

In the time it took Jim to go to his house and come back, the number of people had tripled, and more were coming. She could hear people talking about Longcross and about the sailing deaths at Iocaste Proper. Others were talking about Zumi, how he was here poisoning their town and scaring their children.

Maggie caught a brief glimpse of Laren talking to her trainees – she had arrived along with the crowd – but the four of them were nothing against all the people of Ashveil. The crowd began to surge inward as more and more people built up around the edges.

"This is as good a distraction as we're going to get," Maggie said quietly.

Jim nodded in agreement and pulled the concussion grenade out of his pocket. Longcross had suggested a taser, but Jim had access to these through work and they delivered one hell of a punch, more than enough to knock out a shield.

He hurled two in quick succession.

The first bounced off thin air ten feet from where Zumi stood on the lip of the well before detonating. Zumi looked up startled, as if this was the first time even noticing the crowd gathering around him. The second grenade sailed straight through, landing at Zumi's feet. Maggie saw his momentary look of panic right before it went off.

The concussive blasts almost knocked her off her feet. Some of the people in the leading edge of the crowd did fall, stumbling back into the people behind them, dropping their candles as they lost their footing.

"The kur's attacking us!" came the shrill scream from somewhere in the middle of the crowd.

Pandemonium broke loose. Some people turned to run away.

A few jacket sleeves caught fire as candles waved around in the press of bodies.

Maggie ran forward, Jim and Ava right beside her. She kept her eyes on Zumi, a crumpled shape lying a few feet from the well. A grin stretched her face. Just like Longcross had said, without their Skills, kurs were nothing. In a second, they were at his side. Blood trickled down his temple and from his nose.

"Hurry," Maggie hissed.

Ava pulled the collar from her pocket and looped it around Zumi's neck with shaking hands.

<What are you doing?>

They all flinched at the voice and Ava lost her grip on the buckle.

Maggie lurched to her feet and found herself face to face with an Enforcer. The concussive blast had hit this kur too. She looked dazed, her eyes not quite focusing.

"There was an explosion," Maggie said. "You're hurt." She kept herself between the Enforcer and her friends behind her, willing Ava to hurry up with the collar. "Here. Come with me." She reached for the kur and got a handful of shield. Pain lanced up her arm and she snatched her hand back as if she'd grabbed a hot stove.

"Here! The kur's here!" a random person shouted.

Maggie snapped a glance over her shoulder. The crowd had already reformed itself and was lurching towards them.

"No! Stop!" she shouted but too late, the mob descended.

Jim and Ava were shoved aside.

Maggie jumped forward, trying to push back the reaching hands. They needed Zumi alive for Longcross's plan. Even though he'd been ashed, it all could still work. She twisted fingers, stomped insoles, hit pressure points and diaphragms, but there were too many people. An elbow clipped her in the temple, her feet fouled on something, and she was hurled to the ground. Someone stepped down on her wrist. Another foot caught her in the ribs. A strong hand grabbed her by the back of the collar and hauled her up.

She swung at whoever was holding her and caught Jim in the gut. With all his years of brawling he barely grunted at the hit. She shook him off, turning back to where Zumi should be, but the kur was gone, devoured by the crowd.

"Longcross did want to draw out Ataku," Ava said softly, her eyes fixated on where the mob was thickest. "This will certainly do it."

Longcross had explained that Ataku was the strongest Water kur still on land. The Matriarch and most of the others lived out at sea removing plastic from sea turtles. Since Ataku never left her stronghold in the Water Works she would need to be lured out, and what better way to do that than with her own son? With Zumi as a hostage, Ataku would be forced to negotiate with humans and release her death grip on the water of the Eastern Corridor. Humans would finally have some say in their own lives.

Maggie started forward.

Jim grabbed her before she took two steps.

"We need him alive!" she said sharply.

"He's already dead," Jim answered with a nod to the crowd.

Maggie could hear the shrieks of glee, see the undulating mass of limbs as blows rose and fell. She felt a pit open in her stomach.

"This works too," Ava added firmly. "Longcross wanted to negotiate with Ataku but when she comes, we can just kill her."

"We're just supposed to capture them, to negotiate!" Maggie argued.

Ava came over, forcing Maggie to meet her eyes. "When the kurs came for Callum, do you think a negotiation would have saved him? If you'd come to them with a strong, proper argument, do you think they would have listened?"

Maggie opened her mouth, but no words came forth.

"They're monsters," Ava went on. "And they're never going to give up their power. If humanity is ever going to be free of them, we'll have to fight, tooth and nail."

"I just…" She just what? Whenever she'd dreamed of a better world, she'd always pictured the kurs gone, but had never spent much time thinking about where they would go. As she listened to Ava, she realized the other woman was right. The only way out was through violence. The only way Callum would have lived was for Carnage to be dead. She finally just nodded.

"Now," Ava went on briskly. "We need to get ready for when Ataku comes."

Chapter Twenty

SalNavari

Salasi had prodded Zumi when she saw the crowd forming. <We should go.>

He'd waved her off, not even looking up, his attention just on the well at his feet.

<We really should go,> she said more forcefully, staying just this side of respectful.

<You don't understand,> he answered, a mixture of irritation with her and giddiness to share what he was sensing. <There's something here. Something… unimaginable.>

Salasi struggled with her words for several minutes, trying to find a phrasing that would respect his higher aught rank while insisting that he defer to her age and experience. Before she could speak to him, she was thrown off her feet. Her ears rang, her head felt like it had been stuffed with cotton. She could feel Navari picking at her, demanding she wake up.

Joy at Navari's presence pulled Salasi back to full consciousness. She dragged herself to her feet and felt Navari behind her eyes, offering what little strength and concentration she had.

The crowd had scattered but they surged forward now, their many voices a roar of sound.

A group of three was huddled around Zumi. Salasi recognized the Detectives, but not the other woman who grabbed Zumi by the neck.

<What are you doing?> she demanded.

The blonde Detective was on her feet in a moment, babbling something about an explosion and trying to corral Salasi away from Zumi. She grabbed Salasi and received a shield burn for her audacity.

Salasi moved to shove the woman aside, anger and fear bubbling in her. She'd been tasked with keeping Zumi safe and he'd now been attacked twice on her watch. She needed to get him out of here. He could come back after Squaring the Earth with a full escort of armed, high aught Enforcers. Salasi barely made it a step before the mob surged, descending on Zumi.

The blond Detective rushed forward alongside Salasi, trying to protect Zumi and beat the crowd away, but even with her Skills, Salasi was only a Two. She couldn't stop this many not even with the Detective fighting beside her.

He vanished into the mob.

Salasi's horror echoed back to her through Navari. She threw up a sight shield and threw herself into the crowd of unSkilled. She called in her tonfas, pushing aside all training about how to gently deal with the unSkilled, and started cracking skulls. She used her shields to deliberately burn people, clearing a path through them. With each touch, a piece of her shield fizzled out. She constantly reinforced it, pouring in more power, steadily draining herself of her Skills.

She was vaguely aware of Navari staggering out of bed, shouting for Command.

Salasi forced her way through to the center. Zumi was curled on the ground, his hands over his head. The people around him tried to hit and kick and stomp, but were hampered by so many other pressed in around.

<Zumi!> she said desperately.

He didn't answer.

<Zumi! Come on!> She was running out of strength, in minutes her Two aught shields would fail.

She beat off the crowd with her tonfas and finally had enough space to grab him under the arms and pull him up, wrapping her shields around him as she did.

A cry of alarm went up as he vanished from sight. Several people threw themselves back into those behind them. The unSkilled had no problem kicking an unconscious opponent but were terrified of one that might fight back.

Zumi was dead weight in her arms, so unresponsive she would

have thought him dead if she hadn't heard his heart thundering.

<Zumi! Wake up!>

She could get him onto her shoulders, but then she wouldn't be able to fight free of the crowd. Her shields would fail long before that and then they'd both be dead. They needed his Five aught strength to get out of here.

<Zumi!>

His head lolled bonelessly against her, his neck pressing against hers. A shock like a live wire raced through her, and she dropped him from the sudden pain, clamping her hand to her burning skin. There was no blood, no wound, but the spot where they'd touched felt like a fiery brand.

The unSkilled shouted at his sudden reappearance – her shields had snapped back to cover her alone when she let go – and resumed their attack once more.

She reached down to drag him up again, spotting the innocuous black leather collar as she did. He hadn't been wearing it before, and just looking at it made her senses tingle. She reached to take it off – and it sent searing pain up her fingers. She shrieked at how much that hurt, not only physically, but she could feel it imprinted on her Skills. She refused to reach for it again. Instead, she turned to the nearest unSkilled.

<Take it off!> she shouted.

The woman quailed, her eyes going wide from the thoughtspeak order.

<Take the collar off now!>

If Salasi kept shouting, she'd burn out the woman's mind, leaving her physically unharmed but brain dead. A high aught could burn out an unSkilled with one forceful word, but Salasi wasn't that strong.

<NOW!>

The woman fell to her knees from pain or obedience and fumbled with the buckle. Salasi defended the woman and Zumi as best she could, tonfas knocking away hands and feet that sought to do harm. Then the collar was off.

Zumi's eyes snapped open and he gave her a wild eyed stare.

<Zumi! Shields!> Because all he was doing was staring at her horrified.

No shields came.

Salasi was almost out of strength.

<Hold on,> Navari said. Power poured out of her as she pushed all her Three aught strength into Salasi.

Salasi grabbed it like a drowning woman and hauled Zumi back up to his feet. This time he clung to her. Terror and pain rolled off him.

Salasi wrapped him in her shields again and screamed, <MOVE!> at the unSkilled directly in front of her.

They dropped back, hands clutched to their ears, blood running from their noses. The crowd was unending, a press of bodies no matter which way she turned. With one tonfa and pointed shouts, she fought their way free, finally stumbling out into the cool darkness of the night, the press of bodies behind her.

They were barely any safer here with the murderous mob only a few feet away. Her knees shook as her eyes and Skills looked for any nearby refuge.

Zumi slipped from her weakening grip, sinking to his knees beside her.

She reached for Navari.

Navari reached back, her own power nearly tapped out.

<No one's coming,> Navari said furious and afraid, her desperate pleas to Command echoing through Salasi's memories. <There's too much going on in Iocaste Proper. They've deployed everyone they can to deal with that. You have to keep going. You can do this.>

Salasi felt too tired to keep going but she needed to try. She reinforced her sight shields with what little strength she had left, and pulled Zumi back up. They could get into the neighborhood and hide in someone's yard.

A hand touched her shoulder.

Salasi jerked around, tonfa raised, and met the burning eyes a Fire, gold around the edges and blue around the center, just like a flame.

Overwhelming relief swamped Salasi and she almost sank to her knees. No Enforcers had come as back up but Fire was still Skilled. She would help. <Thank you,> Salasi said gratefully.

The girl didn't answer. Instead she signed with her hands and said very carefully, "You need help?"

It was only then that Salasi registered that the girl had no psychic scent. She looked for all the world like a Fire, but she was as unSkilled as any member of the mob behind them. Tears stung Salasi's eyes and fear grabbed her heart. No one was coming to help her.

"Here," the girl said when Salasi didn't answer. "Come. We will help." She hooked an arm around Zumi and lifted him almost effortlessly.

Salasi staggered after them, following the girl to a disability assistance van that had been left idling nearby. An ancient woman sat in a wheelchair locked into place in the passenger position, a cane across her lap.

<Don't!> she snapped when the girl loaded Zumi in across the backseat.

"Don't fear. We'll get you away from the mob," the old woman said, her voice like dried paper.

Salasi had no trust for these strangers, but she also had no other options. Her legs were shaking. Her Skills so drained she'd lost her sight shield at some point and hadn't even noticed.

<Go with them,> Navari ordered.

Salasi dragged herself into the van, collapsing in the seats beside Zumi, not caring that she sat on his legs.

A moment later the van was pulling away down the street. Salasi watched the circling mob drop back out of sight.

The old woman tapped the girl. She glanced over to watch the woman's hands. The woman signed while she spoke out loud, "To the hospital I think. This one needs help."

The girl nodded and took the next turn.

"I'm Grandma Suri, former Head Librarian and now Captain of Story Time," the old woman said, looking back at Salasi. She had a congenial, toothless smile and dancing dark eyes that put Salasi at ease. "Our driver is my great-granddaughter Ko, recently moved here from Iocaste Proper. As I'm sure you already noticed, she's deaf, but don't let that fool you into thinking she's stupid. She's brilliant, and will share her thoughts with you if you speak ISL."

Deaf. Salasi hadn't noticed but it explained her hand signs.

"Salasi of Enforcer SalNavari," she answered. She tried to keep track of the streets, but she was too tired and didn't know Ashveil well enough to know if they were actually driving to the hospital. Navari was similarly exhausted, sending feelings of encouragement Salasi's way and little else. "And Zumi." She glanced at him. His skin was too dark for her to easily see the bruises, but she could see the swelling. His heart beat too fast and too hard. His breathing was sharp and ragged. He didn't need a hospital so much as he needed a Bone Body Walker.

She opened her mouth to redirect Ko to the Carriage station then closed it again. If Animachea Command hadn't sent help when the mob had been ready to crush her, the chances of a Carriage Driver on standby was low. With how Zumi looked now, he didn't have time to wait. He needed help now, and if that was an unSkilled doctor, so be it.

"Zumi, the son of Controller Ataku," Suri said with admiration. "I'd been told he was coming. I came out tonight to meet and speak with him. I had not been expecting to find a riot."

Salasi nodded. It took several moments for her mouth to catch up with her thoughts. "Why did you want to talk to him?"

"That well has been dry for as long as I can remember but the stories that have been told about it filled my imagination. Now that there's water in it, I wondered if any of those old stories were true. It would please my inner child immensely to find out they were," Suri said with a smile.

"Stories?" Salasi asked. It soothed her to listen to the old woman speak. She had a cadence to her voice that reminded Salasi of the bards of Viridae.

"The stories my great-grandmother used to tell me. That well is supposedly one of a vast network, and that if you look in the right places, you'll find more. Some are out in the forest, overgrown by roots and brambles. Some are even still here in town, but they were capped and paved over when the town was built. If you are brave enough to climb – or swim as the case may be – all the way to the bottom, you'll find a door, and behind that door is a secret kingdom full of wonders."

Such a kingdom couldn't exist. Earth or Viridae would have found it back during the first construction of the town. It was a cute story though, and Salasi was happy enough to listen.

"When I was a little girl, my younger brother and I got a long rope. We tied it to a nearby tree and climbed down as far as we could, but the well was so much deeper then we thought, so we climbed back up and got a longer rope. After many attempts we finally made it all the way to the bottom, and wouldn't you know, there is a door down there. It was small, meant for a person half our size."

"What was behind the door?" Salasi asked when the woman didn't go on.

"That is the question, isn't it? No matter what my brother and I tried, we simply couldn't open it, locked as it was from the other side. We vowed that we would come back and get it open the next time, but one thing led to another and the years past. I have always wondered if the secret kingdom truly did exist."

Bright white light different from the street lights flooded through the windows. Salasi squinted out at them and saw that they were pulling up to the hospital. It took her several tries to get out of the vehicle. By the time she did, hospital staff had come with a gurney but they were all keeping their distance.

"He needs help," Salasi said harshly.

"We're getting help," one of the women answered, her eyes round with fear but her voice steady. "Doctor Lightfoot is coming now."

"You can't help?" she demanded.

Before the woman could answer, Doctor Lightfoot strode out through the door. Salasi almost sobbed in relief. Lightfoot was part-blood Bone.

"What happened?" she asked, walking straight up to the vehicle and looking at Zumi.

“He was attacked in the park,” Salasi answered. “There was a riot.” She could feel the part-blood’s Skills sliding over Zumi, getting a clearer picture of just how injured he was while she felt his pulse with her fingers and listened to his heart with her stethoscope.

“Let’s get them inside,” Lightfoot said.

At her words the unSkilled came forward, carefully loading Zumi onto a backboard and then getting him on the gurney. Another nurse offered Salasi a wheelchair, but she refused. She could still walk. It wasn’t until they wheeled Zumi inside and she tried to follow that she realized maybe she couldn’t still walk.

“Here dear,” Suri said, handing over her cane. “This will help.”

“Thank you,” Salasi replied. “For everything.”

“Of course. I hope that you’re both okay.”

Ko didn’t pull away until Salasi had safely hobbled into the hospital, leaning heavily on Suri’s cane. She followed the scent of Water back into the treatment area. A few unSkilled gave her side eyed looks as she walked by but no one tried to stop her. She wanted to put up a sight shield but didn’t have the strength to raise one.

She reached the treatment area in time to hear Lightfoot say, “Anyone who doesn’t want to help, leave now.”

The Bone part-blood stood toe to toe with another doctor, staring him down. His eyes had narrowed dangerously, his lip curling in a sneer. He reeked of anger. He had a white-knuckled grip on the edge of Zumi’s backboard and looked ready to flip the injured youth onto the floor.

“Harm him and you’ll be explaining your actions to a Tribunal,” Salasi said, her voice managing to come out sharp despite how exhausted she felt.

His gaze flickered to Salasi, taking in her Enforcer uniform, the cane in one hand and tonfa in the other, both raised and ready weapons.

“Kur loving traitor,” the man spat at Lightfoot, before shoving himself away from Zumi and stalking off. He shouldered his way passed Salasi, and she shocked him with a shield as he did, his yip of pain and surprise making it worth the power it cost her.

"Anyone else want to go with Statton?" Lightfoot asked.

"We're all with you Doc," one of the nurses replied firmly, already moving into action.

With swift and sure hands, the nurses were drawing blood, placing catheters and maneuvering equipment around to take pictures of Zumi's insides through his skin.

Lightfoot directed them all, her words clear. Even as she spoke to the nurses, her Skills slipped along Zumi's injuries. Her touch was so delicate and precise that she could knit tiny blood vessels and nerves back together. Salasi had heard of fineBoned Skills before, but never actually seen the Skillset. They were a rarity on the Mountain, less than a handful born every generation and always, *always* high aughts.

Lightfoot called out medications and dosages as the nurses showed her the results of the unSkilled equipment. Between that and her Skills mending the worst of the damage, Zumi's breathing began to ease and his racing heartbeat slow. She finally stepped away from him and came over to Salasi.

"No need," Salasi said, shaking her head. "Not that badly hurt."

"You may not have been beaten," Lightfoot answered. "But you're just this side of auto-dissolution."

Salasi's breath caught. Every Skilled that their limit, the point at which they tapped out their Skills. The higher the aught, the more Skills they could draw on before they pulled too much. If they kept pressing past that point, they'd enter auto-dissolution, when the Skills began to cannibalize the body for fuel.

"You drew too deep," Lightfoot murmured quietly.

"There wasn't a choice," Salasi replied. "It was that or watch him die."

"Not saying you didn't make the right choice, but you need help now."

Salasi resisted for a moment before saying, "Okay."

Lightfoot's Skills ran along Salasi's Skills and body, soothing tension, easing some of the exhaustion and pain. Salasi could even feel it creeping out towards Navari, their Bonded status allowing

Lightfoot to send some healing to Navari despite the distances involved.

"We've got incoming!" a nurse shouted the entrance. "Multiple injuries! Shield burns and ashing!"

These had to be the people in the mob that Salasi had shouted at or forced out of her way. She was a low aught and hadn't shouted at anyone that loudly, the only person who might have long term injuries was the woman who'd taken the collar off.

Lightfoot finished with Salasi and sorted out her nurses, sending all but one up front to help. The one who stayed was also the one who'd announced 'we're all with you' at the beginning. The two of them moved Zumi back into a private room.

"Maris, stay here with them. Don't leave. Don't let anyone in. Don't give any meds or treatments unless you hear it directly from me," Lightfoot said.

"Got it Doc," Maris replied.

With that Lightfoot was gone, off to see the multiple injuries.

Salasi sank down onto the nearby chair, watching as Maris finished setting up all the equipment, connecting all the lines.

<Water knows,> Navari said, her voice little more than a cracked whisper. <Controller Ataku is coming.>

As drained as they both were, Salasi hadn't been paying attention to Navari. With more effort than it should take, she looked through Navari's eyes.

The pain from the migraine twanged violently through Salasi. Navari was lying on the floor, cool stone pressed against her cheek and chest and thighs. She had run from Animachea all the way to House of Water to tell them what had happened. She'd given Salasi everything she had and then still dashed across the Mountain. Now she collapsed, unable to stand or catch her breath.

<Navari?> Salasi shouted. She tried to send strength to her partner, but Lightfoot's healing had done nothing more than pull Salasi back from the brink. She had no strength to give. <Navari!>

A Water gently rolled her over and sat her up, pressing a mug to her lips. Navari greedily sucked down the salt tea.

<We'll be fine,> Navari assured her when the mug was empty.

<Rest now. We'll both be fine.>

The words weren't enough to reassure Salasi. She tried to hang on to Navari but they were both too weak to hold a conscious connection. She could feel warmth and safety coming from Navari, the echoing promise that they would be back together soon.

The people of Ashveil may have had no qualms about picking a fight with a Two, or beating a Five aught youth unconscious, but they would think twice about a Nine aught Water Controller.

Salasi eased herself up and over to Zumi's bedside and told him, "Hang in there. Controller Ataku is coming."

Chapter Twenty-One

Maggie Reeves

Maggie trembled as she leaned against the wall of the hospital. Her legs felt so weak they could be stirred with a spoon. Her back and shoulders burned. She'd prided herself on being in shape but this disaster had shown her otherwise. This late at night, the trolley only ran once on the hour. There was also an overnight taxi service but they didn't have the drivers or the vehicles capable of transporting everyone who needed it. Between the taxi and the few people who owned private accessibility vehicles, the worst injuries were taken straight to Angels Landing. Maggie, along with a few other able bodied people, had carried the rest, and there had been many.

Stupid. She was so stupid. They had taken out Zumi but forgotten his minder. The Animachea Enforcer had ashed and burned people left and right to pull him free.

"Detective Reeves?" a man asked.

Maggie quickly straightened, and nearly fell over, as a doctor walked over. "Volunteer Detective," she corrected.

"Doctor Jon Statton," he said, holding out his hand. He was tall and good looking with a strong grip. She vaguely recognized him. He'd come to True Human meetings but wasn't a dedicated member. His on-call schedule made it impossible for him to make any commitments. "You're the one who carried in the injured?"

"Some of them," she answered. Jim had been right there with her while Ava had coordinated care of the people in the park until they'd been transported to the hospital.

"Can you tell me what happened?"

"We were holding a peaceful candlelight vigil for Doctor Adrian Longcross when the kur attacked us." She'd practiced the lie so often in her head as she'd carried the wounded that it rolled easily off her tongue now. She didn't want anyone knowing what she, Ava and Jim had been up to. Secrecy was the only way they'd be able to try again to catch Ataku now that Zumi had escaped.

Statton's face was grim. "That explains all the shield burns."

"Is anyone permanently…" she couldn't bring herself to finish that sentence. She and the others had acted righteously, to protect humanity, but the thought of anyone dying because of her actions made her stomach twist so painfully she thought she'd be sick.

"No fatalities yet," Statton assured her. "But a few are showing early signs of ashing."

Maggie pressed a hand to her stomach.

"Nothing so bad as Longcross," he added hurriedly. "But it will be a few days before we'll know the extent of the damage. A lot of people recover just fine, but some are left with seizure disorders, migraines, blindness, proprioceptive deficits…" He stopped talking with a concerned look on his face. "You're white as a sheet. Come on. The saviors need to be seen to also."

Maggie wanted to protest that she was hardly a savior. If she'd done her job right, none of this would have happened and Zumi would be safely squirreled away. They'd be waiting patiently for Ataku to come looking for him and begging for his return. Maggie had given all her strength running back and forth between Temple Park and Angels Landing, so when Statton put an arm around her shoulders, and took hold of her elbow with his other hand, she didn't stop him.

He walked her into the lobby where the least serious of the shield burns were still waiting to be seen. Most of them had walked here on their own, cradling burned hands, arms or faces. They all smiled or nodded to Maggie as she passed by and walked into the treatment area.

"You should be seeing to them first," she protested.

"They'll all get seen," Statton assured her and led her back into a private room. He filled a glass with water from the sink and gave her a pair of anti-inflammatory pills. As he did so, he spoke quietly, "In the room across the hall is the kur who did this. Lightfoot believes 'do no harm' includes *them* too."

“Zumi’s here?” Maggie whispered back startled. She’d been sure the Enforcer would have run him right back to the Mountain.

“The Water kur? Yeah. He’s here. I can’t do anything about it but you Detective—” he gave her a meaningful look. “—You can.” With a nod he walked out, leaving the door cracked open.

Maggie popped the anti-inflammatories and chugged the water to free her hands, then swiftly messaged Ava about this development.

Ava messaged back that she’d found the collar trampled in the park, but it seemed to be unharmed.

‘Bring it here now,’ Maggie messaged before texting Jim and telling him to come to the hospital as fast as possible.

As soon as that was sent, Maggie eased off the exam table and moved quietly into the hall, all her aches and pains forgotten. She carefully cracked open the door Statton had mentioned and peered in.

There was Zumi, hooked up to lines and wires and receiving the exact same care as the people he’d harmed. He even had his own private nurse.

“Can I help you?” the nurse asked, moving to stand between Maggie and Zumi.

“Wrong room,” Maggie replied, closing the door quickly before the woman could ask anything else.

The nurse was short, plump with dyed blonde hair and cat’s eyes glasses and far too shrewd a look in her eyes. Zumi himself had been unconscious with half his face swelled up. This would be easy. She could lay out the nurse, then Jim could collar Zumi and haul him out. The plan was still on. This could all still work out, she just needed to wait for the others.

She made her way carefully back to the lobby, staying close to the wall in case she needed it for support. As soon as her leg muscles recovered, she would add daily dead lifts to her training. If there was ever an emergency like this again, she didn’t want to be so easily wiped out.

She surveyed the lobby, trying to pick out Jim among the people gathered there. Everyone she could see looked shaken but alright. A few held ice packs to the shield burns on their hands or faces. None of them were Jim. He’d been hauling people with her, he couldn't have gone that far. Maggie glanced at her meme but there were no new messages.

'Where are you?' she messaged Jim, then stared at the screen for a minute to will an instant reply. It didn't work.

The sliding main doors hissed open and Laren hurtled inside, startling everyone. Her crisp suit was rumpled, her shiny shoes caked with dirt. A few strands of hair had escaped the tight confines of her bun and hung around her face in wild curls. A livid bruise bloomed across her cheek. Despite her appearance, her voice was calm. "Where is Zumi? Tell me he's still alive."

"What's happening?" Maggie demanded, speaking for everyone there.

"Is. He. Alive?" Laren snapped.

"He's fine," Maggie answered peevishly.

"Thank the All-God for small favors," Laren whispered, relief easing the set of her shoulders.

"He hurt far more people far more badly than he himself was hurt," Maggie snapped, angry that Laren, a fellow human, would be more concerned with the kur than the people of Ashveil.

"That can all be dealt with," Laren answered, waving her off.

"These are people's lives!" Maggie said, ire growing at Laren's lack of care. "Their livelihoods! People could have died tonight!"

Laren gave her a strange look and said, "Do you understand what would have happened if Zumi had died tonight?"

We would have been free, Maggie was going to say but Laren kept speaking, cutting off the statement before Maggie could even open her mouth.

"Ashveil would have been placed under extinction protocol. Controller Ataku would have depopulated the town."

Maggie's veins froze hearing those words. She'd been briefed on extinction protocols when she'd joined the force as a volunteer Detective. They were also one of the tropes media dramas loved to trot out, the plucky heroes thwarting the evil kurs and saving the town just in the nick of time. She wanted to say that was just media hype and that extinction protocols didn't really exist but she'd been through the training. She'd read all the material that the Chief Inspector had given her.

"She wouldn't," Maggie said, feeling numb. "Not for this."

"Controller Ataku is the most powerful Water Skilled in Iocaste," Laren replied. "For all intents and purposes, she is the Matriarch because Matriarch Balane never comes in from the ocean. If Zumi had died, the lives of everyone in Ashveil would have been taken in payment and none of the other Skilled would have censured her."

Maggie shook her head, not wanting to believe that, but also the spark of anger returning. The loss of a life was tragic but for thousands to die in retaliation? That wasn't justice. The kurs had to be stopped. An entire town shouldn't fear for their lives because they tried to protect their water supply.

"Ogwo, Smith and Park have already started evacuating people," Laren continued. "If—"

"Evacuating?" Maggie demanded.

"Zumi's alive so there's a solid chance the Controller can be convinced of a lesser punishment. In case she can't, we need to evacuate as many people as possible. All of them if we can."

Maggie shook her head and opened her mouth to point out the absurdity of all this, that the kur didn't have the right to harm anyone regardless of what had happened to her son—

All the lights shut off. The darkness held for a moment before emergency lighting flickered on. Several people in the lobby called out in alarm, asking what just happened. A few pointed through the windows. Outside was pitch black. All the streetlights and stoplights were out.

Laren's lips were pressed into a thin line. "Controller Ataku just cut the power to Ashveil," she said quietly. "She'll be coming soon. Be prepared."

"Zumi attacked us," Maggie said sharply, grabbing onto the narrative she'd crafted. "We weren't just going to calmly stand by and let that happen. We defended ourselves."

"Concussion grenades are not a Skilled weapon," Laren replied pointedly. "Anyone with even basic forensic knowledge will tell you that Zumi didn't throw the first punch."

The nearby water fountain suddenly rattled.

Laren's attention flashed to it, fear flickering across her features before she smoothed her face and suddenly seemed tranquil as a pond.

The water fountain rattled again, then with a shriek of rending metal, the pipe in the wall tore free and water began sluicing out across the floor.

From the darkness of the town, a pale form emerged. It came so smoothly in such silence it appeared as a floating apparition. It was only when she was nearly upon them that Maggie recognized Controller Ataku. Her simple white dress had made her appear like a ghost. Her Water black skin blended in with the night. Maggie could see her eyes and her teeth, and the white dots drawn vividly across her cheekbones and chin and forehead, and little else.

The water on the floor rippled unnaturally.

Maggie took a step back from it, and glanced at her meme, hoping for some message from Ava or Jim. Instead the screen read 'no signal.' She stared at it blankly, having only once before seen that message and that's when she'd been on the train to Iocaste Proper, deep in the tunnel through the Ice Whites.

"Controller Ataku," Laren said moving to stand at the entrance to the hospital and dropping to her knees in entreaty. "May we speak please?" She used a grammar form so formal that Maggie had only ever heard it used when learning about it in school.

It worked on Ataku. The kur stopped, surveying the statie before her with cold blue eyes. **<You may speak.>**

Maggie shivered. That voice didn't hurt the way Zumi's had, but it was as unforgiving as the crushing depths of the ocean.

"Your son is alive and being cared for," Laren said, each word enunciated clearly.

<My son was attacked.>

The words 'my son' reverberated hard in Maggie's head, searing like fire in her mind. She shuddered, taking a step back from the kur.

"Your son lives," Laren replied evenly. "He was brought here and cared for by the people of Ashveil. Please Controller Ataku, do not hold them all responsible for the foul work of a few."

The water pouring from the broken pipe suddenly stopped, the water hanging in midair as if someone had hit the pause button. Completely, hideously unnatural.

"Zumi's attackers will be remanded to you," Laren continued, seeing that she'd gained some traction with Ataku. "But it wasn't the entire town, it wasn't even most of them. Please Controller Ataku, let the town go."

Controller Ataku just stared at her, cold, unfeeling, and alien. Extinction protocol. She was going to kill them all no matter what Laren said. There could be no reasoning with a kur. Maggie wanted to strike first and hard. It didn't matter if she died if she could take the kur down with her and save the rest of Ashveil.

Then – to Maggie's utter shock – the kur nodded slowly. **<Very well,>** she agreed. **<You have until sunset to bring them forward.>**

Something moved in the darkness beyond Ataku, so minor that neither the kur nor statie noticed, as focused as they were on each other.

Maggie saw the concussion grenades come flying. She threw herself to the floor, slapping her hands over her ears a split second before they hit.

The sliding glass door exploded in a shower of glass. The lobby filled with shrieks and screams as the waiting people were hurled to the ground. Laren had been thrown backward, and twitched where she lay, completely stunned. Beyond the doors Ataku—

Ataku *hadn't* been thrown off her feet. The concussion grenades that had so easily taken out Zumi had only caused his mother to stumble.

The kur turned where she stood, face contorted with fury and reached out into the night. She a made a violent 'come here' gesture and two figures flew towards her, hooked by her Skills.

"No," Maggie whispered to herself, scrambling to her feet.

There was only a split second, a moment where Maggie saw them, Ava's eyes wide, Jim cursing and kicking uselessly against the kur's invisible hold, then the kur ripped the water out of both of them and hurled it into the lobby as thousands of finger thick spikes. The deadly icicles ripped through flesh and plastic and drywall with the same power as bullets.

"Controller Ataku," Laren said, dragging herself upright, dazed but still trying to reason with a monster. "Please—"

<Your own people damn you,> the kur spat.

The words hit hard, driving Maggie to her hands and knees. All she could do was watch helplessly as the kur stalked towards her, the water pouring from the broken pipe now rising into the air at her command. It spread like ribbons and bubbles, ominous and graceful as it moved towards the crying, bleeding people that filled the lobby. A ribbon of water slithered straight towards Maggie. She tried to push herself away from it but her head still rang from the kur's final words.

"No," someone new said. "Not here."

The lethal ribbon of water stopped just short of plunging down Maggie's nose and mouth. She ripped her gaze away from it as one of the doctors walked past, her shoes crunching in the glass. She put herself between Ataku and Laren, Maggie and a handful of other people in the lobby.

The kur glared at her, lips peeled back from too white teeth as the doctor stopped just feet from her.

"I saved your son," the doctor said. She spoke respectfully, but with none of the bowing formality that Laren had used. "He lives because of me and my team, and now you threaten us and our families."

The silence between them hung so heavily Maggie was sure the air itself would snap.

<You and yours will be spared,> the kur seethed. **<The rest are forfeit.>**

She emphasized her words by ripping the water out of everyone still in the lobby. Maggie felt the yank – all her organs pulling, her heart seizing for a moment as an unseen force gripped it – but from her place behind the doctor, she and Laren and a dozen others were left unharmed.

The kur hurled the water away from her, the darts and blades it created shredding the vehicles, trees and buildings that got in the way.

Then she vanished from sight.

The doctor immediately snapped out orders for everyone to contact everyone they knew and get them to Angels Landing as fast as possible.

"What happens now?" Maggie said, her voice sounding scratchy and hollow and completely not her own.

Laren pulled herself up. "We get everyone here as fast as possible. This hospital is Lightfoot's territory and Controller Ataku will spare it," she said, pulling out her meme. Her fingers started whizzing across the keyboard before she saw the 'no signal' in the corner and abruptly stopped typing. All at once it seemed that decades settled over her face and shoulders.

"What happens to the people who aren't here?" Maggie asked timidly, wanting to hear a different answer than the one she knew was coming.

Laren didn't look up when she answered flatly, "Extinction protocol. Anyone not here will be depopulated."

Chapter Twenty-Two

Raid

Raid and Mordred waited through the night in Mordred's new set of rooms. As an Inquisitor he had a suite on one of the higher levels. It was about the same size as the suite the four of them had once shared with six Four and Five aught women when they'd left the creche. That space had been cramped with ten of them living there and filled to bursting with the detritus of ten different lives.

These rooms were draped in all the finery of Carnage, the great fireplace filled with smokeless, heat producing high quality gleams from Fire. The smooth stones actually looked like they contained flickering flames, unlike the cheaper gleams that simply glowed. All the furniture had been carved from black wood and polished to a high shine. The art on the walls had been painted by the great Skilled masters. For all of that however, it had about the same heart and soul to it as Raid's apartment. Mordred might sleep here, but this wasn't his home.

Just before dawn, the High Inquisitor finally acknowledged their ping and invited them in. They left Mordred's rooms and crossed down the hall to where the High Inquisitor lived and worked.

Her rooms were decorated the same as Mordred's but far more expansive and expensive. She was seated at a black wood desk, neat stacks of paperwork spread out around her. In her early sixties, the High Inquisitor was just coming into her prime. Her thick black hair was silver at the temples and lines were just starting to frame her face. Despite that, she looked grim, determined, and exhausted.

<You requested an audience,> she said flatly, not inviting either of them to sit.

<What happened to Cain?> Mordred demanded bluntly.

<Squaring the Earth begins in a few hours. This can wait until tomorrow,> she replied, her words a dismissal.

<No,> Mordred snapped.

Raid froze, slanting a look at Mordred.

<You know Arcana and True Human. You know why he died. You know what happened,> Mordred pressed, every word a challenge to her authority. A Seven against a Nine, the outcome was a foregone conclusion.

<Arcana,> Bester said slowly, leaning back and regarding him coolly. <Where did you hear that name?>

<They're all over Daal,> he answered. <And you've spoken about them more than once. You know something.>

The temperature in the room dropped so much the gleams in Bester's fireplace began to steam.

The High Inquisitor noticed, her eyes narrowing. Her focus shifted abruptly to Raid. <Why worry about Arcana when Controller Ataku has invoked extinction protocol and is currently depopulating Ashveil? You have *friends* who live there.>

Raid's heart clenched at both the mention of the extinction of Ashveil and Bester's tone with 'friends.' She knew about Li. What the High Inquisitor knew about Li wouldn't matter though if she was depopulated.

<What's happening to Ashveil?> Raid asked respectfully. He tried to keep his voice under control and sound disinterested but the fear for Li was bleeding through.

<Go and find out,> Bester answered. She then gave Mordred a pointed look. <Unless you want to stay here and argue about things you know nothing about.>

Mordred looked more than ready to fight her even though they all knew he would lose.

<Mordred, please. If something's going on…> He pitched his voice as privately as possible, but this close to Bester and as strong as she was, she no doubt could hear him. He didn't want to use Li's name and put her in danger in case the High Inquisitor didn't know exactly who she was.

Mordred and Bester stared at each other for another moment

before he backed down. <Fine,> Mordred muttered.

Bester smiled and turned her attention back to the reports in front of her.

The wards of Carnage kept them from jumping from inside the House and the walk out felt painfully long. His mind raced out ahead, worrying about Li and wondering what had provoked such a lethal response from Controller Ataku.

As soon as they were through the rose garden and beyond the territory marker, Mordred jumped. In a second they were standing in Ashveil. A dark and silent version of Ashveil absolutely drenched in Water Skills.

Too panicked for words, Raid showed Mordred an image of Li's cottage and where it was in the town.

Mordred jumped again.

All the candles were out in the cottage windows. All the happy little charms had been scrubbed out by Water. The world twisted around Raid for a dizzying moment before righting itself.

<Li!> he shouted, running for the cottage, wanting to find anything other than what he feared. He burst through the door. Water Skills were everywhere even though there was no water. Ataku had come through like a flash flood, then sucked all the water back down the pipes leaving everything bone dry. <LI!> he shouted again, panic building.

He didn't smell death, but he also couldn't smell *her.* The scent of Li he always found so soothing and welcoming had been washed out by Ataku's fury.

Raid found broken dishes in the kitchen. In the studio all the neat vials were smashed or cast about, the handwritten labels now illegible. All the plants left out for drying were scattered everywhere, and ruined after being soaked and then forcibly dried again. All the once living plants were now just husks in pots.

The bedroom was mostly untouched. It still smelled like Li. It also smelled like him. Ataku had come here looking for Li and had run into Carnage instead.

<She's out in the garden,> Mordred said, having taken the time to take a sense of what was around them instead of running inside in a

panic.

Raid was out the back door, leaping down the porch steps and racing into the garden.

<Li!>

He felt the barest wave of her Skills back at him.

In seconds he was under one of the gnarled old apple trees who's boughs hung over the garden fence. Li had climbed as high as she could and was clinging to the branches.

Raid dropped his sight shield. As soon as she saw him, she climbed down, and in a moment was in his arms. Relief so sharp it hurt filled him as he felt her real and warm and alive, her scent twining around him.

"There was so much water," she whispered. "It came out of every faucet all at once. It chased me out into the garden, I was sure it was going to kill me, but then it just… stopped."

It had stopped the moment Ataku had scented Carnage and hadn't wanted to cross his House. "It was Controller Ataku," he said quietly. "She depopulated Ashveil."

Li spasmed in his arms, pulling away enough to look up at him in horror, "She what?"

"Don't know why." He hadn't stayed long enough to ask the High Inquisitor more questions.

"Everyone?"

He could feel Li's heartbeat began to pick up speed, could smell the anxiety curling around her.

<Not everyone,> Mordred answered.

Li looked over Raid's shoulder and froze.

Mordred stood on the porch. He'd dropped his sight shield which wasn't a good thing considering he was still dressed as an Inquisitor.

"This is Mordred. He's…" <You will not hurt her,> he said, switching to private thoughtspeak.

<No,> Mordred said irritated.

"He's not going to hurt you," Raid finished out loud.

Li didn't let go of him. Using formal speech she asked, "You said 'not everyone'?"

Mordred's irritation grew. <Not everyone,> he repeated coldly. <A few houses are fine. The entire hospital is full of people.>

"'A few houses,'" she repeated, her anxiety solidifying into dread. "How many is 'a few'?"

Mordred shared a map with Raid, the untouched houses highlighted. None of them were familiar to him. He didn't mention that Maggie's apartment above her dojo was one of the dark places. The hospital glowed like a beacon.

"We can go to the hospital and find out what happened. The most people are there," Raid said.

Li tightened her grip on him, afraid of what she was going to find out. She didn't say anything out loud, but he knew she was thinking about Maggie. She finally nodded.

Mordred came over slowly, moving carefully and trying to look harmless. Li still tensed, waiting for a blow to fall. Mordred put his hands on both of them and jumped. In a blink they were standing in the Angels Landing parking lot. Unlike the rest of the dark town, it was lit up brightly.

Mordred stepped back and disappeared behind a sight shield which disconcerted Raid. It would be awhile before he started thinking of Mordred as a Seven.

Li took Raid's hand and hurried towards the hospital.

The lobby was in disarray. Broken chairs had been stacked up against a wall. The whole place smell of death and blood, though Raid saw no sign of either. Tucked into a corner on one of the few still intact chairs was a familiar face he noticed a split second after Li did.

"Maggie!" she shouted, dropping his hand and dashing over to her friend. "Maggie what happened?" She knelt down in front of her.

Maggie looked at Li like she was seeing a ghost. "Li?" she whispered. "You're not dead?" She grabbed Li and burst into tears. The scent of regret and dread oozed off her.

Raid hovered nearby, not wanting to intrude but also unwilling to be far from Li.

The story poured out of Maggie about the candlelight vigil for Longcross, and how Zumi had attacked them. The humans had protected themselves and fought back. Upset by their show of defiance, Zumi had called his mother. Ataku had then rushed in and slaughtered everyone.

Raid winced inwardly at the mention of Longcross. He hadn't meant to burn out the unSkilled's mind, but his intentions didn't matter much in the face of the outcome. He would need to tell Li what had happened, but now was not the time.

As Maggie spoke, the part-blood Bone had ambled up, stopping beside Raid and listening to the story.

When Maggie finished, Lightfoot asked, "Leaving out a few things, aren't you?"

Maggie gave a hostile look to the newcomer. An even darker look than she gave Raid.

"Zumi was nearly dead on arrival. He had multiple blunt force trauma injuries as well as injuries consistent with being hit with a concussion grenade. He didn't attack you out of nowhere. Also remember, State Agent Laren talked Controller Ataku into only taking the people who attacked Zumi. It wasn't until True Human attacked her directly that she invoked the extinction protocol."

Maggie's eyes went hard and flinty as obsidian.

Lightfoot gave her a guileless smile and held out a sheaf of paper. "Keep telling the story your way and you're going to give people the wrong idea about what happened here."

Maggie snatched the paperwork out of Lightfoot's hand.

"Those are you discharge instructions. You're welcome," the doctor said amiably and wandered back the way she'd come.

"Is that… true?" Li asked quietly.

"No!" Maggie spat out sharply. "She's lying. Zumi attacked *us*. He was mad that we were gathering to remember Longcross. He was mad that he wasn't getting his way. This is Ceres all over again. Kurs not getting exactly what they want so they punish *us* for it."

Her words had Li pulling back slightly. Raid could see the change. Maggie could too.

"Don't listen to her!" Maggie pressed. "This wasn't my fault! None of this was my fault!"

"I didn't say it was…" Li answered. She struggled with herself for a moment before saying, "Let's get you home."

"NO!" Maggie threw off Li violently enough she nearly fell backwards.

Raid caught her, helping her regain her balance as she stood.

Maggie's eyes darted between the two of them. "Of course you'll take his side," she said coldly.

"What?" Li said bewildered. "What side Maggie? What are you talking about?"

"Just… go away," Maggie snapped bitterly. "Leave me alone."

"Maggie…"

"LEAVE ME ALONE!"

Li looked like she'd been slapped.

"Come on," Raid murmured.

Li resisted for a second, her eyes on Maggie.

The other woman had turned resolutely away, her face awash with anger, her eyes glaring holes at the far wall.

Finally Li turned to Raid and left.

Chapter Twenty-Three

Maggie Reeves

Maggie wound her arms tightly around herself. If she let go, she would spin apart into a thousand different pieces.

This wasn't

This wasn't

This wasn't

This wasn't how things were supposed to be. Longcross had told them that if they caught Zumi, Ataku would come, and then they would catch her too. With the Water Controller under human control, the people of the Eastern Corridor would finally be free. No more water taxes, no more threats of droughts.

They caught Zumi.

Ataku came.

And the kur

And the kur

And the kur

Ava dead.

Jim dead.

Everyone in the lobby dead. Husks. Mummies made in seconds. So light weight with all their water gone. So easy to carry downstairs to the morgue. So different from when she'd carried them alive from the park. When they'd talked to her. When they'd thanked her.

Thanked her for her help.

Thanked her for standing up against the kurs.

Thanked her for making a difference.

All silent now. So light weight.

This wasn't how things were supposed to be. They were

supposed to catch Ataku. Collar her. Jim had the grenades. Ava had the collar. Why didn't it work? Why didn't Ataku fall?

And now

And now

And now this.

Everyone

Everyone so quiet and light weight.

Everyone dead.

No. No. Maggie couldn't believe that.

They weren't

They couldn't be

She would walk out of this hospital and everyone would still be alive and well and fine and alive. All her students. All her neighbors. Her favorite barista at her favorite café who she still hadn't plucked up the courage to ask out yet.

She would ask today. As soon as the sun rose. She would go there and ask.

But she knew.

She knew

She knew

She knew what she would find the second she set foot out those doors. It would be the same as in here. All those husks. Mummies made in seconds as all the water was pulled out of them in a flash. That's why she couldn't go with Li. She couldn't go home. As soon as she did, it would be true. It would be real. Everyone would be gone.

Everyone would be dead.

And it was all because of her.

Because she had tried

Because she had tried

Because she had failed.

Akatu should have fallen.

Why didn't the grenades work? This was supposed to be the dawning of a new day, of a new era. Humans finally taking back Oceanea from the kurs. Humans finally in charge of their own destiny.

Maggie had tried

She had tried

She had tried and she had failed.

It was all her fault.

Her insides felt like lava worms, molten and wriggling and trying to eat their way out. She clutched herself tighter, doubled over, tried to be as small as possible.

It wasn't her fault.

It wasn't.

It couldn't be.

It was the doctor's fault, Lightfoot. She was the one who made the deal to save herself at the expense of the town. She saved Zumi instead of her fellow humans. She saved Zumi and then used that to save herself, save her job, at the expense of everyone else. And even if Lightfoot hadn't been stupid and selfish and vain, it would have been the kurs. If not Zumi and Ataku, then someone. They would do anything to crush humanity under their feet. They were liars and monsters and this was all their fault. Not hers.

She held herself tightly. This was their fault. Everyone who was dead, was dead because of them. This was not her fault.

Not her fault

Not her fault

Not her fault

This wasn't her fault.

Chapter Twenty-Four

Raid

The sky lightened. On the Mountain, the sun would have already broken the horizon. It wouldn't be much longer before the sun touched the Eastern Corridor as well. Raid knew he and Mordred should be going back for Squaring the Earth – the trials would be starting soon if they hadn't already – but he didn't want to leave Li, and Mordred seemed to have forgotten altogether. Raid didn't remind him.

After Maggie's blowup, Raid wanted to take Li back to her cottage and help clean up, but she'd refused. She'd insisted on seeing the extent of what had happened.

"You really don't want to see," he'd said gently.

"I don't *want* to see it," she'd answered grimly. "But I need to."

Raid had gone with her, and Mordred had trailed along brooding behind them.

Controller Ataku had been precise and thorough. In every house they found the people dead, their bodies desiccated husks from infants to the elderly. All the water she had given to them she had taken back. She'd left the animals alive. Worried dogs greeted them at the door. Cats peered out from under beds. There were birds on perches and small furry things in cages. Raid wasn't sure how much of a kindness that was. Normally Animachea dealt with unSkilled livestock and pets, leaving Viridae to oversee their own specific herds, but Animachea was tied up completely in the mess with Mountain Village in Iocaste Proper. Now Viridae would need to catalogue, collect and feed all these creatures until Animachea had the resources to do it. Though none of that would be until tomorrow after everyone had finished celebrating Squaring the Earth.

A few people outside the hospital had survived. The vast majority of them were close friends and family of the hospital staff. At some point Lightfoot had stamped all of their homes with her version of a territory marker and Controller Ataku had respected it. Why a Nine aught Water cared at all about the territory of a part-blood Bone, Raid had no idea. Part of the story was missing, edited out in Maggie's rendition of how kurs did evil for the sake of doing evil.

Some other survivors seemed random, like the ancient librarian Suri and her deaf and dumb caretaker Ko. Controller Ataku had had her own reasons for sparing them. A few, like the part-blood Gemma, had noticed something amiss and had fled before the water could flood their homes, suck them dry, and then retreat.

They found Gemma at home after coming back in from one of the far fields. Her dogs swarmed around her like their own entity. Even after the horror of the night before, Gemma still had the energy to be wary of the two Carnages.

"They're fine," Li had assured her. "They're here to help."

"Since when does Carnage help?" Gemma had asked darkly, her eyes on Mordred's uniform, but she had let them into her house and treated them cordially.

"What do we do now?" Gemma asked, she and Li now settled at her kitchen table.

"I don't even know," Li said, the strain and loss breaking into her voice. "The bodies…"

The bodies would keep the way they'd been dried, but while there was no rush to bury them, neither woman wanted to leave them just lying around. That being said, neither woman seemed that keen on being the ones to start burying them either.

"The state agents will come," Gemma finally said. "They'll know what to do."

Li had agreed with relief and set herself to making tea with what she found in Gemma's kitchen.

<Should we go back for Squaring the Earth?> Raid finally asked feeling that he should bring it up despite his misgivings.

<Why?> Mordred answered bitterly.

<Protocol. Tradition. The High Inquisitor will want us there.> Or she'd want Mordred at least. It would be a blow to her authority if one of her own people didn't show up, but with how Mordred had just challenged her on the Mountain, he clearly didn't care that much about her opinion anymore. The Matriarch would also want them there, but then again maybe she didn't given how many low aughts she'd culled.

<Then she can summon us then,> Mordred said.

<Are you sure?>

Mordred looked at him, blood red eyes piercing. <Do you really miss the trials that much?>

<No.> It was actually a relief not to have to worry about Adira. The trials were only supposed to mimic what Rejo had gone through when protecting Soth, with injuries kept to a minimum. Adira had always pushed those limits, specifically with Nico but even after he'd been culled, she come after one or all of the three of them from time to time instead.

Mordred shrugged. <Then let her come and get us.>

The dawn brightened outside. It felt strange to sit and wait. Everyone came to the Mountain to celebrate Squaring the Earth, even the Witch Angels and the scouts left their posts at and beyond the Border to come back. Animachea Command and all their Enforcers would have paused whatever was going on with the unSkilled in Iocaste Proper to go back to their House and celebrate. Squaring the Earth was when all the Children of Soth came together and rejoiced that the world remade for a third time had lasted another year.

Raid really looked at Mordred. The High Inquisitor had boosted him two additional Skill ranks, but she likely hadn't counted on him challenging her authority as much as he had. It surprised Raid that she hadn't reprimanded him a few hours ago when he'd refused her dismissal.

Mordred noticed him staring.

Raid glance away, turning his attention back to Li and Gemma who spoke in haunted voices about the extinction of Ashveil. Outside the sun continued to rise, and the High Inquisitor didn't come.

Chapter Twenty-Five

SalNavari

<Wake up.>

The gentle voice didn't break through the haze, but the smell of salt tea did. Salasi's eyes were open and focused on the mug before she was aware of anything else. She felt exhausted, sick, and slow.

Salasi snatched the proffered mug and downed the contents. Another was offered immediately. She dropped the empty cup without thinking and took the new one, drinking it down almost as fast. By the time she'd finished, the first mug had been refilled and Salasi switched cups again. By the time she reached the bottom, the salts and minerals began soaking into her cells and her brain began to clear. She recognized her bedroom in Animachea, but had no recollection of returning here. Navari's presence was vague and disjointed, not even the nightmares of before reached Salasi.

<Navari!> she called, reaching for her absent partner, panicked for a moment that she might be well and truly gone, but she was there, sunk deeply into the dreamless healing sleep of Bone.

<She lives,> Salasi's minder said.

Salasi glanced at them and recognized Getch of VaGetch. One of many within Animachea who oversaw the husbandry of the great herds and flocks that kept the unSkilled fed. Also, one of the most beautiful men Salasi had ever laid eyes on, and who had, several weeks ago, shown interest in her courting advances.

<Where is she?> Salasi demanded, her tone less than respectful for someone higher ranked than her and who she was hoping to impress. <What happened?>

<When Command didn't answer her pleas to help you, she ran to House of Water and solicited their aid,> Getch answered.

Navari ran? In her state? Indistinct memories from the night before filtered into Salasi's awareness. Navari hadn't yet recovered from the damage the Matriarch of Carnage had inflicted on her mind and then she had run from *here* all the way to *Water?* Not just that, she'd also drained all her strength to Salasi, giving her the endurance to break out of the mob with Zumi in tow. That... that could have been more than enough to kill her. Salasi's stomach sloshed and she nearly vomited up all the salt tea she had drunk.

<Where is she?> Salasi said, getting unsteadily to her feet. She needed to see her partner *now*, to hold her in her arms, feel her warmth, listen to her heartbeat, reassure herself with every sense she had that Navari was not dead and gone but would recover. Her absence was already a harrowing hole digging into Salasi's psyche.

<In House of Water,> Getch answered. <Too weak to be moved.>

<House of Water...> Salasi sank back onto her bed, her muscles wavering at the thought of such a trek even as her mind was determined to make it. If Navari could run that distance after being psychically mauled by the Matriarch of Carnage, and then draining off all her own Skills for Salasi's use, then Salasi could certainly walk over there and see her. Salasi struggled to stand up again.

Getch held out another mug of salt tea. <Drink more first and recover your strength. If you collapse on the way, they'll just carry you back here.>

She yielded to his firm but gentle words and drank the tea. He had also brought food, all protein rich. She devoured it while he spoke, filling in the rest of what had happened last night. All things she should have known already. The fact that Navari's memories hadn't reached her yet showed just how critically weak Navari had become.

Navari had reached Water and solicited their immediate help. Unlike Animachea, Water had contacted Controller Ataku and apprised her of the situation. She had stabilized the Water Works for her brief absence, and then had gone to Ashveil. By the time she reached it, Salasi had already pried Zumi free of the crowd, and a part-blood Bone doctor had saved his life. For that, the Controller had spared all the doctor's people but had depopulated the rest of the town, getting rid of everyone who had done her son harm, or had known them and hadn't stopped them.

The Controller had brought Zumi back to the Water Works, dropped Salasi off at Animachea, and ordered House of Water to care for Navari until she recovered. Both Zumi and Navari had been seen by Bone Body Walkers. Zumi fared far better than Navari, the part-blood having healed the worst of his injuries. He was doing so well in fact, that Bone planned to go see the part-blood tomorrow and assess her actual Skill level. What she had done was far more than what anyone would expect of an untrained part-blood.

Navari however, had pushed herself so far past her limits that her body had begun the process of auto-dissolution. Unlike Salasi who had been just on the edge and pulled back, Navari's body had actually started breaking itself down.

Salasi stopped eating and had to just breathe for a moment.

When the demands of the Skills exceeded what the body could offer, auto-dissolution started. The complete failure of all organ systems as the body devoured itself to continue supplying power. An excruciating death that Salasi would have shared in before Navari disappeared forever. Salasi couldn't comprehend the other half of herself just not existing.

Accidents happened. There were diseases that even Bone couldn't reverse, and an Animachea partner died long before their other pieces did. In larger groups, those who remained learned to work around the hole that was left behind. When there were just two, like SalNavari, the surviving partner often didn't live much longer afterwards. Taking their own lives, wasting away or simply vanishing without a word.

Salasi reached for Navari, reminding herself that such a disaster hadn't befallen them. Navari lived, wrapped up tightly in the healing Skills of Bone, protected down in the heart of Water.

Getch continued talking.

While that had gone on at Ashveil, unrest still rippled through Iocaste Proper. It turned out the unSkilled who she'd watch steal the boat hadn't been drowned like Salasi had expected, but instead were being held by the Mariners of Water. That, along with the burning out the mind of the True Human founder Longcross, had all the unSkilled up in arms. The candlelight vigil at Ashveil wasn't the only one. Similar ceremonies and protests had cropped up all across Iocaste Proper and in the surrounding towns. Rioters had returned to Mountain Village, and anyone unSkilled considered to be a Skilled sympathizer found themselves under fire from True Human. If it weren't for the Speakers from the unSkilled House of Commons, the entire city may have started rioting.

The Speakers mollified the crowd enough that all of Animachea's Enforcers had returned to the Mountain for Squaring the Earth except for those with animal partners. While many unSkilled showed a lack of self-preservation when it came to dealing with Skilled humans, the visible fangs and claws of Animachea Wolves gave them pause. Besides, those who had animal partners had already shown a lack of interest in human companionship and would not mind missing Squaring the Earth the way the wholly human partnerships would.

Salasi ate until her body felt replenished. Getch vanished what little remained of the food and offered Salasi his arm. She took it out of camaraderie now more than a need for support. She had wanted to spend Squaring the Earth with him, but this was not how she'd pictured enjoying the festivities.

The sun was high in the sky – it had to be past noon – by the time they finally left the compound and stepped into Animachea's main courtyard. She had slept through the morning ceremonies that had commemorated Lalong, the first Animachea, and the heroic deeds she had accomplished with Soth, helping to save the unSkilled from the Cataclysm and the destruction of civilization as they knew it. Now it was all food and festival. Games and plays filled the courtyard. Laughter and joy echoed through her mind as everyone chattered happily with each other.

Vaka came to join them, leaving off flirting with her own interest to check in with Getch.

It hurt to see them together, the conjoined mind and spirit split between two bodies. Another time Salasi wouldn't have minded, she wouldn't even have noticed as every member of Animachea was like that, but all she could focus on was that Navari wasn't here. She wasn't simply across the courtyard absorbed in a play, or even across the Mountain enjoying the company of the Skilled from other Houses. She wasn't even asleep so Salasi could ride in her dreams.

<Thank you Getch,> Salasi said, stepping away from him and bowing. <Will be going to Water to thank them and celebrate there.>

<We'll see you tonight in the Grand Plaza,> Getch replied.

She left swiftly, relieved neither of them had tried to stop her. She'd feared Getch had come with orders from Command when he woke her, but he hadn't, and Command themselves didn't reach out to touch her mind as she hurried from the Animachea compound. All of them had likely set aside concerns about the crisis in Iocaste Proper, letting themselves relax and recharge before wading back into the fray tomorrow.

Squaring the Earth had already spilled out of the Houses and there were groups traveling the roads through the Mountain, some on their way to see friends in other Houses, but most going to the Grand Plaza.

The winding paths of the Mountain had been made by Sebael herself when the Skilled settled here. Sebael had been the blood sister of Soth and the first Earth Skilled. She had laid down all the roads, raised the bridges, and carved the tunnels. Through them, all the Houses were connected and easily accessible even though they all stood on different mountain peaks.

Salasi thoughts slid around from the first Skilled to Navari and this path she had taken last night, exhausted, drained, and injured. She had given everything she had and everything she was to save Salasi and Zumi. She could have died. She still might.

Soth had made a similar choice all those hundreds of years ago. He had walked alone into the Devil's Inkwell to face the unNamed. He had given everything he had and everything he was to save his people, Skilled and unSkilled alike. Soth had died, but they had all lived.

Soth had died.

Salasi shook off the foreboding that brought to her. Soth had died but that didn't mean Navari would. Soth had faced the unNamed and died for his triumph. Navari had simply run too far and pushed herself too hard. She hadn't been trying to save an entire civilization, just two people. Plus Getch had said Bone had reached her in time to stop the auto-dissolution from progressing.

Around and through the mountain peaks. How fast had Navari run to get from Animachea to Water in time? Salasi should be running to her side right now, but her legs were still like cotton even after everything she'd eaten. Anything more than this leisurely stroll felt impossibly hard to achieve but she kept going and House of Water revealed itself as she walked along the final curve of the path.

House of Water had been built in and around an alpine lake. It rose out of the water, multi-tiered and grand. Waterfalls cascaded down from one level to the next, forming pools and obscuring doors and windows. Trees grew from its rocky façade, their roots snaking down toward the ground, grown and tended in such a way that their roots and branches formed natural stairs and bridges.

All of the people of Water were out celebrating. They dove off cliff faces into the pools and lake below. Their bodies arced and spun in the air before plunging into the water with barely a ripple. Less coordinated children hurled themselves off after the older members of their House, hitting with tremendous splashes. The smallest children had been tied to buoy boards, splashing along with everyone else and resting on their boards when they were tired.

Salasi wondered briefly at the children. She had a faint recollection of all Water children being sent out to sea to be raised by the Mariners in their creche on the ocean. She must have remembered wrong because there were many children here of various ages.

The path to Water plunged into the lake, and continued out to the island House under six inches of water. Salasi stopped just short of stepping into it, watching the revelry. They played games with hoops and sticks. Some were just fun and physical but other required Skills. Tendrils and spikes of water picked off targets as they spun through the air, drawing shouts of dismay or joy as each one was nailed or missed. A few groups sat or lay on the surface of the water simply talking or eating while the others cavorted around them.

The water nearest Salasi rippled. She took a step back right as a woman with Four aught Skills rose seamlessly from the lake. Rivulets of water ran down her black skin making her glisten brightly in the sunlight. The blue leggings she wore clung to her, covering her from waist to knees. Stripes of a similar blue shade had been painted along her breasts and belly and arms, and were slowing rubbing loose despite their water resistant nature. Heavy blue beads hung at the end of all of her braids and clacked as she tipped her head and appraised Salasi.

<We are Salasi of Enforcer SalNavari,> Salasi said respectfully introducing herself. <We were told Navari was here under the care of Water, we would like to see her.>

The woman flashed a brilliant smile and her entire face lit up. <You are the one who saved Zumi! Come and be welcome!>

The water pulled back, leaving the path dry for Salasi to follow. <Your kindness and generosity are appreciated.>

<You and your partner are the ones who should be thanked. What you did was no mean feat.>

As they crossed the bridge, the woman announced her. Cheers and great splashes of water rose from the already celebrating Waters. By the time she reached the far end of the bridge, she was soaked through by their exuberance. Her escort drew the water off with a deft flick of her Skills, sending it back into the lake and leaving Salasi completely dry. The path they followed then curved up behind one of the great waterfalls before passing under another. Her escort waved a hand, pulled the falling water back like a curtain and gestured Salasi through.

Salasi could feel the wards of the House cascading down with the water. Once she entered, there would be no leaving without Water's permission, but that had been true since the moment she set foot on the bridge. A Water surrounded by her element was far more powerful than an aught of the same rank from another House. There was simply no arguing with the elemental power of Water. Salasi walked through the waterfall curtain and into the House.

Unlike the Water Works that had been cavelike, the House of Water was more like a rainforest sinkhole. The roping roots of trees draped down walls while their boughs stretched up towards natural skylights. Brightly colored birds called to each other and fluttered in and out of the sunshine. There were ponds filled with fish and salamanders, and water ran freely in rivulets down the walls and floor.

The passageways all appeared naturally carved, dipping and turning at seeming random intervals. As she walked, Salasi could feel Navari growing closer. Her escort finally pulled back a reed curtain to a warm, dark room.

Salasi could feel the Bone Skills the moment she stepped inside, brushing across her mind like spiderwebs. She paid them almost no attention as she hurried to Navari's side.

Even under the blankets Salasi could see that Navari was far too thin. Her cheeks were hollow, her closed eyes sunken. Her Skills had burned through her fat stores and had started digging into muscle to supply the strength they had both needed last night. Salasi gently brushed Navari's cheek with her fingertips, almost afraid to touch her.

Despite the healing sleep of Bone, Navari turned her face into Salasi's touch. Salasi let all her love pour through the bond between them.

Navari shifted briefly within the healing Skills, a slight acknowledgement that she knew Salasi was there with her and was glad.

Salasi curled up around Navari, wrapping her shields around both of them feeling at peace for the first time since they'd been sent on that stupid census call. Beyond their little cocoon, the rest of the Mountain celebrated.

Chapter Twenty-Six

Raid

The day passed remarkably uneventfully. Li didn't want to stay still, so they had left Gemma's farm, but there was also nowhere she wanted to go. She wanted to care for the dead but also didn't know where to start. Raid finally convinced her to stop for a moment and rest. She didn't want to go back to her cottage or back to Gemma's, so they ended up at his apartment. It appeared untouched, mostly because there wasn't much there to start with, and because the presence of Carnage Skills had deterred Ataku. The scent of Water Skills was strong in the bathroom and around the kitchen sink, the farthest Controller Ataku had entered before realizing this was a Carnage space and withdrawing.

Li cried herself to sleep in his arms.

Mordred drifted off on his own. Raid could feel him nearby, haunting through the empty town. Mordred's presence reassured Raid, keeping an eye out like this was the kind of thing he'd done in creche.

Raid nodded off himself, waking up again when Li started stirring. The last of the sunlight faded from the sky as evening set in. They'd been asleep for hours.

<Mordred?> Raid asked tentatively.

<You're awake?>

<Yeah,> Raid answered, relieved to hear him. He hadn't disappeared while they slept.

The power to Ashveil had been shut off along with the water. Raid simply sharpened his vision to see in the dark, then called in a gleam when he remembered Li couldn't. She navigated her own cottage so well that it took her moving with exaggerated care through his apartment to remind him. She held the gleam tightly in her hands though this one was for light only and not warmth. Her tears had dried, but her face was puffy and her eyes red rimmed. All of her Skills had curled up tightly within herself.

Raid went through his pantry but the cupboards were mostly bare, reflecting the fact that he spent so little time here. He had no food he could offer her. He wrapped his arms around her instead, pressing his lips to her hair. After a moment she leaned into him.

"We should find something to eat," he murmured.

She shuddered, repulsed by the thought of food or more likely, the finding of food. The cafes and restaurants over in the plaza would all be well stocked, their industrial grade freezers and fridges still holding in the cold. Doing that however would involve seeing – and stealing – from the dead.

"I can't," she whispered.

Raid tried to decide the best way to point out that the dead had no need of their food any longer when Bester's presence washed over him. The High Inquisitor had finally arrived.

"What is it?" Li asked, feeling him tense.

"The High Inquisitor's here."

Li pressed more tightly against him, as if he could protect her from a Nine.

Bester's impatience rolled over him, already aggrieved that he'd kept her waiting.

"Wait here," Raid said quietly. The High Inquisitor had implied she knew about Li, but that was different from her actually laying eyes on the part-blood.

Li clung to him for a moment longer, before letting him go.

The High Inquisitor stood in the empty plaza, not far from the Carriage stop. Mordred was already there, the two of them staring at each other in a way just shy of open hostility.

Despite being impeccably dressed, the High Inquisitor looked rough. She had a split lip and a black eye, and held herself carefully as if there were more bruises and cuts under her uniform. The trials had not been kind to her. It made Raid wonder who she had fought against as few in Carnage could land such blows on the High Inquisitor.

<Neither of you were there this morning,> she said when Raid

appeared.

<There was no reason to be there,> Mordred replied coldly.

Raid flinched, expecting the High Inquisitor to strike Mordred for his impudence.

A flicker of irritation crossed her features but then she just looked tired. More than tired, hollowed out. Alarm washed through Raid for a moment at seeing such weakness in someone so powerful.

<You wish to know about Arcana, do you not?> she said, tone acerbic.

Mordred looked like he'd rather swallow glass than agree but he answered sullenly, <Yes.>

<These are their headquarters downtown. If you believe they had something to do with Cain's death, go prove it.> With that she jumped away, forestalling any questions.

<What did she show you?> Raid asked once she was gone.

Mordred passed the information. It was the image of one of Iocaste Proper's many skyscrapers. Its architecture harkened back to pre-Cataclysmic styles; a tall, spiraling tower of glass. It lacked the gravity defying, wondrous quality of the Ancestors, and instead seemed more like a child's attempt to recreate an adult's design.

Raid called Li, telling her it was safe and asking, <What do you know about Arcana?>

"Arcana Industries?" she asked tiredly when she reached them. She still had the gleam clutched tightly in her hands. "They're a medical manufacturer. Drugs, implants, devices…" She shrugged.

"You said once you didn't like them," Raid said, vaguely recalling a conversation they'd had months ago.

"Their R and D kicks out a lot of experimental things," Li replied. "Things that look great on paper that they claim will change the world, only once people start using them, turns out they actually cause serious harm. They had one implant that was supposed to stop seizures by shocking major nerve bundles. It stops your heart instead. There was also no way to remove it once it was implanted. People were told 'well, if your heart stops, just get to a hospital as soon as possible.' Several people died. There are other stories like that one."

<How are they still in business?> Mordred demanded.

“Good marketing,” Li answered simply. “Besides, it's cheaper to pay off the families of the injured and dead and have them sign a non-disclosure agreement then it is to pay for legitimate double blinded safety studies.”

Raid remembered some of this as Li talked. They’d discussed it because someone from Ashveil had just suffered heavy metal toxicity from a replacement hip that Arcana had produced. He’d been horrified and asked why everyone didn’t just request the help of a Bone Body Walker. Something like smoothing out hip arthritis would have been nothing for one of them. That had then turned into a long discussion of just how much the unSkilled didn’t trust the Skilled in this day and age.

“Why do you want to know about Arcana?” Li asked.

“They fund True Human,” Raid answered. “And they may have been involved in Cain’s death.”

<Let’s go find out if they were,> Mordred said, reaching for Raid.

“You’re leaving?” Li said, alarmed at being left alone.

“You can come,” Raid answered.

<No she can’t,> Mordred snapped.

<She knows more than either us,> Raid snapped back.

Mordred flicked his shields in irritation.

“Where are you going?” Li asked.

“Arcana downtown. Then we’ll figure it out,” Raid replied.

Li glanced around the empty plaza, her town of Ashveil so recently depopulated. She nodded slowly. “Yes. Let’s go. I need to… concentrate on something else for a while.”

<Fine,> Mordred said exasperated, then grabbed them both and jumped.

Chapter Twenty-Seven

Maggie Reeves

"Hello Volunteer Detective Reeves."

Maggie startled violently. She was on her feet, a second away from punching Laren in the face before she recognized the statie.

Laren didn't even look phased by Maggie's reaction. She looked exactly as she had when Maggie had first met her, crisp black suit, shining shoes and slicked back hair in a tight bun. She looked as if the attack last night had never happened.

"You have been sitting in this lobby since last night. It is safe to assume whoever you're waiting for isn't coming," Laren continued.

Maggie looked around and realized she was still sitting in the ER lobby. Various muscle groups began to cramp or tingle as her awareness returned, all of them reminding her that she had been sitting here unmoving for hours. She drew in what felt like the first deep breath she'd taken since she'd sat down here after the last of the bodies in the lobby had been carried down to the morgue.

So light weight. So quiet.

Maggie shuddered and pushed away the thought. "What do you want?" she demanded coldly.

"The Inquisitors and Enforcers will be coming to investigate what happened here last night. As you are the only remaining member of the police department, were present at the inciting events, and were present when the Controller was attacked here, they will want to speak with you. I came—"

"What do you mean 'the only remaining member'?" Maggie demanded.

"Exactly that," Laren replied. "You are the only remaining member of the Ashveil police department, volunteer or otherwise."

The world suddenly felt cold and small around her. "What about Jim? He was with me the whole time." Wasn't he? He'd been at the park when Zumi attacked, and had helped her carry the victims here to the hospital. He'd—

He'd been cursing, ripping at the air, trying to break free.

Maggie shied away from the horrible image.

Laren gave her an odd look and said quietly, "He's dead. His body is in the morgue with the others. You carried him down there yourself."

Maggie sat back down abruptly, her legs giving way beneath her.

"The Inquisitors and Enforcers will be coming here soon," Laren said, her voice gentle. "They'll want to talk to you—"

"I don't want to talk to them."

"You unfortunately won't have a choice. Not with an extinction protocol."

Extinction protocol. Maggie's stomach churned violently and she pressed her fist hard against it to stop herself from throwing up.

"What do you know of Skilled Protocol?" Laren continued.

"That they kill entire towns," Maggie said bitterly, throwing her hand towards the door and the bright sunset that filled the world with brilliant oranges and deep blue shadows.

"Not extinction protocol specifically, but Skilled Protocol in general," Laren clarified.

"It exists," Maggie answered. Supposedly it was the laws that all kurs followed, but there were convenient ways around it so the kurs always got what they wanted in the end. Ataku no doubt had a neat excuse for why she destroyed Ashveil when her son had been the aggressor just like Earth had explained away Ceres.

Laren sighed. "Protocol is etiquette and codes of conduct. It is what they rely on when dealing with each other, and it will make things go more smoothly for you if you use it as well."

Maggie didn't want to hear any of this but she was afraid she'd vomit if she tried to stand and leave.

"As you know, for us unSkilled, there are three speech forms, casual, respectful and formal."

Maggie nodded. Casual for friends and family. Respectful for superiors and elders. Formal that was taught in grade school but she had only ever heard used once before last night.

"Among the Skilled there are twelve," Laren continued.

Maggie choked. "*Twelve*?"

"You will not be expected to know them or when they apply. However, be aware of them and remember to always use respectful speech forms with the Skilled, and should someone like the High Inquisitor speak with you, use formal. Always use titles. Avoid single, first person pronouns—"

"What?"

"Avoid single, first person pronouns. Don't say I, me, my, mine, myself, etcetera."

"I thought that was a joke." Maggie had heard that rule before but had dismissed it as an exaggeration from the media of just how bizarre kurs were.

"No. The only time a Skilled will use single, first person pronouns is to take complete responsibility for an action, or to stake a relational claim. Controller Ataku referred to Zumi as 'my son' last night to make very clear the depth of her upset. Unlike most Waters, she did not send him out to sea to be raised in the creches on the ocean, but raised him herself. She has a far stronger bond to him then most Skilled parents feel for their offspring. It also makes her far more dangerous around him because of the lengths she will go to defend him, as you can see." Laren nodded over her shoulder to indicate the empty town beyond the walls of the hospital.

Mommy to the rescue after he picked a fight he couldn't win.

"They will use thoughtspeak, however you can request an interpreter. There are low aughts who will speak aloud to you should you feel too uncomfortable to hear thoughtspeak."

"Uncomfortable," Maggie muttered darkly. Thoughtspeak wasn't just uncomfortable. It hurt like a wicked bitch and gave the kurs the excuse they needed to go rifling through someones private thoughts, or ash their mind like what happened to Longcross.

"Do you have any questions?"

"No."

Laren nodded. "The hospital administration has been gracious enough to allow the agency to set up headquarters here, as Angels Landing is the only building that still has power and running water. You are welcome to stay here as well or return to your home. However, do not leave Ashveil until this investigation concludes."

"There won't be any investigation," Maggie said bitterly. "The kurs will discover whatever it is they want to find and make up whatever story suits them best."

"Do not use derogatory slurs," Laren replied without missing a beat. "Should you choose to stay here, please check in with Administrator Song." With that, Laren walked away.

Maggie stared blankly after her and wanted nothing more than to just sink back into this chair. Now that her cocoon of silence had been disturbed however, the aches of sitting still so long were making themselves known, not to mention the hunger. After several tries, Maggie pulled herself to her feet and walked stiffly out into the coming night.

Chapter Twenty-Eight

Raid

Arcana Industries had looked ugly in Bester's memory of it and wasn't any prettier up close. Its imposing front of glass and concrete loomed over the sidewalk and light rail tracks, both of which were nearly overrun with unSkilled. Everything lit up so brightly by streetlights that the night was driven back.

Li pressed herself into Raid as someone carrying a large sign nearly crashed into her.

"Sorry!" he shouted over his shoulder without looking back.

<They're headed for city hall,> Mordred commented, scanning over the heads of the crowd.

<Why?> Raid asked a moment before he saw another sign. Instead of the typical True Human garbage, this one proclaimed: JUSTICE FOR ASHVEIL! He shouldn't have surprised that word of the depopulation had already reached Iocaste Proper, memes spread information faster than wildfires could burn.

Mordred snapped a sight shield and aural shield over all of them, ensuring that no one would be able to see or hear them, before picking the lock on the front door and shorting out the alarm system in the process.

The lobby was cavernous. Marble and steel and giant plants in giant pots. Longcross's house could fit in here. This was what Raid didn't understand about True Human, they said they needed more space because there wasn't enough space for the unSkilled, but then they had buildings like this one. How many people could live here comfortably? How many people could live in Longcross's house comfortably? They didn't need more space, they just needed to get better at dividing up what they already had.

<Did the High Inquisitor say where we should start looking?> Raid asked. This building was massive, and he wasn't thrilled with the idea of searching every floor.

"Check the directory?" Li said softly, nodding at the directory made of black marble embossed with gold lettering.

Raid started towards it just as Mordred said, <There's half as much building under the ground as there is above it, and then… nothing.>

Raid paused and took a better sense of the building around him. Restaurants and little boutiques filled the rest of the ground floor. Offices spread through the floors up above him. Down below was parking for personal vehicles along with basements and subbasements filled with the pipes and wiring that kept this place operational. Both above and below, the building stretched beyond his ability to sense it.

Raid focused again on Mordred, not feeling anything amiss.

<You didn't feel it?> Mordred asked.

Before Raid answered, Mordred passed him the memory.

It was identical to what Raid had felt, only with the sharper detail and the farther reach that came with a higher aught set of Skills. The outlines of the basement and sub-basements stretching down until… nothing. It didn't turn back into earth or rock like he would expect it to, it just… ended.

<What is that?> Raid asked with a frown.

"What is what?" Li echoed softly.

<Something that shouldn't be there,> Mordred answered grimly. Which was enough of a reason to go take a closer look.

Raid described it to Li while they crossed the lobby, the feeling of nothing, a gaping cavity in the reality of the world.

At the center of the lobby stood a statue of a well muscled man carved from white marble, holding up a staff with a serpent and using it to force back a figure carved from black with a skeletal face and hands. *The Miracles of Medicine Will Conquer Even Death* was carved in bold letters along the plinth the two figures stood on.

They passed an unmanned security desk and headed back to a huge vault of elevators. They all had numbers indicating the floors they connected to except for one. It didn't even have buttons to summon it, only a keycard scanner.

"Authorized personnel only," Li murmured as she looked at it.

<We're authorized,> Mordred answered, using a flick of Skills to mimic the swipe of a card.

<Neat trick.>

<Learned it from Bester,> he said as the elevator doors slid open without a sound. Once they were inside, Mordred hit the button of the lowest level. The doors closed smoothly, and the elevator began its descent.

It wasn't a surprise that the High Inquisitor would know how to fool electronic locks. She would have had to expand her Skillset to include the new advancements of unSkilled technology. A hundred years ago, the news about Ashveil would have spread only to the closest towns, if at all. Weeks or months would have passed before the information made it all the way back to Iocaste Proper and the unSkilled House of Commons via cow cart delivery. Even if mail had been sent by Wind couriers it would take a few days to reach its destination.

<Do you think Bunny was a Wind?> Raid asked suddenly, his brain making the tangential connection. Just because he'd never felt anything like her Skills before didn't mean they hadn't existed at one time.

<Bunny?> Mordred asked.

Raid tossed him a memory clip, the woman with the rainbow reflective ski goggles who had brought the white moths of oblivion with her.

<No,> Mordred replied once he knew who Raid was referencing. <She's something else.>

<A new House?> Raid asked doubtfully.

<Weird things pop up from time to time,> Mordred answered. <Matriarch Thaydra claims her granddaughter is an Ice stronger than a Ten, with a body temperature so cold she can't be seen in public without melting.>

<That's a convenient excuse not to have to prove your claim,> Raid pointed out.

Mordred shrugged. <There have been others like that over the

years.>

Raid had to agree. He'd grown up with those same stories, Skilled who had been born with uncommon or overwhelming abilities, many of which included serious downsides; like a body temperature so cold they would melt in normal temperatures. Bunny the Oblivion must be one of those outliers, an amalgamation of part-blood Skills that had come together in a horrifying way, including eyes so sensitive to light she needed to wear ski goggles inside.

<It's coming,> Mordred said tensely.

Raid, who'd let his senses stretch down below him, felt it a second after Mordred spoke. The basement floors that had been passing them by gave way abruptly to nothing. The elevator didn't slow as it approached. Raid pulled Li close, bracing for impact as the void yawned open and rushed up to meet them.

The nothing reached them, engulfed them. His ears popped and the world inverted. Suddenly he could feel nothing above him, it all just disappeared. Instead, now he could feel the facility below that had previously been hidden. The shift gave him intense vertigo and claustrophobia. He battered his Skills on the roof of the reality bubble above him and couldn't find a way back into the world, all of his attempts folded back in on themselves. The entire universe had suddenly become a single city block four floors deep.

Li's hands were on his face. Her voice reached him. "Look at me."

It took a moment to focus on her words, then on her eyes. Her Viridae Skills had reached for him curling around him like the gentle tendrils of bean sprouts. She was real and solid and loving and warm and here. She grounded him long enough to get his bearings.

Something about this place hid it from the world and hid the world from it. All he had to do was take this elevator back up a floor and the world would be there waiting.

He kissed Li's palm. "Thank you."

She nodded and glanced through the open elevator door uneasily. "I don't like this place. It's unnatural."

"Yeah." It reminded him strongly of Bunny's oblivion, only on a larger scale. Instead of being trapped within his own head, he was trapped within this bubble world. At least his Skills still worked. <Are you alright?>

Mordred had a wild look in his eyes, his face had gone pale and clammy. He'd called his knives in. <Can't jump out of it,> he said shakily. <Can't jump within it.>

That left the elevator as their only means of escape.

<What do you know?> Mordred asked focusing in on Li. <You know Arcana.>

"I don't *know* Arcana," she countered. "But if I had to guess with the way this is buried and the way it's shielded, they're doing things down here they don't want anyone to know about."

<Like?>

"I'd start with ethics and animal welfare violations, and watch it get worse from there," she answered grimly.

All three of them just stared out into the empty hall, no one taking a step to leave.

<The High Inquisitor works with Arcana; do you think she knew about this?> Raid asked.

Mordred looked troubled. <No?>

"We can keep speculating, or we can go look," Li said moving towards the door. "You think Arcana had something to do with Cain's death, right? Let's see if that's true."

Raid hadn't felt anyone present in the facility but that didn't mean there weren't unSkilled there, the paper dolls gone flat and blending into their background. He stayed at Li's side as she stepped out, Mordred's shields – regular, sight and aural – protecting them. The elevator was in its own little nook. They turned the corner and—

The main hall was **white.** The fluorescent lights brightening the shining paint to a painful edge. Raid dulled his vision, shading away the brightness so he could look without being blinded. Mordred did the same while Li shaded her eyes with her hand. All individual smells had been wiped away with bleach but he still caught a whiff of something underlying it. He ferreted out the scent, trying to get a better sense of it—

<Shit!>

Mordred was immediately on the defensive. <What?>

<Bunny the Oblivion was here,> Raid replied tensely.

Mordred followed his attention and said after a moment, <It's not just Bunny. That's more than just one.>

<More than one Oblivion?> That thought was horrific.

"Oblivion?" Li asked.

"Do you remember Longcross's assistant? The one with the rainbow ski goggles?" When Li nodded, Raid went on. "She had Skills. She had the ability to bring Oblivion… to negate other Skillsets." The memory of the softly fluttering moth wings made him shudder.

"I didn't know that was possible," Li said surprised.

"Neither did we."

Raid caught the fleeting scent of Oblivion as they moved through the floor. All offices and conference rooms, all of them empty and lacking personal effects. There weren't even paintings hung up. If he hadn't seen the wearing around the edges, the scuffs on the floor or the repainted dings on the walls, he would have assumed this place was newly moved into.

"How long as this building been here?" Raid asked.

Li pulled out her meme. "No service. Should have figured that," she muttered before putting it back in her pocket. To him she said, "I don't know. Somewhere in the last ten or twenty years? I haven't heard about any big construction projects but I also don't keep close track of what goes on in Iocaste Proper."

<What the fuck have they been doing down here all this time?> Mordred said, eyes narrowed.

<Nothing good,> Raid answered, thinking of what Li had said about hiding from ethics violations, and also what she'd said earlier. If Arcana was openly selling products that hurt and killed their consumers, what the hell kind of terrible thing were they hiding?

They toured the rest of the floor but found nothing useful. Li had made a point of checking all the drawers of every desk but never took anything.

"What are you looking for?" Raid asked.

"A work tablet," she answered. "Even a notebook. Something we could take with us and use to get into their systems."

"Maybe they lock it all up when its not in use."

"Maybe," she agreed, but she didn't look convinced.

Beyond the offices, the hallway ended in a thick, heavy, reinforced door. It was set into slab concrete several feet thick. Arcana really didn't want anyone going down to the level beyond.

Mordred swiped the keycard with Skills and the heavy lock disengaged, making the whole thing useless. Whoever had built this hadn't wanted any high aughts to pass through the walls or doors, but they hadn't considered the keycard slide would be a weakness. With the reality bubble hiding the whole place, maybe they'd simply assumed no one would ever make it down this far.

On the other side were blast door, currently retracted in the walls and ceiling. These were so thick that even someone strong enough to pass themselves through solid objects might not be able to pass through those.

<Why do they need blast doors?> Raid asked.

<To keep us from getting in,> Mordred answered. <This whole place was built to keep the Skilled from finding it and getting in.>

Down the steel stairway that also had the too bright lighting but at least the walls weren't painted reflective white. There was another set of blast doors on the landing and a third at the bottom of the stairs ready to snap shut and protect another keycard locked steel door.

Raid braced himself for the worst as Mordred swiped the keycard lock and let them through. Here the scent of Oblivion hit him in the face, almost as hard as the searing bright lights that glared down from the ceiling.

Li hissed and blinked in reaction to the dazzling glare, her hands almost completely covering her eyes as she peered between her fingers. "Who needs this much light at night?" she muttered.

Raid dialed back his own vision further, details coming into focus as everything else dimmed.

At first, he'd thought the floor was entirely open, but he realized the walls were just made of inch thick acrylic. Layers and layers and layers of it. It took a few minutes to make sense of what he was seeing.

Row after row after row of small cubicles, just long enough to lay down in and tall enough to sit up, stacked four high from floor to ceiling, with a lock on the outside. In each was a narrow bed made up of reflective, crisp white sheets. The smell of laundry detergent was in the air, along with food smells from a nearby cafeteria, and the rubber and sweat he associated with a gym. Stronger than all of it, was the psychic scent of Oblivion, whispering of caves and darkness and huge echoing spaces. The complete opposite of what he was seeing.

<Arcana has them trapped here,> Raid said suddenly. Bunny with her ski goggles to protect incredibly light sensitive eyes. If he found the lighting here in Arcana painfully harsh, what would it have been like for her? For any Oblivion if they shared her same trait? <How many can they house here? Hundreds? Thousands?> That's why Arcana had built a shield to hide this facility, they were hiding an entire enslaved House.

"And here's the ethics violation," Li said with grim humor and a horrified look in her eyes.

<Where did they come from?> Mordred demanded. <How did Arcana come up with a Skillset that doesn't exist?>

"Better question," Li cut in. "Where are they all now?"

Raid reached down into the lower floors with his senses and came up empty, but then he hadn't felt Bunny's psychic presence until he'd been standing over her. It could have been because she was a low aught Oblivion, or it might be another part of Oblivion Skills, someone who could pass as a paper doll until you were close enough to see that they were actually three dimensional.

"We have more than enough for a full Inquisition," Raid said. Not to mention all of Animachea Command and a Matriarch Tribunal. They could leave now and let the Tens deal with this monstrosity.

<And Cain?> Mordred asked. <Bester is involved with Arcana. If she knew about all this and comes in with a full Inquisition, she'll destroy anything she doesn't want found.>

<But she was the one who sent us here. If there's anything that will implicate her, won't she want to keep it hidden?> Raid replied.

"Unless it's a trap," Li said quietly.

Several moments passed uneasily. If it was a trap for them,

they'd walked straight into it without pause.

<Even if it is, if they're involved with Cain's death, now's our chance to get that information,> Mordred answered.

"Let's keep looking then," Raid said. The bright white was bleeding in at the edges of his perception and blending with the shield that kept him from the rest of the world. It was hideous and uncomfortable, and he didn't want to stay down here. He also didn't want to give up any chance of finding out what happened to Cain if Arcana really was involved. "There has to be information somewhere."

The cubicles made up most of the space. At the far end they found the small cafeteria and gym, and a communal bathroom. White towels and white coveralls were neatly stacked on acrylic shelving. There was no other color anywhere, and no place to hide from the blinding lights.

There was another stairwell with its own keycard scanner and its own set of blast doors. Raid had thought for a moment that the previous stairway was another method to keep the Oblivions under control, but this nearly identical setup made him believe their first thought was the right one, Arcana didn't want anyone Skilled getting down into their facility.

"This is where the Oblivion came from," Li whispered as they stepped out onto the third floor down.

Bright white, immaculate walls. White laminate floors. Lots and lots of shining stainless steel medical equipment. Some things he recognized vaguely from unSkilled hospitals and labs. Most he didn't recognize at all.

<What do you mean?> Mordred said sharply.

"Cloning," Li answered, her eyes skipping from one room to the next as she walked down the main hall, glancing in through all the observation windows. "Vat breeding. This is all the equipment you need for that."

"How do you know that?" Raid said, caught more off guard by the fact she was saying it than what she was saying.

"University agriculture classes. Even after a thousand years not all livestock does well on Oceanea. They were never able to get horses or sheep to adapt. The camelids have done pretty well. Goats— we all know how that went with the goats. Cows and pigs, they need to keep reengineering. When they get a strain that does well, they clone and vat breed so they can have entire herds that will still be fit for consumption while they try to continue the bloodlines in more conventional means."

<Arcana bred an entire House in a *vat*?> Mordred seethed. The temperature dropped and ice rilled up the closest windows.

Li shrank back from him. "I mean… Biology's not my specialty but just looking at all of this… I don't know what else they'd be using it for. If they were simply cloning animals, they wouldn't need to hide it. Human cloning though, that's always been illegal."

An entire House grown and raised and hidden for Soth only knew what reason.

<What's their point?> Mordred demanded. <There isn't enough space upstairs to train them. They barely even have space to walk around.>

<They don't need to be combat ready because they don't need to fight,> Raid answered. <They just need to get close enough to let their Skills take effect.> If he hadn't had his knives in hand when Bunny had walked up to him, Longcross would have been able to dissect him with a butterknife. He wouldn't have been able to defend himself. Even after Bunny had died and his Skills had returned, he hadn't been able to pull up a shield to protect himself for several minutes. If Mordred hadn't popped in when he had, there was still a chance the men in armor would have taken him.

<Maybe they tried to grab Cain,> he went on, remembering his disorientation. <Mad said that Arcana was always in Daal, that they were treating Kaolin. Maybe he got too close to an Oblivion, and they figured out he was Carnage.> If he'd been under the influence of Oblivion, he wouldn't have been able to reach Raid through thoughtspeak, but that wouldn't have stopped him from physically trying to reach Raid.

<There's one more floor,> Mordred said darkly. <Let's see what else they're hiding.>

Li darted into a few of the medical rooms as they walked.

“Looking for another tablet?” Raid asked.

She nodded. “Looks like just about everything is automated. The offices upstairs may be empty because there are only a handful of people currently involved. Just put the orders into your meme and it connects to the equipment and fulfills them.”

<Can you connect?> Mordred demanded.

“No,” Li answered. “You’ll need specific software, maybe even a specialized meme to connect. There’s going to be all kinds of security around this to keep random people from getting in.”

The final stairway unsurprisingly had its own sets of blast doors, but it opened into an almost completely empty floor. The air had to be close to freezing. Li crossed her arms and started shivering. Raid put an arm over her shoulders and drew a thermal shield around them. It would keep the cold out, but it would also drain him faster than the other more basic shields would.

Four ten-foot by ten-foot white cubes rested at the center of the room. Huge pipes and heavy cables snaked down from the ceiling attaching to the top. The center two glowed softly with intense light pouring from the narrow view ports. The other two were dark. That light had to be hell on Oblivion eyes.

“Those look like prison cells,” Li murmured.

Mordred crossed the floor without another word. Raid and Li followed. The floor was like ice under his shield.

They reached the first cubes. Heat radiated off it, the glowing white sides just shy of burning. No wonder this room was kept so cold. These cubes drew a tremendous amount of power.

The three of them peered through one of the observation ports. Inside there were four workstations that all faced towards the center. At the center was a tube filled with a pale liquid. Suspended in the fluid was a woman. Tubes ran from her nose and mouth and vulva. Smaller tubes were wired into her arms and legs. Her muscles were atrophied, her face gaunt, her skin sallow, her head shaved. She looked like she hadn’t moved or seen daylight in years. She could have passed as a skeleton if her stomach hadn’t been bloated. She could have passed for dead if he hadn’t seen the flutter of her heartbeat at her neck, the slow and steady rise and fall of her flat chest.

Raid reached for her with his Skills, but they didn't penetrate the thick walls of the cube.

<How long has she been in here?> Raid whispered horrified.

<Too long,> Mordred answered and knocked sharply on the window. The sound echoed loudly and hollowly around them. Raid flinched. She didn't twitch. The rest of the room remained quiet and still.

<An Oblivion?> Raid asked.

<Maybe,> Mordred replied. <Can't get a feel of her through here.> He tapped the side of the box with his Skills.

"There's a door," Li murmured.

They went over to it, but it wasn't keycard access like the doors in the stairwell. Instead, there was a numeric pad that required a code. <Can you pick the lock?> Raid asked.

Mordred ran his Skills over the keypad and shook his head. <Not without tripping an alarm.>

"You can't leave her like that," Li protested when Mordred turned to the other of the two lit boxes.

<Not planning to,> Mordred answered. <Let's see who's in here first. Then we'll come back for both of them with the Inquisition and a Body Walker.>

"She's going to need more care than we can give her," Raid said quietly when Li lingered. A Body Walker would be needed to disconnect all of that safely without killing the woman who floated there.

"What did she do to end up here like this?" Li murmured.

"We can ask her once we get her out," Raid replied. And then they could track down whoever had snatched her and stuffed her into this box along with the Arcana assholes that were holding her down here.

<FUCK.> Horror spiked from Mordred so strongly that Raid felt nauseous and he grabbed Li so hard she squeaked. Raid reeled back from the cube and started toward his brother, not wanting to know what Mordred had seen to cause a reaction like that.

And then there was joy and a mounting tidal wave of fury.

<What?> Raid said, reaching the porthole and bracing himself

for whatever even worse atrocity was waiting beyond.

There wasn't a tube with a floating captive, surrounded by consoles. This cube was barren except for a cot and two basins, all bolted to the floor. A single person sat pressed in a corner, knees drawn to chest, hands so tightly clasped at the elbows that his knuckles were white.

He was so unexpected, so completely out of context, that it took Raid a moment to recognize him.

Staring starkly back at him was Cain.

Chapter Twenty-Nine

SalNavari

Salasi's dreams filled with rain. It followed her no matter how she tried to escape it until she finally woke up enough to realize it was a Water, gently trying to rouse her. She blinked herself fully awake. She and Navari were twined around each other on a cot, somewhere within the House of Water. Navari still slept deeply; the healing Skills of Bone having worked wonders in the last several hours.

<Your kinsman has come for you,> the Water said as soon as he felt Salasi wake.

She blinked owlishly at the Two aught who stood in the doorway watching her. He struggled to remain respectful and not impatient, but she easily felt how much he wanted to go to Squaring the Earth, and he couldn't leave as long as SalNavari was still here.

<It's nearing midnight and everyone has gathered in the Grand Plaza,> he continued quickly.

<Navari isn't well enough to move,> Salasi answered, wanting to curl up with her and go back to sleep for a few more hours.

<Controller Ataku has agreed that your partner can remain in Water until she is fully recovered,> the Water replied. <And your kinsman reported that your Matriarch has also agreed that Navari can rest. Your attendance, however, is required.> His excitement continued to pluck at Salasi, wanting her to hurry up and leave so that he could leave with her. He felt anxious about being the last one in the House while all his friends had already left to celebrate.

<She's to be left alone?> Salasi demanded.

<The wards of the House will keep her safe,> he reassured her. <And the Bone healers are still monitoring her progress.>

Neither of those gave her confidence. The wards would keep

Navari safe, but that wasn't the same as having a person here watching over her. Likewise, the Bones would be celebrating along with everyone else, how close track would they truly be keeping? Not that any of her concerns mattered. The Matriarch had required Salasi's attendance, so Salasi would attend.

She let Navari know where she was going and that she would be back as soon as she could. She checked what she could of the healing Skills before finally stepping out into the hall.

The Water pranced anxiously a few steps ahead of her all the way out of the House. The cavorting Waters from earlier had long ago left for the Grand Plaza, leaving their lake quiet and calm. As soon as she set foot on the sandy beach, her escort took off, his long legs eating up the ground as he hurried along the path to the Grand Plaza.

Getch had stepped out of one of the nearby gazebo pagodas that dotted the lakeside. Some of Salasi's ire lifted at seeing him.

<The Matriarch sent you as escort?> she asked, sounding more annoyed than she meant to.

<Would you have preferred someone else?> Getch replied.

<Would have preferred Navari here.>

He brushed her with his sympathy. <Yes,> he agreed. <She will be alright,> he added when Salasi glanced back towards House of Water. <In a few days she will be recovered, and tonight, you can fill her dreams with joy and festivities.>

Which was exactly what Salasi had wanted yesterday. Now it felt foolish and selfish. Now all she wanted to do was stay with Navari until the worst had passed and they were back in the field together again responding to noise complaints, fallen trees, or newly formed potholes. She reached for Navari. Her dreams were pleasant, filled with waterfalls and dappled shadows. The underlying feelings a far cry from what they had been before. Salasi reminded herself of all the reasons why Navari would be fine, but she still couldn't shake the feeling that something terrible would happen in her absence.

The paths and bridges through the Mountain were all lit up with gleams. Their white light poured from the claw-footed lanterns that held them suspended. For Squaring the Earth, someone had place incense along the paths as well, the sweet smoke filling the air with haze and adding a surreal quality to the night.

The thoughtspeak chatter grew in Salasi's mind as they drew closer to the Grand Plaza. She could hear the laughter and singing, could feel the goodwill pouring off everyone. Salasi could feel herself relaxing despite herself, her worry and tension steadily melting away.

The gleams ended with the path and the Grand Plaza was lit only by the light of the moons. White Thebus waxed nearly full, gilding everything in silver light, while green Kuu was just a sliver of a crescent grinning down at them. Salasi paused there at the edge, looking out at the throng.

The psychic scents of all the Houses mingled as the thousands of Skilled came together. The smell of food and wine and stronger spirits blended with the incense that drifted from lotus shaped holders that floated above the crowd, held up by Skilled charms. Strains from guitars and flutes floated in the air along with physical shouts and laughter that echoed the rumble of so much thoughtspeak. People danced. Elders stood with canes or sat on air, held up by their Skills. Infants with serious expressions peered at everything from the safety of their caretakers' arms while the older children laughed and squealed, meeting up with friends they hadn't seen since the last Squaring the Earth and chasing each other through the crowd.

Getch tugged her forward.

Fire with their long black hair decorated with brilliantly colored feathers, and red or gold thread. Viridae dressed in beaded and painted leather, and flowers tucked behind their ears. Austere Ice dressed in white and silver, standing out so vividly against everyone else that they seemed to glow. Carnage in black and blending in to the shadows. Earth with their metal and stone jewelry that clanked and clicked as they gestured. Water with their faces and bodies highlighted with white and blue and red paint. Bone with their curly hair twisted up into elaborate headdresses.

They all looked and dressed so differently, moved and interacted and spoke differently, but they were all here together. All of the Children of Soth. Similar in all the ways that mattered most.

Getch brought Salasi to Vaka and a group of Animachea Shepherds. The drab uniforms styled to make the unSkilled feel comfortable had been abandoned in favor of bright fabrics decorated with even brighter embroidery or shining disks of metal and glinting chips of semi-precious stones.

Salasi became keenly aware of the Enforcers uniform she still wore, and the fact that she hadn't changed it since yesterday. She hesitated at the edge of the group. They might all be Animachea, but they were Shepherds and Getch's friends. What would they think of her showing up without her partner, smelling of the blood and smoke and sorrow of Mountain Village?

Vaka came over, wrapping her fingers around Salasi's free hand.

<We've all heard the updates of Mountain Village, and Getch has told us about what you and Navari did for Water and for Zumi. You are incredible.> Her approval washed over Salasi, and her smile was bright and welcoming.

<They say the humans are still attacking the Mountain Village. The Wolves have had to bite several people,> another of the Shepherds said.

Salasi tensed. Her chest ached dully reminding her she'd been shot. Bone had healed all the bruising, but a few vestiges still remained.

Getch noticed and waved off the comment. <The animal bonded Enforcers will keep the unSkilled in check,> he said firmly. <Tonight, we don't need to worry.>

Vaka took her cue from him and began telling stories of the brand new crias just born to the barn she oversaw. Images of the day-old camelids flickered across Salasi's thoughts as Vaka shared her memories. Long-necked, long-limbed, woolly little creatures that hadn't properly unfolded yet after birth.

One of the other Shepherds supplied her own images of the piglets she oversaw, more than a dozen of them running laps around their giant mother as she dozed in the shade of her pen.

Story by story, Salasi began to relax again. She fell into the cadence of the Shepherds, listening as they talked at length and with great love for the animals they tended. She sent the stories and the images to Navari, and felt them echo back in her partner's dreams.

Maybe once Navari had healed, they two of them could go visit VaGetch at the barn they tended and see the camelids in person. She wanted to bury her hands in their fluffy wool and see if they were as soft as they looked.

A ripple of unease moved through the crowd, the conversation guttering out for a moment in its wake.

Salasi turned her senses towards it but already the moment had passed, the happy chatter and cavorting of the crowd back to full swing.

<What was that?> she asked.

<Some old grievance brought back to light,> Getch answered easily.

Salasi made herself relax. With all the Houses together, old rivals ran into each other the same way old friends did. Injuries were kept to a minimum but that didn't stop shoving matches from taking place or the occasional fight from breaking out. She was just jumpy after what had happened at Mountain Village and Ashveil, after what had happened to Navari, and that she was here alone.

She leaned into Getch.

He leaned back, his strong arm pressed to hers, their fingers twined together.

Glee washed off Vaka. She wanted very much for this courtship to work. She wanted to bring Enforcers into their circle, especially ones with as solid a reputation as SalNavari.

Salasi blushed at feeling Vaka's praise.

<You shouldn't be surprised she likes you,> Getch murmured to just Salasi, letting her feel his delight at having her here with him. <*I* like you.>

Giddiness flooded Salasi, enough that she felt an echo of it from Navari, even deep within her healing dreams. Salasi prepared to answer him right as his delight faded away from her. She clamped down hard on the words she'd been about to speak.

A moment later Getch's delight faded back in, though it was now mingled with puzzlement.

<Do you feel that?> he asked.

A moment snow began to fall. Snow flurries this late in the

year weren't uncommon. More likely an Ice thought it would be fun to start a snowball fight and douse everyone around them.

<The snow?> she asked back, but her words sounded flat. She started feeling light-headed as the snow fell harder. She could still feel Getch pressed close beside her, and Vaka on her other side, but her sense of them faded to nothing but the physical. <Getch?> she asked alarmed.

He didn't answer.

She realized suddenly the crowd had faded into silence. No laughter. No chatter. No calls of alarm. The snow blanketed everything, making it hard to see. It muffled every sound. Salasi let go of Vaka and batted at the snowflakes, trying to clear it away but it did no good.

<Navari?> she called, panic growing. <Navari!>

Navari stirred at Salasi's growing fear, but then the snow buried even her. The bond between them disappeared, leaving nothing but white.

<Navari!> she shouted again.

A flicker of movement drew her attention. A woman walked towards them. She wore black coveralls and light body armor. A shining black face plate obscured all of her features, showing nothing but Salasi's contorted reflection. For a moment the world narrowed down to nothing but the two of them, Salasi and this woman, standing alone in a place of nothing but snow. Then even the woman was buried in the flurry of white, and Salasi knew nothing else.

Chapter Thirty

Raid

Raid stared. For a moment his heart stopped. The world stopped.

Cain's wary stare wavered. Then he was rolling to his feet in an easy motion that Raid recognized so well. Raid's heart thundered in his chest. The world came back into focus, too bright, too cold, to be real.

<Cain!> he shouted, but there was no answer. <CAIN!>

Cain reached the viewing port. He looked haggard. His blond hair was long and ragged. He didn't look like he'd shaved in weeks. Only his eyes were the same, bright blue that no one believed belonged in Carnage.

<CAIN!> Still nothing. "Can you hear me?" Raid demanded out loud.

Cain shook his head. He gestured to the window, to the rest of the cube, and shook his head violently.

<You said he was dead!> Raid roared, turning on Mordred.

<He was dead!> Mordred snapped back. <Animachea brought him in a coffin! He was sung back to the land!>

<Then who's that!> Raid jammed a finger at Cain who desperately stared at them through the window.

<You were there! You felt his scent at the well when we went!>

"Clones," Li cut in. "The whole floor upstairs is dedicated to cloning."

Mordred gave her such a scathing look she took a step back.

<He's not the clone,> Raid said, knowing that absolutely. <And we're not leaving him here.>

<No shit,> Mordred answered in angry agreement. He stepped back and took the measure of the cube, looking for weaknesses.

Cain pointed to another side of the cube, but Mordred was already moving, examining the door. Thick, heavy, airtight. It looked like it was never meant to be opened. Raid could feel Mordred's Skills sliding around the electric lock that was more than just a keycard slide, trying to find a way around the number code. His Skills were getting a sense of the rest of the cube also, pressing and picking at weak points.

Cain came up on the other side, watching them through the viewport. His tiny window to the outside.

<There are a lot of fail safes built in here,> Mordred said quietly. <If the code isn't entered in the exactly right way, the box will kill whoever's inside it.>

Raid stilled.

Cain's eyes darted between the two of them, his agitation growing.

<You can't open it?> Raid asked, keeping his voice low even though Cain couldn't hear them.

Mordred's Skills traced the mechanism again. <It's… It wants a long sequence of numbers.>

Too many for Mordred to guess, and if he didn't get it right… Raid looked up at the wires and tubes that were fixed to the cube. If they didn't get it right, would the entire box electrify and kill Cain? Would it be pumped full of poison gas? Or suck out all the air? Could they irradiate him the way the unSkilled did with their food when they used wave cookers?

<Be ready to run,> Mordred said.

<What?>

Mordred's Skills surged. The viewport iced over. Even in the already cold room, Raid felt the punch of the freeze.

With the screech of rending metal, breaking plastic and popping wires, Mordred bypassed the lock entirely, and just ripped the door off with nothing more than brute force.

All over sirens began to scream. The huge floodlights came to life with a brightness that rivaled the face of the sun.

Cain was on him in a flash, hands knotting into Raid's shirt, trying to prove to himself that Raid was really there. “Take it off,” he hissed. “Take it off. Take it off.”

Raid just caught a glimpse of the black leather collar before Mordred reached over and iced it. With a hard yank, it shattered into a dozen pieces of delicate wiring and electronics hidden beneath the leather. Mordred flicked his fingers and grimaced as if the thing had burned him.

Despair like Raid had never felt punched him as Cain’s Skills were freed. Raid staggered under it. Cain’s inner shields nearly collided with his own in Cain’s desperation for connection. That Raid was there. That the world was still there. Cain was shaking, sobbing. His thoughts were incoherent.

Raid’s reassurance washed over Cain. Raid was here. Mordred was here. Cain was with them now, and they were all leaving together.

<Get him on his feet, we have to go,> Mordred prompted. <They know we’re here now.>

Raid hadn’t realized that he’d dropped to his knees with Cain, holding him close, trying to ease that soul deep pain somehow. Raid stood, pulling Cain up with him. He was so light, too thin beneath the coveralls he was wearing. There was nothing but bones where there should have been muscle. He couldn’t walk far; he probably couldn’t even stand for that long.

Li’s hand was on Raid’s shoulder, her part-blood Viridae Skills striving to reassure him, while he bolstered Cain.

Mordred hovered nearby, looking like he wanted to join them and having no idea what to do.

<Now would be a good time to jump,> Raid said as he looped one of Cain’s arms over his shoulders.

<Can’t, remember?> Mordred answered. <Not within this bubble. There’s nothing to grab to make the jump. No landmarks.>

Shit. <Then help,> Raid snapped.

Mordred went to Cain side and looped Cain’s other arm over his shoulders. As he did, Raid saw that ice now rimed the cuffs of his jacket. The four of them then bolted back the way they’d come, Li leading the way. Raid barely spared a glance for the other cube and the woman suspended inside it. They would tell the Matriarchs about her. The Inquisition would come, the Tribunal, she would not be left here to suffer.

Across the room. Back to the stairs—

The blast doors had started to drop. No, they had dropped. Raid could hear their gears squealing as they tried to drop against the shields that were holding them open.

Li was under first, reaching back for Cain. Raid dragged him through, then Mordred. As soon as he was cleared, the shield released, and the door dropped with a thud of finality.

<You're keeping them open,> Raid said. It wasn't a question.

<Yeah,> Mordred answered, his voice strained. <So let's hurry.>

Up the stairs, through other blast doors, each one thudding down as soon as they were through so Mordred could dedicate his power to propping open the ones that still cut them off from the exit.

Down the hall of the third floor with its cloning equipment and chemical smell. It seemed even brighter now than it had been before. Raid shaded his eyes as much as he could, giving up the details of the world to keep from being blinded.

Li had a hand over her face, squinting between her fingers. Raid could still feel her Skills, the happy little cloud trying to do anything to make this better.

Cain stumbled, his fear spiking. He suddenly fought against Raid, tearing away from him and Mordred.

<We're here. We're here. We're leaving,> Raid said, wrapping Cain in reassurance, trying to ignore the terror that was bleeding through his inner shields. <You'll be safe, but we have to keep moving.>

Cain was shuddering, breaths still heaving. A vague sense of agreement among the desperation to get out. Get out. GET OUT!

The desperation ran along Raid's nerves, and he poured out as much reassurance as he could to combat the despair that was coming off of Cain. <We're getting out. We need to go,> Raid grabbed his arm. Cain tensed for moment before allowing himself to be pulled back to his feet and then along again, stumbling down the antiseptic corridor, past the labs and the surgical suits. Straight into Arcana's guards in military type armor coming down the hall towards them.

<Watch him,> Mordred said. He strode forward, and Li took his place, looping Cain's free arm over her shoulders. Mordred's sight shield keeping them all invisible.

"Cube three is down," the guard said sharply into his radio. "I haven't had a chance to assess the damage. We need reinforcements here now."

"We're starting mop up," came the response. "Forces are being dispatched. They'll be there within two hours."

"We don't have two hours if one of those things is loose."

Mordred slit his throat. Straight through the windpipe and severing the big vessels, so deep into the meat of the neck, the edge of the blade slicing into a vertebra. He nearly took off the man's head in his rage.

"Jamison's down! It's on level three!" The other guard shouted into the radio. Then he too was down and bleeding out.

<Now they really know we're here,> Raid said unnecessarily.

<You think?> Mordred snapped.

Raid could feel the effort pouring off of Mordred. Even as a Seven, keeping all those doors propped open started swiftly draining him down to his reserves. Cain tripped and stumbled, too weak and hurt to keep up. Li didn't waver once, her years of ripping out roots and hauling heavy pots and bags of compost making her sturdy and strong as she kept Cain up and moving.

They reached the stairs, Mordred taking out two more guards as they went. This set of blast doors was noticeably lower than the last set.

<How much strength do you have left?> Raid demanded privately so as not to panic Cain or alarm Li.

<Enough,> Mordred answered as if through clenched teeth, and the blast door crunched down behind them.

Onto the second floor with its plastic fishbowl cubicles and overwhelming scent of Oblivion.

A hideous, high-pitched shriek cut straight through Raid's ears and deep into the core of his thoughts. He shut off his hearing and peeled himself up off the ground. Mordred had taken a similar hit. Cain was crouched, knees to chest, head to knees and his hands clamped over his ears. Pain and fear oozed out of him. He hadn't tried to dial back his hearing. Of all of them only Li had kept her feet, hands pressed to her ears, wincing through the blinding light at whatever was coming.

<Use your Skills, shut off the sound!> Raid ordered.

Cain grimaced and then relaxed fractionally. A moment later, his shields went up, wobbly and unsure. He was no longer solely dependent on Raid and Mordred to keep him safe, which was good because a half dozen men in heavy armor with long range rifles were now stalking towards them, down the acrylic halls.

Under the blazing lights, Raid couldn't sharpen his vision to pick up the details of their armor without also blinding himself, but all armor had weaknesses. The neck. The joints. It wouldn't be as clean a kill as it had been for the four men downstairs, but they would die if they tried to stop Raid and Mordred from getting Cain out of here.

<The doors are down,> Mordred said grimly. He'd lost his grip during that piercing wail. That had been the whole point of the sound, to stun anyone with sensitive hearing.

<They know how to hurt us,> Raid answered.

"It's worse than that," Cain said in a hoarse, disused whisper.

Memories bled off him. Raid blanched at the fragments coming through.

<Tell us about it when we're out of here,> Mordred cut him off.

"Whatever you do, don't let them catch you," Cain went on, fear and fury mingling in equal parts. "Make them kill you first."

Raid didn't have time to respond to that. The armored men opened fire.

Their rounds pierced straight through the acrylic like it wasn't even there, lacing the world with spider web cracks.

Raid grabbed Li and dragged her to the ground with him. Shields could stop bullets, but it took power. The more bullets his stopped, the faster his Skills would drain. If his Skills were drained past his reserves, his shields would fail, and those bullets would be as lethal to him as to any unSkilled. Better to simply avoid them.

The six men fanned out, four closing the distance fast while the other two hung back with their rifles raised. They looked ready to shoot through the backs of their own comrades if that's what was required to stop the Skilled.

Any other time, Mordred and Raid would've had no trouble cutting them down, but Mordred had drained a good deal of his Skills keeping the blast doors open. They also had Li with them who couldn't shield, and Cain whose shields kept faltering as his panic grew.

<Can you hold a blanket shield?> Raid asked. If Mordred could stop any bullets from getting down the hall and hitting Li or Cain, Raid could go after the men and kill or disarm them before their bullets fully drained his shields.

<The ceiling isn't as reinforced as the doors are. It's full of ducts and pipes,> Mordred commented.

<And?> Raid demanded. <What does that matter?>

<Up and out,> Mordred replied.

Concrete and plaster exploded in every direction and showered down in the wake of Mordred's punch of Skills. Raid didn't have a chance to gape at the hole in the ceiling before Mordred was punting him up through it. Jagged ends of pipes and hissing electrical wires bit into his shields as he scraped along the edge of the hole. A moment later he cracked into a wall. He was on his feet, reorienting to where he was now. One of the clean, neat, empty offices, now in disarray and covered with dust and debris.

Cain was hurled through the hole a second later, followed by Li.

<Get him out of here,> Mordred ordered. <Be right behind you.>

Raid didn't hesitate. He and Li hauled Cain up to his feet and ran for the elevator and the only escape from the reality bubble. Carefully he turned up his hearing. The screeching wail was gone but bullets were tearing up the floor behind them as someone shot up into the ceiling. No one guarded the elevator, presumably they had all headed straight down with the expectation that the blast doors would keep the intruders contained.

To summon the elevator required a keycard.

Raid stared at the magnetic strip for a blank moment. He'd just watched Mordred do this a half dozen times. He flicked the keycard slide. The light remained red; the elevator doors didn't open. He tried it again with similar results. He wanted to swat the stupid machine but that wouldn't do any good. Gunshots blazed on the floor below, punctured by the occasional scream. Cain was shaking uncontrollably, draped over Li's shoulder.

"You got this," she said encouragingly, even though her face was stamped with worry.

Raid focused. He'd learned from Mordred all the time when they were in creche, mimicking Mordred's style and actions because he'd always been so confident in what he was doing. Raid took a slow breath and tried again, using Skills to trick the magnetic slide.

The light went green, and the elevator door slid open.

Cain shrank back, claustrophobic images of being locked in the cube flicking from him, along with other, darker things.

<This is the only way out,> Raid said. <There aren't stairs.>

Li's Skills worked to smooth away the sharp edges of Cain's fear.

He hissed out a breath and walked forward unwillingly, Li keeping him upright.

Raid reached for Mordred. <We're at the elevator. Where are you?>

Distracted acknowledgement, followed by a concussion that made the floor shake. <Keep going,> Mordred said through gritted teeth. <Right behind you.>

Shit. No, he wasn't.

Raid hesitated. Mordred needed an assist, but Cain was in no shape to do anything. Even with Li's aid, the two of them weren't going to get far, not with how deeply hurt he was.

<We're getting out of here,> Raid said. <Once Cain's safe, we'll come back for you.>

This time Mordred barely acknowledged him.

Raid punched the button for one of the lower sub-basements.

If the unSkilled were planning an ambush, it would be at the ground floor and the garage levels, closest to the exit with the most space to maneuver. They couldn't cover every floor though. He hoped.

He double checked the shield and sight shield around the three of them and put another shield up over the door to deflect any bullets should someone shoot before looking.

<We're coming back for you,> Raid said to Mordred. A second later his ears popped as they passed up out of the shield bubble and all of the rest of the world came rushing back in.

Cain crumpled like a puppet with the strings cut, nearly dragging Li to the floor. His relief and joy at finding the world still existed flooded out of him as powerfully as the despair a few minutes earlier. Safe. He was safe. He was going home.

Raid turned his focus to the Mountain, planning to raise the Inkwell and all of the unNamed if he needed to in order to catch someone's attention. The Mountain was close enough it shouldn't take that, but it was also Squaring the Earth so who knew how much it might take for anyone to notice.

His demands for immediate aid curled up and died in his throat. The Mountain was gone. All the Houses were gone. Where once had been the living, breathing, vibrancy that was all the interactions and interconnections of the Skilled, now there was nothing. It was like someone had taken away the Mountain and replaced it with a painting. Flat and bereft of life.

He pinged High Inquisitor Bester. No response.

He pinged her again. Still nothing.

In growing alarm he pinged all of the Inquisitors, even Adira, hoping for some explanation for what he felt.

<High Inquisitor?> he called. His voice shook.

Nothing but roaring silence.

He tried the Enforcers. Animachea Commands were all Bonded groups of four or more. One of them had to be listening. They didn't answer either.

His mouth had gone dry. His heart thudded so hard in his chest it hurt.

The elevator dinged, startling him momentarily out of his

horror.

"What?" Li demanded, her eyes darting from him to the concrete corridor of the subbasement and back again. "What do you hear?"

"Nothing." His voice sounded far away and too harsh.

"Raid?" she prompted when he didn't go on. She managed to sound calm despite everything.

He shook his head and pinged everyone again. All the Inquisitors. All of Animachea Command. He tried the Viridae forestry service that he knew through the unSkilled construction crews he worked with, and then the Bone's emergency Body Walker requests. He even tried the Matriarchs. He would have welcomed the censure that came with disturbing them if it meant someone would answer. Only silence.

Not the silence of being ignored, but *nothing.* All the people he would expect… just gone.

He reached back down for Mordred, but his Skills smashed into the disruption field. He reached out for Carnage one more time, as if suddenly there would be a different response, something besides this yawning chasm of nothing. He could feel the House itself, its wards still old and deep and strong, but the people who filled that building, who made it Carnage, they were gone leaving a Carnage shaped hole in the fabric of the world. A *Mountain* shaped hole in the fabric of the world because it wasn't just Carnage. All the Houses were gone. There were no Skilled left to answer him.

"Raid," Li said again, more sharply this time.

"Nothing," he heard himself answering her. "There's nothing to hear. The Mountain is gone."

Chapter Thirty-One

SalNavari

The snow tried to freeze her from the inside out. A parasitic cold that crept up from below and tried to suck her down and bury her. Navari fought it. She bit and clawed and screamed and dug. The cold didn't become any less cold, but the snow released its hold on her. She rolled out of bed and crashed onto an unfamiliar floor. Water Skills surrounded her. The constant crashing of waterfalls filled the House with background white noise.

Navari pulled herself to sitting. With that managed she struggled to stand. That took more effort than it should have and left her winded.

No snow surrounded her. No cold. Blankets puddled at her feet from where she ripped them out of bed with her, still warm from where she'd been sleeping.

She reached for Salasi and the cold bit deeply into her. She tried to look through Salasi's eyes and saw nothing but white.

<Salasi!> Navari cried.

The quiet of snowfall greeted her. Terror gripped her, deeper and sharper than anything she had ever known before.

<SALASI!> She plunged into the freezing drifts, pushing them aside. Tearing at the snow with will, battering it away with her thoughts. She screamed her partner's name, begging Salasi to answer.

Silence where there should have been laughter or ire or exasperation or delight. Silence where there should have been sight and sound and memory and thought. Silence where there should have been a person.

When SalNavari had been young, a set of older children managed to obtain the memories of those who had lost their Bonded partners. The memories were worn and faded, having been passed down through generations of minds. The unrelenting pain of having been torn in half. The stark emptiness of suddenly being half a person. It had filled SalNavari with horror. For both to die would be tragic, but to lose only one would be atrocity beyond reckoning. Those remembered feelings tore through Navari, resonating with her dread and strengthening it.

Salasi's voice was gone. Her feelings were gone. The underlying murmur of her subconscious thoughts were gone. There was no one but Navari alone and this snow and this white.

<SALASI!> Her mind rang with the force of her shriek.

The barest flickering of a battered image flared in the snow. Navari fought her way to it, the only thing in this white unchanging landscape that should be Salasi and found herself looking through Salasi's eyes.

No snow fell in the Grand Plaza. The haze of incense hung in the pleasant night air. She'd collapsed beside Getch, her head tucked in the crook of his arm, her eyes fixed up at Thebus and Kuu in the clear starry night. For a horrifying moment Navari thought she had invaded the corpse of her partner, but her heart still beat, her lungs still breathed.

<Salasi!> Navari shouted, trying to shake her awake, shake her into moving. <Get up!>

Salasi didn't answer and didn't move, but someone else did.

Out of the corner of Salasi's eye, someone walked, picking their way slowly forward. Navari pressed her will into their bond begging Salasi to respond. After a long, long moment she did. Salasi blinked slowly, her eyes turning just enough to watch.

People walking, all of them dressed in black. Men in heavy armor with rifles. Women with black reflective masks instead of faces. The men laughed and talked to each other, but their words sounded as if underwater. It was one thing to share Salasi's senses when she was alert and present, it was something else to ride along in her dreams while she slept. This was something altogether other.

Where Salasi should have been was nothing but snow and this one little snip of sight. Not dead, but unconscious in a way Navari had never experienced. Even the passed down memories of those unlucky enough to lose their partners hadn't experienced this.

A gunshot ripped sharply through the white. Navari startled before focusing on the sound. One of the riflemen lifted his gun lazily having just shot someone lying on the ground.

Someone nearby made a comment.

Weird, warped laughter filtered back to her and then he shot someone else.

<SALASI!> Navari shouted as he drifted towards her, shooting again and again. In the background, she could hear other gunshots echoing this one. Everyone in the Grand Plaza was being massacred by an unknown enemy. Salasi would die if she stayed.

Navari shrieked her name over and over until her throat bled, screaming out loud while she screamed in Salasi's mind. Navari threw herself at the snow and whiteness, trying to thaw it, break it, send it away, anything to release Salasi from its grasp.

Nothing. Nothing roused her.

More gunshots.

The riflemen slowly drifting closer, taking his time to point and shoot, like he had all the time and not a care in the world.

Navari screamed at Salasi. She screamed at the snow. She screamed at her useless body that was painfully staggering down the slick halls of Water, braced against the wall, trying to reach Salasi even though it had nothing left to give. Navari didn't know who these people were or why they were there, but she *would not* let them take her partner. She had saved Salasi last night and given everything she had to do so. She would do the same again right now and give up even more.

Everything from the last few days, the exhaustion and struggle, the attack by the Matriarch, the horror of Mountain Village, the atrocity that was happening now, and her impotent helpless rage at all of it, tripped something inside her. Something primal and long dormant – unneeded for many generations, passed down through the bloodlines from the oldest of her ancestors – woke up.

<Get up!> Navari screamed. <And run!>

Even though her mind remained encased in snow, Salasi leapt

to her feet. So did every other Animachea still alive in the Grand Plaza. Navari was aware of all of them, running scatter shot in every direction.

The riflemen shouted in alarm and anger. Bullets hailed down.

Animachea ducked and wove, surefooted as they sprinted across the ground, leaping the bodies of the fallen and the dead. The women in the black reflective masks watched Salasi come. One held out a feeble hand to stop her, but Salasi shoved by her and kept going. Out of the Grand Plaza, beyond the beams of the flashlights, into the forest, and gone.

Almost immediately the snow began to melt. Salasi's awareness thawed, and she came back to herself in frightened, wide-eyed pieces. Relief flooded Navari that Salasi was alive, even as Salasi's own panic washed back through her.

As Salasi regained control of herself, her steps faltered, tripping now over unseen obstacles. She stumbled to a halt, her breath ragged, her fear growing. She couldn't come up with words, just feelings and images. The snow falling, the world fading away. Not just the physical world either, but everything. No thoughtspeak. No connection to anyone or anything else. She hadn't even been able to feel Navari. She had been so completely alone, a half person drifting unmoored, lost forever.

Navari reassured her. She was safe now, no longer alone—

Branches snapped under booted feet and tinny voices hissed back and forth through the radio.

Salasi froze as fear seized her again.

Navari whispered encouragement to her, reminding her that she could shield and climb and run.

Salasi's legs trembled.

<Keep going,> Navari whispered urgently. <Get away from the Grand Plaza. Come back to Water.>

Salasi tried to pull up a sight shield and failed. The snow may have melted from her mind, but it's cold still ran deep.

The footsteps were coming closer. Someone shouted and opened fire. Bullets tore up the trees around Salasi.

<`You need to move,`> Navari snarled, her fear punching

up right along with Salasi's. <Now.>

Salasi bolted. She wove her way between the trees, too quick for the hunters to keep up with her. The white moonlight of Thebus dappled the ground as she ran on nearly silent feet. The bullets stopped as the riflemen lost sight of her. The voices faded away behind her as she put more distance between herself and them. Up ahead she saw the gleam lined road. She tried again to draw a sight shield and this time it came, wavering for a moment but holding. Hidden from sight, she ran. Along the elegant curves and soaring bridges, each step more putting more distance between herself and the snow and the riflemen and the women in their black masks. Every step bringing her that much closer to Navari.

Navari hurried to meet her, one arm braced agains the wall to stay upright. Her body protested with each step and the Bone healing Skills kept insisting she lay down and rest. She would rest once Salasi was safe. Then they could rest together.

They both saw each other at the same moment. Salasi raced down the path towards Water, splashing into the lake and slowing only when the wards tugged her ankles. Navari reached the entrance waterfall, stopping just short of plowing straight into it, the wards having made it as solid as any wall. Navari paced to where the waterfall was thinnest and looked at Salasi through it.

Salasi paced back and forth on the submerged path, unable to move forward and unwilling to retreat. Navari stood still, barely managing to keep to her feet. They couldn't physically reach each other, couldn't touch, but that did't stop them from being a Bonded pair.

Thoughts and feelings swirled back and forth between them. The snow that wasn't snow. Salasi who had been lost in it as if dead. The riflemen shooting. The women in the masks. Everyone in the Plaza collapsed to the ground.

<An attack,> Navari said, the first to pull enough away from the fear and desperation to form words. <They attacked us.>

<Who are they?>

Flashes of memory snapped between them, there than gone. The riflemen shooting. The women in their black masks. Tinny voices hissing in the darkness.

Navari's attention shifted as she reached for the Grand Plaza, Salasi twined along behind her eyes.

They recoiled.

Death. There was nothing to see but death.

The Skilled had all collapsed where they'd been standing, cut off from everything the same say Salasi had been, then they'd all been shot where they lay. Their jewel bright eyes now as empty as glass. Some had run like Animachea, and had been riddled through with bullets. Blood slicked the great paving stones, soaked into the beautiful formal clothing and hair. The hunters stole from the dead, stripping rings and bangles and necklaces. A few even that the gall to cut off hand or heads

Salasi wrapped her arms around herself, barely holding herself together. Navari managed to stagger back a few steps before collapsing, her spent body unable to bear her up in the face of so much horror.

<They killed everyone,> Salasi whispered.

And SalNavari still didn't know who 'they' were or why they had come.

<And they're not done yet,> Navari replied, her voice just as quiet.

Salasi followed her attention. The riflemen and the faceless women had abandoned the Grand Plaza and its horror, breaking into groups and marching ominously towards the different Houses. One set now headed straight for them.

<You need to hide!> Navari shouted.

<Not without you! Not leaving you here!> Salasi snapped, her foot inching forward despite the Water wards that tightened their grip on her ankle.

<They can't pass the wards,> Navari replied.

<You don't know that!>

<There isn't another choice! Hide!>

Salasi reeled back. Up the path. Along the shoreline. Over to one of the gazebo pagodas that dotted the lake shore and up it. Up its walls and into the beams. Up higher still. Cramming herself into the upper most corner she could reach. Bracing herself there in such a way that if the snow came again, she wouldn't fall.

Navari pressed herself to the wall behind the waterfall, letting the spray of water curtain her from view. The group came striding down the path. Even hidden, she pulled up a shield and sight shield. Both wobbled ominously. Bone had drawn her back from the brink, but she was far from healed. Even this little she did to protect herself strained her recovering Skills.

One of the men barked an order and pointed to the submerged path that led to House of Water. A woman moved forward at his command and walked down the path.

Navari held her breath. The wards of a House were far stronger than the wards of a single Skilled, having been laid down over and over, generation after generation by the strongest members of the House. It had given them a sort of sentience and made them far more aware than any unSkilled building. The faceless woman seemed confident in her ability to cross, and as she approached, snowflakes wafted across Navari's vision.

The snow may have incapacitated Salasi and every other Skilled in the Grand Plaza, but House of Water was having none of it. The woman reached the point at which Salasi had stopped before and walked right past it. With a splash and a ripple, she vanished from sight, the wards dragging her down to the bottom of the lake.

The man ordered another faceless woman to follow the first. The second hesitated for a moment before starting down. She stopped when the wards threatened her and shook her head. The man screamed at her to keep going but she silently shook her head again and refused. With a flurry of colorful curses, her ordered her back to the shoreline. A second later they all opened fire. Rock chips rained down as the bullets chewed up the front of House of Water.

Alarm exploded from Salasi.

Navari flattened herself down against the rock walkway and bolstered her shield while sending reassurance back to Salasi. Fine. She was fine. Salasi needed to stay where she was, she was far more at risk now than Navari.

Memories of the bullet riddled house from Mountain Village

swirled in Salasi's memory, and the smell of blood that had accompanied it. Those people had died in their own home, thinking they were safe.

Navari whispered reassurance, and flattened out her hearing, turning the deafening roar of ammo into something more like aggressive rainfall. The men could shoot all they wanted, they'd run out of patience and bullets long before these wards came down.

On that count, Navari was wrong.

The men were still shooting when Controller Ataku's presence filled House of Water. The attackers only noticed her arrival when her Skills wrapped around them, and with less effort than it took to blink, she ripped the water out of them. The husks of their bodies teetered for a moment before clattering onto the beach.

<Controller Ataku,> Navari said carefully, respectfully, both afraid of drawing the Nine aught's attention and equally afraid of what would happen if Controller Ataku came across her without proper prior announcement.

The Controller's flicked acknowledgement at her, but her focus was outward. <What happened here?> she demanded, her Skills skimming not only House of Water and its lake, but all of the Mountain beyond.

<We don't know,> Navari replied quietly. <They came from nowhere. They killed everyone.>

<And now they're setting fire to the Mountain,> Salasi added grimly.

Through the waterfall, Navari could see and smell nothing, but as Salasi dropped back down to the ground from the top of the pagoda, she could see the orange glow coming up over the mountain peaks and smell the smoke on the breeze.

<This…> Ataku's words failed as she saw the destruction the two of them had experienced. <There is almost no one left.>

<No,> SalNavari agreed, their words overlapping each other as did their own horror at what this night had brought.

For a long moment Ataku stood tall and silent, then her long hands curled into fists, and her shock condensed into fury. Without a word she gathered Salasi and Navari with her Skills and jumped. In the blink of an eye, the burning Mountain was gone, and they stood in a room, the stone around them saturated with Water Skills.

<This is Cyanea Under the Lake,> Ataku said. <You will be safe here.>

<Your hospitality is appreciated—> Navari didn't have a chance to finish before Ataku jumped away again.

Salasi rushed over to Navari. They wrapped themselves around each other, ear to ear, face to shoulder, all inner shields dropped and wound around both together. As close as they could reach each other. They were alive. They were together. For the moment they were safe.

The sound of footsteps had Navari lifting her head and looking for both of them, ready to face whatever this new threat. Her eyes locked on Zumi, wrapped in a heavy, wool lined coat that fell to his knees. He stood hunched and vulnerable, but still looked a far sight better than the last time Salasi had seen him in the unSkilled hospital.

<You're okay,> Salasi said, not looking up or letting go of Navari as she spoke to him.

<Because of you,> he answered very respectfully. <Thank you.>

<You're welcome,> Salasi replied.

After a moment Navari added, <Do you know where Controller Ataku went?>

<She's gone to the Mariners to petition the Rain Maker tribe to put out the fires on the Mountain,> he said, his voice strained and scared.

<That worries you,> Salasi said, sensing that his concern for his mother was far greater than his concern for the Mountain.

He hesitated before saying, <The Mariners don't always give people back.>

Salasi's memory of the wave swamping the sailboat and washing away the unSkilled filled SalNavari's mind. The ones the high aught Enforcers had been bargaining to get back. Controller Ataku was a Nine of Water though, not some petty unSkilled.

<She'll be back,> Navari replied confidently. Along with Matriarch Balane and those of Water who lived far out to sea. The

fools who'd attacked the Mountain wouldn't last long when the remnants of House of Water returned.

There would be a reckoning.

Chapter Thirty-Two

Raid

Li stared at Raid. "What do you mean the Mountain is gone?"

He couldn't find the words to explain it. The Skilled had all been connected to each other and to the world around them. A web that touched everyone and everything. Even the unSkilled with their paper doll lives were connected, though weakly. It was something so ubiquitous in everyday life that he rarely paid attention to it. Its absence now was crushing, like the sky itself had been erased. A Mountain sized hole had been cut out of the fabric of reality.

"The Houses they're..." He couldn't hear or feel Carnage or any of the others. "...gone."

Cain laughed bitterly, a harsh, barking sound. "So, she pulled it off."

Raid turned on him. "You know what happened?" he demanded.

"Her name is—" Cain choked, hands clenching, as if just speaking her name caused him distress. He gathered himself for a moment and spat, "Her name is Reefa Mazuli. The Doctor."

"The head of Arcana's Research and Development," Li said.

And Longcross's friend. Raid regretted burning out the man's mind. As much as he'd deserved it, what he could have told them about Mazuli would have been invaluable.

"She's been planning this for decades," Cain answered.

Those words caught Raid off guard. "How? Someone would have noticed."

Cain shook his head, that bitter look still twisting his face. "No they wouldn't have. Wind were the mail carriers. When they died out, the Inquisitors and Enforcers took over, but they didn't scrutinize it in the same way. Then the unSkilled switched to electronic communication and no one at all was watching that. They have entire networks now on their memes that no one pays any attention to."

Raid just stared at him, trying to comprehend how meme messages could turn into the entire Mountain disappearing.

"Her greatest achievement were the Shields," Cain went on. "She somehow developed a Skillset that negates all other Skills. She's been tinkering with their genetics and education for years, and now has enough tame and loyal copies to see her plan through."

Shields. The ones like Bunny. What Raid and Mordred had been calling Oblivion.

"So what, she just… marched onto the Mountain and killed everyone?" Li said aghast.

Cain nodded with a look of despair on his face. "You felt what it was like within the disruption field, now imagine that only you can't even reach beyond the edges of your own mind."

Raid didn't have to imagine. He shuddered at the memory of Bunny and the mind moths that had swarmed him. "Met one before," he said softly. "It was… awful."

"But… the whole Mountain?" Li asked, contradicting them out of her desperate need for this not to be true.

"The Doctor has been planning this for decades," Cain repeated. "She had contingency plans. She knew who she was going to keep alive to keep the infrastructure running until it could be switched to human control. Slaughter all the rest."

"She told you all this?" Raid asked.

"She likes having an audience and…" His feelings spiked. Jagged memories that had Raid recoiling. Cain touched his neck where the collar had been.

"And she never thought you were going to escape," Raid finished.

Cain gave Raid a stark look. "Gave up hope that you were ever going to come looking. After days, and then weeks and months… figured you and Mordred had… forgotten. Moved on."

Months. Raid felt his heart seize and then sink. "You've been here for months…" Which meant all that time he'd been talking to a clone. He couldn't wrap his mind around how Arcana had pulled off such a switch. He couldn't understand how he himself hadn't realized there'd been a switch. He wracked his mind trying to remember the last time he'd seen Cain in person, the last time they'd talked in thoughtspeak. Their communication had all been occasional, spoken conversations over meme. If there'd been any noticeable difference, Raid would have chalked it up to the medium they were using.

"We didn't know you were missing," Raid admitted, guilt washing through him. "There was a clone and… We came looking for answers after he died. We thought he was you. We didn't realize…" There were no words or excuses to make up for this. They should have noticed. Raid should have gone to see Cain in person. If they'd been face to face, Raid would have recognized the replacement as a clone. He should have known.

"Of course, there was a clone." Cain's haggard face became even more shadowed. "You probably liked him better. He was a better brother."

<No!> Raid said adamantly, grabbing Cain. <There is no one better.> He opened his mind, sharing all the memories of their childhood. The four of them in creche, learning to shield, learning to fight. Cain and Raid sneaking off together, leaving Nico to be bossed by Mordred. Exploring the Mountain as they grew older, sneaking into the Hollow Hill that had once been House of Wind.

Openly sharing memories went both ways.

Cain's memories flooded back into Raid. The box. The collar. The ring. The Doctor with her crocodile smile. Fighting her demands, refusing to give into her until it finally just became too hard. Under the strain of such overwhelming aloneness, it had just been easier to give her what she asked for. When she was talking, it was easier to forget that he was trapped in the confines of his own mind…

Raid recoiled from the horror of it all.

Cain jerked away from him, looking away from Raid's reaction.

<Cain…>

He shook his head.

Raid groped for words to bridge this sudden chasm between

them. Something as simple as 'sorry' wouldn't even begin to cut it.

<Mordred?> he asked hopefully, sending the thought back down toward the disruption shield instead.

"He's not coming," Cain said dully.

"He's a Seven now," Raid answered.

Cain just shook his head. "It doesn't matter. Those collars can contain a Ten. If he's smart, he didn't let them take him alive."

"And if they did?"

Cain laughed bitterly. "Then he'll wish he was dead."

They need to go back for him. Raid was ready to say as much when Li came hurrying back. She'd retreated down the hall to give them space.

"Someone's coming!" she hissed, keeping her voice low.

Cain shrank back.

Raid called in his knives, sharpened his hearing and shifted his perception from Cain and the missing Mountain to the concrete corridors that surrounded them. The quiet echo of booted feet. Voices whispering softly to each other through the radio. The occasional fluttering wings of white moths. The unSkilled hadn't guarded all the basements but they now swept them thoroughly. They knew Raid, Li and Cain were still in here somewhere.

<This way,> Raid murmured to Cain and Li, leading them away from the guards and towards a ladder leading up to the next floor.

They'd barely made it ten steps before they were forced to backtrack. The presence of the Shields and their Oblivion Skills made it impossible for Raid and the others to sneak passed under a sight shield. Down a different hall and then down another emergency ladder to avoid the Shields. They finally managed to slip around a group and climb back up, gaining back the two floors and then another.

The next several hours were more harrowing than anything Raid had faced in the trials. The null coronas of the Shields extended up and down as well, affecting him even if they were on a different floor. Their white moths became continuous, at least one always fluttering across his vision or in the corner of his eyes. A dull headache began to beat behind his temples, keeping time with his heart.

For every floor they gained, it felt like they back climbed two more, staying just out ahead of the Shields and the guards who carried high powered rifles along with the black leather collars.

Finally, the last door opened, and they stepped into the parking garage, the air feeling fresh after the canned air of the basements. One landing worth of stairs and they would be at street level. An armored black SUV came peeling down the ramp too fast for Raid to react to. Moths swarmed his vision. Li called out to him, but her voice was swallowed by their beating wings.

Nothing but emptiness. The moths so thick they covered the world over in white. Cut off the world. Just white. Just moths. Just nothing.

Color sparked. Sound roared. The moths retreated, disappearing into the blinding daylight and the crowd.

Raid was buffeted on all sides by paper dolls. The unSkilled laughed and cheered, their voices scraping over his brain like sandpaper. Their detergents and deodorants waged personal assault on his nose. He dug in his heels, nearly dragging Li off her feet.

"Can you hear me?" she hissed.

<What happened?> he demanded. Even her voice was too loud.

"Keep moving and I'll explain. They're right behind us."

He allowed Li to tug him forward. Her other arm looped through Cain's, dragging him through the crowd as well.

"You collapsed," she said, keeping her voice low. "That vehicle came screaming around the turn and you went down."

"One of the Oblivion was in it," he answered, that last moment of cogent thought before everything went white coming back to him. A strong Oblivion for him to hit him so hard and fast from that distance.

"They noticed when your sight shield failed," Li went on, casting a glance over her shoulder. "And they came after us. At least they're not willing to shoot into a crowd."

The moths had completely vanished now, but the headache and disquiet remained. Raid glanced back himself and saw a pair of guards shoving their way through the throng but there were no masked Oblivion with them.

"What is this crowd?" Raid asked, pulling up a shield. It wobbled for a moment. As soon as it felt solid, he extended it around Li and Cain. The guards weren't willing to shoot into a crowd *yet.* Raid wasn't going to trust his life or those of Li and Cain to that dubious goodwill.

"They're celebrating the fall of the Mountain," Cain answered flatly.

The fall of the Mountain. The death of everyone and everything he'd ever known. His heart kicked painfully. He reached out for the Mountain, pinging everyone he could think of as he'd done before.

No answer. There never would be again.

Raid pulled up a sight shield, inciting cries of alarm from those nearest. Before the guards or anyone could respond, they'd already moved on.

Li's happy cloud Skills had eased her way through the crowd, allowing her to stay ahead of the guards even though she'd been carrying Raid's deadweight on one arm and most of Cain on the other. Raid now shouldered his way through, using his Skills as a cowcatcher to get everyone out of his way. Leaving them whining about shield burns in his wake.

They reached a train station, the platform blissfully empty. Everyone was coming into Iocaste Proper to celebrate. They were the only ones trying to flee. The departing car was empty save for a homeless person stretched out across several benches sound asleep. The three of them huddled down near the door, where Raid could keep an eye on anyone entering, and they could make a quick escape if need be.

Li pulled her meme from her pocket and began scrolling. She pressed her hand to her mouth, eyes wide. Cain had collapsed in one of the bucket seats, head resting against the window behind him, staring out at the buildings flashing past. His breathing came ragged, his heart hammering, but both sounds smoothed out the farther from Arcana they drew. Raid leaned against Li's shoulder, looking at the meme with her.

Image after image of cruelty and glee. Arcana's men with their armor and helmets and their guns, holding up dead Skilled by their hair, the same way they'd hold up a dead deer by his antlers. The Inquisitors had all been lined up and shot execution style to the back of the head. One guard with his arms spread wide, stolen necklaces and bangles decorating him from shoulder to fingertip, a wide grin on his face. Picture after picture of the Grand Plaza and all the dead there.

Comments whizzed by under every post. Violent delight. Glee. Exuberant congratulations.

The only good kur is a dead kur.

This is the Cataclysm that every kur deserved.

This is the way forward.

This is the future.

Freedom for humanity.

True Human wins.

Raid clenched his hands so hard his palms bled, the only thing he could do to stop himself from calling in his blades and killing every unSkilled he came across.

Cain let out a strangled laugh, his emotions a weird blend of desolation and dark humor.

Raid glanced at him, then followed his gaze through the window. The train had passed through all the buildings of Iocaste Proper downtown and out into an open space, giving them all a clear view north. A clear view of the Mountain.

A clear view of the Mountain as it burned.

Flames licked up its sides and smoke poured off its peaks.

Cain laughed bitterly again and said a parody of the real words. "Squaring the Earth. When the Doctor remade the world for the fourth time."

Chapter Thirty-Three

Maggie Reeves

Maggie spent the night wandering. She'd taken one of the police vehicles out to Li's cottage, then spent an hour sitting out front working up the courage to walk up the front steps. Maggie just needed Li to understand that none of this was her fault. It was bitter relief when she found the cottage empty. She didn't have to justify anything to Li, but Li also wasn't there for her to pour her soul out to.

She tried Gemma's farm, waking up the old shepherd, but the woman hadn't seen Li for hours.

Grudgingly Maggie tried Raid's place but found it just as empty.

Surely Li wouldn't just leave without telling her. They said horrible things to each other in the past, especially as teenagers, but they'd always worked through it. That bastard Raid had probably dragged her off someplace, insisting that Ashveil was too dangerous now that it had been depopulated.

Depopulated. That word slithered into her awareness and sent a shiver down her spine. A tide of faces flooded her mind. Her students and their parents and friends. Her neighbors and their children. Her favorite barista with the gorgeous smile. Ava and the rest of the True Human members. Jim Dawes who'd finally found his purpose in life again. All of them gone. Every last one of them gone.

She went back to her apartment and began lighting incense. One stick for her mother who'd died before Maggie's first birthday. One stick for her father who'd spent every waking hour out logging or with the union until a freak accident felled him two years ago. One stick for Sensei Callum who'd been more present and engaged with her than her own father had ever been. One stick for Doctor Adrian

Longcross who inspired her to believe that the world could be better. One stick for Jim. One stick for his son. One stick for Ava. One stick for…

Maggie stopped and stared dully at the twisting lines of incense smoke. They supposedly lifted the names of the dead and the prayers for their well-being up to the All-God, the god the Ancestors had brought with them from the Moon. The god her mother had worshipped.

The god who hadn't saved her mother.

The god who hadn't spared the Ancestors.

The god who'd allowed the kurs to cause the Cataclysm and steal the world from humans.

The god who'd let Callum die.

The god who'd let Ashveil die.

Screaming with wordless rage and pain, she swept the shrine to the ground. The incense and effigies scattered across the carpet. Useless worthless god.

She stormed back downstairs. The contemplative quiet of the dojo settled so heavily on her shoulders it crushed her. The trophy case with all its useless stupid awards. How could she ever have thought any of this mattered?

Back onto the street where the stillness and quiet of the dawn did nothing to ease the crushing feeling. The sun mocked her by rising, casting its light over what should have been an endless night. She wanted to walk, to run, to be somewhere else, anywhere else, but her feet felt like lead. Suddenly it took all her effort to simply stand up. Even if she could move, where would she go? To her bachelor uncle? Her mother's brother who had given her her mother's shrine for her fifth birthday, and who she hadn't seen in over a decade? Maggie's entire life had been in Ashveil. Everything she cared about, everyone who mattered, had been here.

She wanted Li. She wanted to collapse in her friend's arms and pour out all her heartbreak. Except Raid had stolen Li away, and left Maggie alone with all the pain and crushing quiet.

The sound of tires broke the silence and Maggie latched onto the sound like a dying woman. She rushed towards it, her eyes finally alighting on heavy-duty all-terrain vehicles that barely fit through Ashveil's narrow streets.

Maggie watched a convoy of over a dozen vehicles drive down the main street, their wheels straddling the rails where the trolley car would never run again. One of them pulled to a stop next to her and the window rolled down.

"Hey!"

Maggie stared at the guy hailing her, her mind sluggishly trying to place him. Statton. Jon Statton. The doctor at Angels Landing who'd told her about Zumi. True Human.

"Hey," she answered. Her voice came out dull but her heartbeat quickened. True Human.

"This is Maggie Reeves," he said over his shoulder to those riding with him. "She's the girl who tried to kill the kurs and free Ashveil."

Maggie heard the door on the other side of the vehicle open and slam close. In a second, another man had walked around the hood to face her. He was taller and broader than Jon and more rugged in the face, but they were similar enough in looks that the two men had to be related.

"That true?" he asked.

Maggie shrugged and said bitterly, "It didn't work, did it."

"In war there will always be casualties," he replied. "What matters is that you were willing to fight for your people. Not many people would be willing to do what you did. To sacrifice what you sacrificed."

She latched onto his words and to the meaning he offered her.

"I'm Sheridan Statton," he said, holding out a thick, square hand.

"Maggie Reeves," she replied as she shook it, feeling the calluses on his palm.

"Now that the Border has fallen, we're heading east to Whichess Down. We're going to reclaim the city of our Ancestors in the name of humanity, and from there, the rest of the world. We could use some solid people like you."

"The Border has fallen?" she repeated, not sure she'd heard

right.

"It fell with the Mountain," Jon said with a grin.

Maggie gaped speechlessly, her eyes darting between both men, waiting for an explanation.

"Last night," Sheridan said. "True Human slaughtered all the kurs while they were partying and took the Mountain." He pulled out his meme and showed her all the images he'd saved to his phone. All the kurs dead. Humans triumphant. "The Border is open. The world is ours."

It took a moment for those words to sink in, but when they did, giddiness flooded her body and for a moment, Maggie thought that she could float. Screaming rage came directly on its heels. The kurs had all died last night.

Last.

Night.

A day too late to save Ashveil.

The unfairness of it all lodged in her throat and choked her.

"So," Sheridan said with a grin. "You coming?"

Ashveil was dead. Li may as well have been. Maggie's entire life lay crumpled at her feet. With Sheridan's words, the future unfurled before her. Furious and fierce determination settled around her. A wolfish smile stretched her face. She may have lost Ashveil, but she could still help True Human reclaim the world.

"Yes. Let's take back the world."

Epilogue

Kasia Laren

Agent Kasia Laren walked out of the Witch Angels' compound. Ogwo and Park both sagged with relief when they saw her. They'd lost Smith back in Ashveil. He'd been depopulated as he'd helped evacuate the town. Early reports suggested they'd been successful in getting out a little over ten percent of Ashveil's population. That failure had weighed heavy on her until last night when she saw the flames licking up the side of the Mountain, and media sites exploded with pictures of the slaughtered Skilled.

She'd raced out here with Ogwo and Park – switching out drivers so they'd never have to stop – hoping against hope that losing the Mountain didn't also mean losing the Witch Angels. When all of her requests for an audience had gone unanswered, she'd made her way inside. Her unSkilled presence within the compound should have provoked a potentially lethal response. Instead, nothing.

White noise roared in her ears as she walked by Ogwo and Park and looked at the huge gate that separated Iocaste from the Wilds. The only official connection between humans and the Natives of Oceanea.

Out loud she repeated the words her mentor had told her many years ago when she had first laid eyes on this gate.

"Always remember that Skills are exponential, not additive. A Ten aught isn't just ten times stronger than an aught, they are ten *billion* times stronger. Every Witch Angel is a Ten aught Carnage, and *every single one of them* is always sent to the Border to defend it."

True Human had made such a show about the Border holding back humanity, but the Border had never been about keeping people in.

"Now imagine what's out there in the Wilds that requires the Skills of every single Ten aught Carnage to keep out."

Neither Ogwo nor Park made a sound.

The Mountain was gone. The Border had fallen. Every single Witch Angel was dead. Iocaste had no defenders left to protect it and the Natives would know soon if they didn't already.

Laren said grimly, "The Monsters are coming."

Acknowledgements

This story is one that has been with me for years and bringing it to life isn't something I would have been able to do without the help and support of some fantastic people.

Martha Steele, all the hours we spent brainstorming together has helped lay a strong foundation. Some of your white rabbit ideas were truly epic and inspiring. Thank you for reading one of the earliest drafts and helping to get the plot on track.

Thank you Dean Scott for answering all my questions about navigating the world of self-publishing, and for being a first reader. You are a real inspiration, and your insight has been invaluable.

To my other first reader Rudy, thank you for taking the time to read it while working overnight, and dealing with a format that started you over again, every time you opened the story, at page one.

Will Fife, thank you for being my tech support and updating my software so I could complete all the formatting. I would not have been able to get that all done alone.

A big thank you to all the professionals who have been involved. To Andrea Hurst whose editing, comments and insights were key in strengthening and streamlining the narrative. To the talented Kim Dingwell who created such a wonderful cover and gave this story a face.

For Lulu who always reminded me that walkies are super important, and that I need fresh air and exercise, and for Mikey, Bandit, Pusheen and Spatzle my moral support and blanket patrol.

About the Author

K. T. lives in Portland Oregon with her dog, cats, plants, and overflowing library full of books.

Made in the USA
Columbia, SC
06 November 2024

45826040R00146